Family Secrets
A Family Epic

by

Sherry Derr Wille

Published by
Melange Books, LLC
White Bear Lake, MN 55110
www.melange-books.com

Family Secrets, A Family Epic, Copyright © 2012 by Sherry Derr Wille

ISBN: 978-1-61235-363-0

Published in the United States of America.
Second Edition

Cover Art by Caroline Andrus

Family Secrets
A Family Epic
Sherry Derr Wille

In the late 19th century, orphans became a ward of the county. When that happened to my grandmother, she was sold as a bond servant, setting the course of her life into motion. At the age of 18 the man who held her bond had taught her to read and write, be a good Christian woman, and the mysteries of housekeeping. Giving her a watch, a bible and $10 she was on her own for the first time since she'd been bonded at the age of three and a half.

In the midst of the depression, my father found himself on his own at the age of twelve. His life was one of a little boy lost.

Last but not least, is the way in which my family impacted my life. This is our story and one that would not survive if I didn't take the time to tell it.

* * * *

Cover pics:
Upper Left – Norma & Ralph Derr
Upper Center – Harriet & Ralph Derr
Upper Right – Amy & Ruben Derr

Second Row:
Ralph as a child
Ralph as an adult
Sherry Derr-Wille

Third Row:
Freddie – Amy – Ruben & Ralph Derr
Freddie holding Ralph with Harriet standing at his side.

Fourth Row:
Harriet & Ralph Derr
Ralph Totton standing behind Ella Mercer, Harriet Mercer Oswald standing behind her husband Ted, Ruben Derr standing behind Amy with Freddie at her side

To My Readers

I hope you enjoy this book. I know it is much different from my usual style, but thankfully Nancy Schumacher is planning to take a chance on it.

One thing to remember is that this story takes place in a different place and a different time. Beginning with my Grandmother's story in 1892 and ending with my story in the present day. My hope is to bring not only reading enjoyment, but also an understanding of the past as it was lived by my family in Southern Wisconsin.

Last but not least, I dedicate this book to my parents, Ralph and Norma Derr. No matter what my father's life was like before he met my mother, he turned into a very caring and generous man. I love you, Daddy.

Part One

The Bond Servant
Lafayette Co.
Village of Gratiot, Wisconsin
June 1892

Amy

Prologue

June 1892

Mary watched from the uppermost corner of the council chambers of the county court house. It was the only thing she'd asked of God and St. Peter when she entered heaven. To gain eternal rest, she had to know the fate of her youngest daughter, Annabelle, and her oldest son, Ralph.

After twenty years of marriage to her first husband, Charles, he died suddenly, leaving her alone on the farm. Her daughters were married with families of their own and little time for their half-breed mother.

She'd survived the winter by milking her cows and sending the milk to the dairy in town. She also tended her flock of chickens and sold the eggs at the general store.

Knowing she could never handle the planting alone, she considered selling the farm and moving to town. Of course, she knew she wouldn't be welcomed there. Her high cheekbones and coarse dark hair did little to disguise her Indian heritage.

In the past, whenever word of an Indian uprising in the west reached Lafayette County, Wisconsin, she'd borne the brunt of her neighbors' outrage. She had no control over the actions of the Sioux, Comanche, Cheyenne or Apache, but it didn't seem to matter. She was caught in the middle of a war not of her making.

With spring, her nearest neighbor, Henry Totten, came to visit. He was about her age, and had never married.

"I've come with a proposition for you, Mary," Henry said. "I need a wife and would like to have children. What you need is someone to run your forty acres. I want to marry you and take care of you."

Henry's proposal came as a shock. Mary hadn't considered taking another man as a husband, but he did make sense. She couldn't continue to run the farm alone and the thought of more children was enticing. "I'll have to consider it. I mean…"

"If you're speaking of your Injun blood, it means little to me."

Mary knew the tears filling her eyes should shame her, but they didn't. Only Charles loved her unconditionally. Their mother's large boned build and coarse features shamed her own daughters. She'd always been grateful her children favored Charles' German mother.

To her amazement, Henry loved her unconditionally. He wasn't as handsome as Charles, who had swept her off her feet and captured her heart when she was but fourteen, but he was sincere.

Within the month, Mary and Henry were married and the two farms joined as one. So as not to make either of them uncomfortable, Henry built them a new house in the middle of the two acreages.

Although her daughters were outraged at her remarriage, Mary knew what she did was as necessary for her survival.

Within no time she gave birth to her first son, Ralph, in 1884. Two years later Bertha Mae was born and her life seemed to be complete. When Mary learned she was again pregnant, she embraced the news with a mix of joy and trepidation. Her daughters from her first marriage wanted nothing to do with her first two children and she knew this one would be no different.

The first snow of November blanketed the area when Henry announced he was going to town for supplies. Although she argued the roads were treacherous, he only laughed at her fears, and then kissed her lovingly before leaving.

Later that afternoon, well past the time when Henry should have been home, the sheriff came to her door. When he told her of Henry's death, he went into great detail.

On his way to town, several young men had surrounded his sleigh, taunting him about his half-breed wife. When they spooked his team, Henry lost control. In the accident that followed he'd been thrown from the seat and the runners of the sleigh cut his throat. Death was immediate.

For the second time in her life she was alone. Not only was she again a widow, but she was also pregnant with a late life child and responsible her two small children.

Now, just over three years later, pneumonia had taken Mary's life, leaving Ralph, Bertha and Annabelle alone, orphans who were destined to become wards of the county. What would be their fate? She was pleased to know that Bertha had been adopted shortly after her death, but the oldest and youngest of her children remained unwanted wards of the county.

"You have seen the children one last time, Mary," the angel who stood beside her said. "Henry and Charles are waiting for you. Ralph and Annabelle are no longer your responsibility. It is time for you to rest."

Reluctantly, Mary followed the angel. Someone else would lovingly comb Annabelle's long black hair and smile when Ralph mastered the manly tasks demanded by life on the farm. Someone else would tuck them in and listen to their prayers. It was, indeed, time for Mary to rest.

Chapter One

Annabelle sat on the big wooden chair in the crowded room. It was hot and the room smelled like Ralph did when he'd been out working in the fields and came in for the noon meal. When Ralph sweat, it smelled sweet because it came from hard work, but with so many people, the room smelled sour, the way Mama said Ralph would smell if he didn't wash up before he came in to eat. She knew the people smelled because even with the breeze coming through the window it was way too hot in the packed room to be comfortable.

In the chair next to hers, Ralph sat, looking forward and not saying a word. Every once in a while he would cover her hand with his and lean over to whisper in her ear saying everything would be all right.

With the logic only a three-and-a-half-year-old child could possess, she relaxed. It was enough to hear her brother promise everything would be all right for her. It gave her hope to know even without their mother, they would be together. Nothing else mattered. What more could happen to them? Mama was in heaven with Papa, at least that's what Ralph said.

"We are here today to decide the fate of Ralph and Annabelle Totten, orphans and wards of the court," the man in a black suit said.

Annabelle did not like the man. His face was all red, like he was mad at everyone. Instead of listening to him she pulled her doll close to her chest and put her thumb in her mouth. No one could take away her one-degree of comfort, no matter how hard they tried.

"Letty Ostrum, you have been caring for these children. Is there a reason you do not wish to continue to do so?"

Annabelle watched as her older half-sister, the one who came to live at the farm when Mama went to heaven, got to her feet. "My mother left the farm to me and my sisters. She didn't say nothin' about Ralph and Annabelle. My pa worked hard for that place for us, not her. I got my own younguns to raise. I can't be bothered with her to say nothin' of the boy. He eats as much as all my younguns put together. I just can't afford to feed him. Me and my sisters just want to sell the farm and get our money."

"And what of these children, Mrs. Ostrum?"

"They ain't anything but trouble to us. They're orphans. That makes them your responsibility. My pa didn't work all his life to have to leave his farm to those two who ain't even blood kin. Let the county take them in."

Annabelle watched as Ralph got to his feet, "Half the farm belonged to my pa"

"Your pa died and left the land to my ma," Letty shouted. "What belonged to her now belongs to us."

"Doesn't what she left include Annabelle and me?" Ralph asked.

"No, it don't, 'cause the farm belonged to Ma's real husband, my pa. Besides, Ma was a half-breed and everyone knows Injuns can't own property."

"Then, am I to understand you want nothing to do with your brother sister, Mrs. Ostrum?"

"Half-brother and sister," Letty reminded him. "We was all against our ma marrying white trash like Henry Totten. We told her no good could come from it, but she didn't listen. She was so afraid of being alone she let him put three brats in her belly. I guess that's just the Injun in her. They ain't picky about who takes them to their beds. It's just a good thing Bertha got adopted right after Ma died so we didn't have to take care of her along with the other two."

Annabelle began to cry. She didn't like to have people yelling. The fact she disliked Letty made things worse. Ma never spoke to her like Letty and she never hit her. Letty spanked her every day since Ma died, but she never knew why. She tried to be good, but no matter what she did she managed to anger her older sister.

"If this is the way you feel, Mrs. Ostrum, we have found families who will buy Ralph and Annabelle's bond, once you sign these papers relinquishing your claim to these children, the property in question will be deeded to you and your sisters. Once the paperwork is finished you will be free to leave."

Annabelle didn't understand why her sister was saying mean things. Of course, she wondered every day why her mama went away and never came back. No matter how hard she cried, no one would tell her how far it was to heaven. No matter how many times she asked, no one would take her there to see Mama. She knew Mama must be very lonely without her, just as she was lonely without Mama at her side.

Without looking in Annabelle's direction, Letty got to her feet and walked over to the desk where the man with the red face sat. Annabelle watched as the man held out a pencil to Letty. She took it and made some marks on the paper before turning to leave. For the first time since Letty came to the farm after Mama went away, Annabelle saw her smile.

"I want to go with Letty," Annabelle cried as she got to her feet to follow Letty from the room.

"No you don't," Ralph said, taking her in his arms. "She don't want us. That's why she signed them papers."

Annabelle began to cry. Never in her short life had anyone ever said they didn't want her. "I want Mama," she wailed.

"I do too, but she can't come back to us. She's in heaven with Papa. You're going to have to be a big girl now."

"But I'm not big, I'm little."

"Silence that child," the red faced man demanded.

"I'm trying, sir," Ralph responded, "but she don't understand."

"Perhaps if she had a reason to cry she would understand."

Annabelle looked up to see the man pull a willow switch from behind his desk. With her fear changed from being left by her sister to the threat of being switched, she swallowed her sobs.

"That's better. Now, Mr. Peters, are you still willing to buy the bond of this boy?"

William Peters spat a stream of tobacco juice to the floor before coming over to examine Ralph. "He looks scrawny, are you sure he can work?"

Ralph pulled away from Mr. Peter's grip on his upper arm. "I've been helpin' my run our farm since my pa died three and a half years ago."

"I want him, Will," Mamie Peters said. "Since our boy died…"

"All right, Mamie. I will take him for you, but he best be able to work. Can you read and write boy?"

"Yes sir, I can. Ma made certain I went to school and did my lessons."

"If that is the case, I'll take him home. The price of his bond is high but if it makes Mamie happy again it will be worth it." The man turned back to face Ralph. "Mind you, I will expect you to keep up with your lessons, but not until you do your chores."

"Yes sir. I promise I will do my work before I do my lessons. What about my sister?"

"I've already got too many girls. She won't be far away. Heard tell Joseph Coble is buying her bond."

Ralph turned from the man who just paid cash to take him home. "I'm goin' with Mr. and Mrs. Peters. He says you're goin' with Mr. and Mrs. Coble. They're good folks. We'll see each other, but you'll have to be good. They're gonna be your mama and papa now."

"But I don't want a new mama and papa. I want to go with you."

"You can't. Mr. Coble is a good man."

* * * *

Joseph Coble looked at the child who would be his bondservant for the next fourteen and a half years. He turned his attention back to the contract he was signing. In it, he read he would be taking on complete responsibility for the little girl who no longer had a mother or father to care for her. He took a moment to read over exactly what would be expected of him. He understood he would teach the girl to read and write, to be a good Christian and instruct her about the mysteries of housekeeping. In return when she turned eighteen he would give her

7

ten dollars, a Bible and a watch. Combined with the cost of buying her bond from the county, this child would cost him a small fortune, not to mention the money he'd be spending to raise yet another child.

Those tasks were all ones he could accomplish; even the money wouldn't be a problem. He only hoped the girl would respond well to his strict discipline. If he could believe Letty Ouster, the girl was spoiled, but that would have to change. It had to. The girl would give up her spoiled ways even if he had to beat them out of her.

"Are you going to be my new papa?" the child asked as she tugged on his hand.

"You will be living with us, and you will call me Mr. Coble," he replied, his tone stern. "From now on your name will be Amy Bell."

"But my name is Annabelle."

"You have to understand my wife and I already have a daughter named Ann. It would be too confusing if you were Ann as well. It will be easier for you to get used to a new name than for us to call for Ann and have two little girls come to us."

Bitter tears filled Amy's eyes. He knew she didn't understand, but he couldn't think about such things now. She would be living by his rules, therefore she needed to start now. "You can stop your crying, right here and now. I don't abide by my servants blubbering like babies."

Amy sniffed loudly and wiped her nose and eyes with her sleeve. At least she understood the necessity of doing as she was told.

"I want to say good-bye to my sister," Ralph said, as Joseph was leaving the courthouse with Amy in tow.

Reluctantly, he pushed the child toward her brother. In time they would forget each other, but for today he would allow them this time alone.

"Do you think this is wise?" William asked. "I don't like the idea of the two of them seeing each other. I have work that needs to be done at my farm. I don't need Ralph runnin' over to your place to be with his sister."

"Today is the last time they will be together. I trust you will keep Ralph busy enough he won't have time to come and bother my family.

Amy is young, in time she will forget he ever existed. You have to make him realize that it's best if he do the same."

* * * *

"Don't cry, Annabelle, we won't be far apart," Ralph promised.

"He says that I'm not Annabelle anymore," she said, pointing at Mr. Coble. "He says I'm Amy now."

Ralph looked up at the man who waited to take his sister home. "How could you change her name?" he asked.

"It will be too difficult for her to be called Anna when I already have a daughter with the same name. Because of her age, it will be easier for her to adjust to a new name than to be the center of confusion in our household."

"But…"

"But nothing, young man. I have bought Amy's bond. Until she's eighteen, she belongs to me. Say good-bye to your sister. You will have more than enough to keep you busy at William Peters' place. I'll thank you to keep your distance from my farm. Amy needs time to adapt to her new life. If you insist on coming around it will only confuse her."

"She's my sister and…"

"And she is now my ward. It is in my house in which she will live. I will tell her whom she may see and what she must do. I know where to find you when I deem it proper for her to see you. I have nothing more to say to you. When your presence is desired, you will be summoned." My Coble looked deep into Ralph's eyes. He knew the boy was eight, nine at the oldest, but he seemed to be an old soul. He would have a problem making Amy forget she ever had an older brother named Ralph.

Mr. Coble turned his back on Ralph, indicating their conversation had ended. Even though Ralph knew his bond had been purchased so he could do physical labor for Mr. Peters, he had hoped Annabelle would have gone to a loving family. Instead, it was plain that as Joseph Coble's ward, she would be a true bondservant in the same way he would be for Mr. Peters. She would be expected to learn to do housework rather than play. Almost thirty years earlier the north had

9

fought the south to eliminate the owning of slaves. Yet his sister had been sold into a bonding that would span the next fourteen and a half years.

* * * *

Amy watched as Ralph climbed into Mr. Peter's wagon and drove out of sight. When she turned back, she saw Mr. Coble load her meager belongings into his carriage. Once he finished, he picked her up and sat her on the plush seat. For a moment, Amy felt like a fairy princess but her fantasy soon dissolved.

"You will be living with us now, Amy," Mr. Coble began. "You will sleep in the attic, under the eaves. Tomorrow morning you will begin learning how to do the housework. You will work with Katie, our hired girl. There is more work than she can handle. Your duties will be to do the dusting, set the table and dry the dishes. In time you will learn to polish the silverware and sweep the floor. In other words, you will be expected to work for your room and board within my home."

Although Amy was a bright child, the words Mr. Coble spoke made no sense. Ralph had chores to do outside, but Mama always did the work inside the house. Amy never did anything other than play.

The room beneath the eaves was very small. In places, Katie couldn't stand upright. For Amy it was a virtual playground. In this room Katie mothered her and allowed the child in her to come through. Here she was still allowed to cradle her doll in her arms and pretend her mama was still alive and would come to take her back home. It was only when she left the room to begin her daily routine that childhood vanished.

Katie woke her before the sun was up each morning. After helping Amy dress, they went down to the kitchen. While Katie prepared breakfast, Amy set the table. Being so young, she needed to stand on a stool to reach the cupboards where the dishes were stored. When the meal ended, Katie washed the dishes and Amy dried them before putting them back onto the shelves. Only then did Katie give her the piece of bread and butter that would suffice as her breakfast.

During the long summer days, Amy watched as Mr. Coble's

children played for hours on end. She envied them their games of hide and seek as well as tag. In the evenings, they chased the ever-present fireflies and watched as their tiny lights blinked on and off. As much as Amy longed to join them in their play, her work in the kitchen seemed to be never ending. Once the evening dishes were finished, she helped Katie set the bread for the next morning, before once again cleaning up the kitchen. By the time their work was finished, Amy was far too tired to do little but climb the ladder to the loft and fall into an exhausted sleep.

Summer slowly faded into fall, but the only change for Amy came as the Coble children returned to school and Mrs. Coble brought a large box from the other side of the attic where Amy and Katie slept. From it, she produced clothing her daughters had outgrown and now, with a few adjustments would fit Amy.

Her new wardrobe included a good dress for church, two skirts and two blouses for everyday as well as two pair of shoes, one sensible for everyday and the other good for church. Amy loved her new clothes and promised to keep them in good repair so in time they could be handed down to another needy child.

Chapter Two

Amy's third summer in the Coble household came to an end. Instead of packing lunches for each of the other children, she packed a lunch for herself. She would be going to school with them and learning all the things they learned.

Each of the Coble children carried lunch pails made by Mr. Coble. In contrast, Amy's pail was one that had once been used for the rendered lard used in the kitchen for cooking. Even with her hand me down clothes and shabby shoes, she was proud of the new slate she'd been given. She was ready for school, ready to learn.

Although she hadn't seen Ralph in the entire time she'd worked in the Coble household, she did remember him coming home at night and laboring over his homework assignments before doing his chores. She could see herself sitting at the table along with the other children to do her schoolwork. She would be able to read books and lose herself in the stories the way the other girls in the family did.

"Who is the new first grader?" one of the older girls asked Ann Coble.

"Oh, she's one of our servants," Ann replied.

Amy wanted to run and hide, but Ann had spoken the truth. She was a servant, even though she thought of herself as one of the members of the Coble family.

"Pa says the contract he signed when he bought her says she has to go to school. I don't see why she has to be educated just to do housework, but Pa won't do anything against the contract."

The mention of the contract Mr. Coble signed brought to mind the day she'd sat in the courtroom while her fate was decided. That had been the last time she'd seen her brother.

The lessons started, and Amy tried, with all her might, to forget she was a servant and concentrate on the lessons being taught by the teacher.

Above the board, the alphabet was neatly printed in upper and lower case as well as in cursive. Since there were only two new first graders, they were each given a lined piece of paper with their name neatly printed at the top.

The teacher concentrated on the first graders, pointing out the letters for each of their names on the chart. "Our new first graders are Amy and Mike. The letters for Amy's name are A – M – Y."

Amy repeated the letters and looked at them on the paper. The teacher had printed a capital A and the other letters were lower case. While the teacher turned her attention to Mike, Amy traced the letters first with her finger and then tried to make them with the new pencil Mr. Coble gave her this morning before she left for school.

Holding it between her middle finger and thumb the way she'd seen the other children in the family doing, she worked hard to make the letters look exactly the same way her teacher had written them.

When she watched the other children, they made it look so easy, but in fact it was difficult. When she finished her awkward attempt, she looked over at the paper on Mike's side of the desk. As the only other first grader, he would be her desk mate for the remainder of the year. She wanted to cry, when his letters more closely resembled the ones the teacher wrote than hers.

"It's okay, Amy, my ma taught me to write my name," Mike whispered in her ear. "I've had more practice."

Determined to make her letters look like those of the teacher, Amy wrote them over and over again on the paper. By the time they went outside for recess, she had filled both sides of the paper with her awkward scrawling. By the final time she wrote her name, she could see the letters looking more like the ones on the board.

For the remainder of the day, Amy worked at learning all the

13

letters written above the blackboard. Even though she couldn't make them correctly, she knew the name connected with each one of them.

With school over for the day, Amy hurried home, anxious to tell Mr. and Mrs. Coble all the wondrous things she'd learned in school. Being much younger and therefore smaller than the other children in the family, she was the last to arrive back at the house. By the time she rushed into the kitchen, Ann, May and their brothers, Will and Robert were all trying to talk at once to tell everything they'd learned at school.

Katie motioned for Amy to join her in the kitchen. She listened attentively as Amy told her about school, while the two of them worked to prepare the evening meal for the family.

From the dining room, Amy could hear the other children telling their parents about their day and preparing to work on their studies. "When can I tell Mr. and Mrs. Coble about my day at school? When can I practice my letters?" Amy questioned.

"You can't child. Your duties are here in the kitchen with me. If you are not too tired, you can practice your letters once we go to the loft for the night. Unfortunately, although Mr. Coble signed a contract saying you had to learn to read and write and do your sums, he is not interested to know anything of your progress in school. Whatever you learn you must do so in school, for in this house there is no time for you to study or practice that which you have learned."

* * * *

Over the school year, Amy did, indeed practice her letters and sums in the cramped quarters of the loft she shared with Katie. Each new accomplishment in school brought praise from the older servant. Unfortunately, the time of study never seemed to be enough for once the kitchen chores were finished it was usually late into the evening.

At school Amy didn't join the other children on the playground at recess or lunch hour, opting to stay inside. During these times of solitude, rather than cultivating the friendships of children her own age, she practiced her writing and did the homework there was no time to complete at home.

"I don't like the idea of you not going out to play with the other children," her teacher admonished more than once.

"I have no time for play," Amy always responded. "I don't have time to do my schoolwork at home. This is the only chance I get to do what is required to get a passing grade so I can be promoted."

The teacher, upset by Amy's words, finally went to Mr. and Mrs. Coble with her concerns. "I worry about Amy," she said when she arrived at the farmhouse.

"I don't see why you would have these concerns," Mr. Coble replied, his tone stern even to the ears of the teacher.

"She tells me there is not time for her to do her studies at home. I watch her every day when the other children go out to play and she sits at her desk doing the exercises I have assigned to the other children to do at night when they go home."

"You have no right to question the running of my household. Has Amy complained to you about anything?"

His words came as a complete shock. "Of course she hasn't. She is a very quiet child with a quick mind. She says staying in at recess and lunch is her choice. She is a joy to have in my class."

"Do not spend too much of your time dwelling on my ward. When I contracted for her, I agreed she should learn her sums, to read and write, and be a good Christian woman, and that is all. If you do not want to follow my instructions, I will see you are replaced as soon as possible."

Outraged at Mr. Coble's harsh words, the teacher left the farmhouse, silently vowing to help Amy as much as she could while the other children played. In the future she would no longer voice her concerns over the child aloud. With the help of God, she would give the sad little girl the education she seemed to crave.

* * * *

As the years went by, Amy continued her education. As she learned in first grade, the only time she had for study was during recess and lunch hour. Many teachers came and went and although they knew the capabilities of their bright student, they could not persuade her to

15

join the other children as they played outside during the breaks.

The result of Amy's imposed study habits left her with no friends among the children at school. She knew the situation delighted the Coble children, as they didn't want any of their friends to associate with someone they considered inferior.

By Amy's thirteenth birthday, she had taken on many more of the household chores in addition to the schoolwork she never brought home. As long as her report cards said she was making satisfactory progress, Mr. Coble never questioned her lack of homework, which his own children did on a nightly basis.

The end of her eighth grade school year meant she would no longer be able to escape her daily chores by leaving the house each day. With the graduation ceremony to be held on the steps of the county court house, Amy inwardly fussed about what she would be wearing to the festivities. She'd heard the other children bragging about the new clothes their parents purchased for this important day, but she knew she had nothing appropriate to wear. Her dark blue Sunday dress would have to do.

On the morning of the graduation, Mrs. Coble called Amy aside. "You have done well in school," she began. "I realize it has been difficult for you, considering your lack of study time. Mr. Coble and I would like you to have this dress for today's festivities."

Amy opened the box with the name of the general store in town printed on the cover. To her amazement, it held a beautiful pastel yellow dress that would accent her coloring well. She immediately knew it was not something one of the other girls in the family wore previously, since she did all of the ironing for the family and would have remembered such a beautiful dress.

"I—I don't know what to say," she gasped. "It's the most beautiful dress in the world."

She hurried up to the loft to dress and was surprised to see Mary Coble, the oldest of the girls in the family waiting for her.

"This is such a special day. I want to give you a grown up hairstyle."

Amy could hardly believe her ears. No one had ever taken time with her hair before. When she'd been little Katie braided it for her, but as she grew older, she found she could do the job herself.

Obediently, she sat down on the bed and allowed Mary to undo the braids Amy put in last night after she washed her hair in preparation for her special day. The tug of the brush pulling through the tangles of her hair came as a bit of a surprise. Usually the only time she combed it was when it was wet and the comb went through easily.

"You're a woman now," Mary said as she fussed with each strand of hair. "You must adapt a new hairstyle. Braids are for children in school, and since you will no longer be going to school, I'll teach you how to put your hair up in a bun. Of course, for today, we'll let your hair hang loose around your shoulders."

When Mary finally finished, she allowed Amy to look in the cracked mirror hanging over the old dresser in the loft. To Amy's delight, her black hair hung loosely around her shoulders with several strands pulled away from her face and secured with a bow that matched her dress perfectly.

"I don't know how to thank you, Mary," she said. If she could have mustered the nerve, she would have hugged the older girl, but she knew it would be inappropriate.

In the mirror she saw not only her reflection, but also that of Mary Coble. They stood in direct contrast to one another. Mary was delicate and very thin with long blonde hair hanging in ringlets. Amy, on the other hand, was big boned, with coarse features and jet-black hair. Mr. Coble told her it was because her mother had been a dirty half-breed and the Indian showed through dramatically in Amy's features. Whatever the reason for the difference, she wished with all her might that for one day she could be as beautiful as Mary. Unfortunately, she realized this was one wish she would never see fulfilled.

The yard of the county courthouse was filled with chairs for the parents and a small stage held more chairs for the graduates of the many one-room schools in the county. Amy hung back shyly. In school she'd been called Amy Coble, even though she repeatedly told herself she was really Amy Totten. Because of her last name starting with a "C" she stood close to the beginning of the line of children waiting for the music to start so they could take their seats on stage.

She listened as the top students were called forward so they could accept their medals for scholarship. In her heart, she wished she would be one of those called, but knew her average grades were not outstanding enough for recognition.

"And finally, the award for penmanship goes to Miss Amy Coble."

Hearing her name called came as a complete shock. On unsteady legs she got to her feet and walked across the stage to accept the medal for perfect penmanship. Her fingers trembled as she grasped the medal. It signified the one thing in her life at school she'd been good at. Even though her grades weren't the tops in her class, her penmanship had been something she prided herself on. Now her hard work finally paid off.

With the awards distributed, Amy, along with the rest of her class listened for their names to be called in order to receive their diplomas. When Amy's name was called, she walked confidently to the podium to receive the piece of paper saying she'd completed the eighth grade and had finished her formal education.

The ceremony ended and each of the graduates went to be congratulated by their proud parents, grandparents and siblings. Only Amy stood alone. Mr. and Mrs. Coble had dropped her off at the courthouse and then gone into town to do their weekly shopping. They told her they would return after the ceremony so they could take her back home. Once there, she knew no one would give her a party like Mr. and Mrs. Coble had for their own children. She would be expected to peel the potatoes to be mashed to go with the roast of beef Katie would be preparing. Together they would also prepare the last of the winter stash of carrots.

"The name on your diploma should be Annabelle Totten," someone said from behind her.

All thoughts of potatoes and carrots, even of dinner dissolved from her mind. Turning to face the man behind the voice, she was frightened. Who could have known her real name? The man standing behind her was tall and very slender with a long narrow face, shaggy brown hair and penetrating blue eyes.

"I don't think I know you," she finally managed to say.

"I'm sure you don't," he said, his face brightening with a smile. "I'm your brother, Ralph Totten."

The name resonated through Amy's mind. It was the same name she silently mentioned in her nightly prayers. Over the years she'd even forgotten her connection to Ralph Totten but she never stopped mentioning his name in her prayers.

"Br-Brother?" she stammered.

"Don't you remember?" Ralph asked. "I was with you on the day Mr. Coble bought your bond. Just like Mr. Peters bought my bond. My bond was finished four years ago but Mr. Peters was always good to me. He kept me on as a hired man. Not being bound by the bond, I was able to find out where you went to school. When I didn't have work to do on the farm, I checked up on you. I knew you were graduating today and it might be the last time I'd get to see you before your bond is finished."

"But why?"

"Because Mr. Coble said we could have no contact. As long as you're bound to him, I have to honor his wishes. I knew he wouldn't recognize me, so that's why I came here today. I told Mr. Peters why I wanted off and he agreed it was important for me to be here for you. The fact Mr. and Mrs. Coble didn't stay gave me the courage to come over to congratulate you on your accomplishment. From what I heard, Mr. Coble is a hard master."

Ralph's face became more familiar. She'd seen him watching from the woods along the road from the school to Mr. Coble's home. At the time she'd thought him to be someone living in the woods or perhaps an area farmer collecting wood for the winter. As she stared into his face, she recalled the day she'd been ripped away from him. Tears sprung to her eyes as she remembered Mr. Coble telling her from now on she would be called Amy Belle. For the first time in nine years she heard someone call her by her real name, not the one she'd been taught to answer to.

"I'm very proud of you Annabelle. I want you to know that. No one can ever take away the education you've received, just like they can't take away your medal for penmanship or your diploma. I only wish the name on it would have been the correct one. Are you happy?"

"Happy? What a strange thing to ask. I know nothing more than being Amy Belle Coble. That's my name and who I am. From what I have seen at school, I am lucky that Mr. Coble is strict, but he has never been cruel to me. There was a girl in one of the lower grades who came to school every day covered in bruises. One day she didn't come at all and I heard her father had finally beaten her to death. You don't have to be a bond servant to live with a cruel master."

"What will you do now?"

Tears welled in Amy's eyes. She wanted to say she would find a young man and be married, but she knew she still had five years left on her bond. "Katie, she's Mr. Coble's hired girl, is going to be getting married, so I'll be taking over all the household chores."

"What are you doing here, young man?" Bill Coble's voice boomed.

Amy trembled.

"I came to see my sister graduate from the eighth grade, Sir," Ralph replied.

"I thought I made it quite clear when I bought her bond I wanted you to have no contact with her."

"And I've complied with your wishes. I couldn't allow her to graduate without her family here. I noticed you dropped her off and left to do something other than rejoice in her accomplishments. If you had stayed, I wouldn't have approached her. Just seeing her receive the medal for excellence in penmanship and get her diploma would have been enough for me. As it was, you didn't stay and I saw no problem in congratulating her."

"The problem, young man, is that Amy is my ward. I have chosen not to allow her to have any contact with you. What she does once she is of age is up to her, but for now, she will do as I say and I say she will not see you again."

"Mr. Coble, please," Amy pleaded. "You know I've been obedient. Won't you allow me a few more minutes with the brother I haven't seen in the past nine years?"

20

"Joseph, the child is right," Mrs. Coble said. "She has never given us a moment of trouble. You should be proud of her winning the penmanship award and completing her education. As you promised that day at the courthouse, you have given her a good education. I can see no reason why she shouldn't be rewarded by being able to be with her brother for the remainder of the afternoon. I trust you have a way to get Amy home in time for supper."

"Yes Ma'am, I do. I appreciate you allowing me this time with my sister."

Amy looked to Mr. Coble for confirmation of his wife's offer.

"My wife is correct. This is a special day for Amy. We would be honored if you would be able to join us for supper, Ralph."

Amy shifted her gaze to her brother. "I will have to ask my employer. I'm to do the milking tonight. If I can make arrangements to be gone longer than I anticipated, I will join you. If not, I'll have her home in time for supper."

Amy thanked Mr. and Mrs. Coble before allowing Ralph to take her arm and stroll toward the buckboard he'd brought into town. Once seated, Ralph slapped the reins against the backs of the team and headed out into the country.

Instead of taking the road leading south to the Coble farm, he took the east road. "I want to show you the farm where I've been working," Ralph said.

Amy merely nodded. She enjoyed being away from home and the inevitable chores she should be doing. Even though she worried about leaving the lion's share of the work for Katie, she knew soon Katie would be leaving it for her to do.

After meeting Mr. and Mrs. Peters, Ralph took her home. It saddened her to think her brother hadn't been able to arrange to be gone for the evening milking, but she understood. Work came before socializing and at least they were able to spend a pleasant afternoon together before getting back to the lives and the chores awaiting them.

Chapter Three

Although Amy enjoyed the afternoon spent with her brother, she knew it would not become a common practice. With Katie gone, the work left to Amy had doubled. She now prepared all of the meals for the family and with the exception of going to church on Sunday morning rarely left the farm.

It wasn't that Mr. and Mrs. Coble mistreated her. On the contrary, they made certain she had one good dress and several housedresses so she always looked presentable. They were usually replaced on her birthday in February as well as at Christmas time.

Although she and Katie had shared the chores while Amy went to school, Amy found she could handle most of them alone, with the exception of bringing in the wood for the cook stove. Knowing Katie always chopped the wood and filled the wood box, she asked Mr. Coble about how she should handle this new chore.

"The older boys can take over that duty. I realize until you get used to working alone, it is a lot to ask. To be truthful, before you came to ease Katie's load, I took care of filling the wood box. In time you'll learn how to do it for yourself."

Amy smiled at the thought of John chopping the wood for her. Even though she never joined the other children at recess or lunch hour, she did hear the other girls commenting on how handsome John was and how they hoped he would speak to them. To Amy, the fantasy was of John asking her to be his wife and treating her in a special way. Of course, she knew it was nothing more than a dream. She was a servant and he was a wealthy young man. He looked at her as her brother and he saw her as nothing more than a hired hand. Anything romantic between the two them would be impossible.

On Amy's sixteenth birthday, she received a note from Ralph. He wanted to let her know he was leaving the area in search of work, since Mr. Peters died suddenly and his son-in-law no longer wanted Ralph working on the farm. His note went on to say it was for the best as he and the son-in-law didn't agree about the running of the farm. Secretly Amy knew there was more to his leaving than that. Ralph told her, in secret, of his love for Nancy Peters and the hope of winning her hand in marriage. When she married someone else, it had to have come as quite a blow to his ego.

Instead of dwelling on the fact her brother would be further away from her, she realized they hadn't been close and probably never would be. He was someone who had crossed her path and been important to her for a brief period in her life, nothing more.

At Mr. Coble's request, they hadn't stayed in contact with one another. In all the time she'd been in the Coble home, she'd seen Ralph only once and received one note. Nonetheless, he was her half brother and so she kept his letter in her treasure box, tucked into the back of her dresser drawer.

She often thought of her half sisters, the grown women with families of their own who wanted nothing to do with Amy. She knew she had nieces and nephews, even though she didn't know their names. Each night, her sister's names crossed her lips in prayer and yet she couldn't remember what their faces looked like.

It would have been easy enough to travel the distance between the Coble farm and the one her mother used to own, but she knew it would do no good. The truth of the matter was it had been sold years ago, or at least that was what Mr. Coble told her when she broached the subject several years earlier. Only God knew where her sisters now lived or what their lives were like. It was evident they wanted no contact with her and it was best if she continued on not knowing anything about them.

Just after Amy's sixteenth birthday, she went out one morning to collect eggs. It was one chore she enjoyed, since going out to the henhouse allowed her a moment of freedom. Even the subfreezing temperatures of early March didn't make the trip any less enjoyable.

"I thought I'd find you here," she heard someone say from behind her.

She turned to see John Coble, Mr. Coble's son, standing behind her. "You startled me. Don't you have chores to do in the barn?"

"Maybe I do and maybe I don't. I want to be here with you and nothing else matters. You know, Amy, you've turned into an attractive young woman."

Before she knew what was happening, John pulled her into a tight embrace and kissed her. "I've wanted to do that for a long time," he confessed.

Amy pulled away. "It's not proper. You're like my brother."

"Ah, but that's where things change. I'm not your brother and I've wanted you for a long time. Meet me in the barn tonight and I'll make a woman out of you."

Terrified, Amy picked up her basket of eggs and ran to the house. All the way she worried that Mrs. Coble would know how badly she'd sinned by allowing John to kiss her and she would be punished.

For the next week, John waited for her in the morning at the henhouse. Each day his request was the same. Finally, Amy could stand it no more. "I know I'm not your sister, John, but that's the way I feel about you. What you want to do isn't right. You hear what the preacher says in his sermons. Relations between a man and a woman are for after marriage. I can't even consider doing such a thing with you."

The words she spoke virtually broke her heart since she'd been secretly in love with John for years, but she knew by the look in his brown eyes he didn't share the same love for her. He wanted to do things to her for his pleasure and his pleasure alone.

* * * *

Over the next two years, both of the Coble girls married and moved away from the house. It gave Amy great pleasure to prepare the wedding dinner for both of the couples. These girls were the closest things she had to sisters, even though they looked on her as little more than the hired girl.

Just prior to Amy's eighteenth birthday, John announced he was going to marry Martha Cornwell who lived on the next farm over. Amy remembered Martha from school, but her memories were not fond ones. Martha was a bit of a shrew and treated Amy with contempt whenever she could.

"I don't want Amy working here when I bring Martha into this house," John said one evening over dinner.

"Amy is my ward until her eighteenth birthday," Mr. Coble protested.

"And if my calculations are correct, that birthday will be in February," John countered. "I'm planning to marry Martha in March, so that should give her ample time to find other employment and be gone. Martha wants to take over the running of this house."

"What about me?" Mrs. Coble questioned.

"Your station in this household will remain the same as it always has. Martha is quite capable of running the household and she certainly doesn't need any help from Amy. If you remember, they were never friends in school. Martha doesn't want Amy to have any role here once she moves in as my wife."

The words hit Amy like a slap in the face. Even though she was in the kitchen preparing the dessert and coffee for the family, she heard everything loud and clear. Where would she find work in the middle of winter? February was only a month away. If Mr. Coble abided by John's wishes, she would be on her own with nowhere to turn.

With supper finished, the family retired to the parlor where Mr. and Mrs. Coble would play a spirited game of whist while John would more than likely read one of the books contained in Mr. Coble's library.

Left with the chore of cleaning up the kitchen after supper, Amy set the water on the stove to heat while she cleared the table. Once the dishes were neatly stacked on the sideboard, Amy filled two dishpans with the hot water from the stove.

She'd just plunged her hands into the soapy water of the first pan to begin washing the glasses when she felt a presence behind her. Before she could turn to see who had joined her in the kitchen, she felt someone grasp her upper arms and place a kiss on the back of her neck.

"If you play your cards right you could be my mistress and not have to leave when Martha and I are married. I know I can convince Martha it would be better to have a hired girl than to have to do all the mundane work around the house. Just say the word and you won't have to leave."

Amy's mind whirled. If she gave in to John's request she could continue to stay in the attic room and do the work she'd done since she first came to this home almost fourteen years earlier. It was tempting and yet she knew it was wrong. As his mistress, she would bear his children, if any of his seed took root in her belly, in shame. She couldn't stand that. When she had children, she wanted them to be a product of a loving marriage rather than the lust of a man who reserved his love for his true wife.

"No John, I'll be gone as soon as you and your wife are ready to move in. You don't love me and I don't love you. It wouldn't be right. Anything that might happen between the two of us would be out of your lust. That's not what I want for my future. I'll start looking for work as soon as possible."

"You little fool!" he snarled. "I could give you a good life. I know you don't want to leave this house. What will Ma do without you?"

Amy finally twisted from his grip and turned to face him. "Your mother will have Martha to do the chores I've done all my life. It's time I moved on. There is no reason for me to stay here as your mistress. What would that make any children we might have? I can tell you. They would be branded bastards and since I'm sure no one would know of our arrangement. I would be called a slut or even worse a whore. I don't choose that kind of life for either myself or my children."

Anger flashed from John's eyes. "I said it before and I'll say it again, you're a fool. Leaving this house is not as easy as it sounds. Who knows what kind of people will employ you? At least here you know you will be treated well."

Without warning, John lashed out and struck her across her face.

Memories of the short time she spent in her sister Letty's home flashed through her mind. In all the years she'd been in the Coble home, she hadn't thought of her older sister or the fact she spanked her on a daily basis.

She put her hand to her cheek and trembled in fear. "You're right, John, until this moment, I have been treated well. I wasn't a member of the family, but at least no one ever hit me. All of that has changed tonight. In two weeks I will be eighteen and my bond will be completed. I've worked for this family for almost fourteen years. I am grateful for the training I've received while I've been here. As soon as I can, I will find employment elsewhere. In no way will I be your mistress and have to be subservient to your wife. I wish you no ill, but..."

"There are no buts, Amy. I want you to stay. I want you to be my mistress. I will speak with my father, I'm certain he will agree with me and not allow you to leave this house. You are a bondservant, bought and paid for and as such you are the property of this family. You will do as I say or you will suffer the consequences."

"It will be a cold day in hell before I become your whore. I want nothing to do with you or your lovemaking. I will be happy to leave this place behind. Any fond memories I have of my life here have been tarnished by your proposition tonight."

"Just what is going on out here?" Mr. Coble asked as he stormed into the kitchen. "I could hear the two of you quarrelling all the way into the parlor."

"I was trying to tell Amy she belongs in this house. She was spouting some nonsense about finding employment once she turns eighteen."

Mr. Coble turned to Amy and gasped as he paid close attention to her face. In no way could he avoid seeing the area of her cheek that burned like fire from John's blow.

"What happened to your cheek, Amy? I don't remember seeing a red mark on it when you served us our supper."

Amy looked up and saw the look of anger in John's eyes. Taking a deep breath, she did as she had been trained to do in this household, she told the truth. "John wanted me to stay here and become his mistress once he's married. I do not approve of such a relationship and told him so. When I did, he slapped me. Never before have I been treated badly in this house. Starting tomorrow I will begin looking for employment elsewhere when my bond is up in two weeks."

Without finishing the dishes, she turned on her heel and ran up the stairs to the second floor and then up to the attic. Once in her room she closed the door tightly and pushed the only chair in her room under the doorknob so no one could come into her room during the night. For the first time, she feared for her safety in the Coble home and the sooner she could escape from here the better it would be for her.

Throughout the night, the sounds she once found comforting now frightened her and kept sleep at bay until the first rays of morning light came through her window. Remembering the dishes she'd left in the dishpan, she quickly washed and dressed for the day. At least at this early hour she wouldn't have to contend with John. If he wasn't already out at the barn doing the morning chores, he would soon be getting up to start his day and help his father.

To her surprise the dishes from the night before were done and put away. She had no idea who would have finished them for her, but she said a silent thank you for whoever took pity on her after last night's confrontation with John.

The bread she'd set to rise the night before was ready to be made into loaves so she set to work, taking a bit of the dough to make a coffee cake to go along with the bacon and eggs she planned to serve the family this morning.

"Something certainly smells good this morning," Mrs. Coble said when she entered the kitchen.

Amy turned to acknowledge her employer. The look on the woman's face was the same one she's seen in her own eyes only this morning when she looked into the mirror as she pinned up her hair. The bruise covering her left cheek stood out almost as much as her eyes belied her lack of sleep the night before.

"I am so sorry this has happened to you, Amy. My husband told me everything last night and together we finished cleaning up the

28

kitchen. I have a friend who is looking for a hired girl. Considering what happened between you and John last night, I will take you to meet her as soon as we have finished with our breakfast. I realize we do not have to find a position for you but I feel obligated to you."

Mrs. Coble's concern touched Amy. In all the years she'd lived and worked in this house, there had rarely been a kind word from this woman. Instead of being a child in the household, she had been an unpaid servant for the family.

Chapter Four

On the morning of Amy's eighteenth birthday, she prepared breakfast as she always did. Once she finished cleaning up, Mr. Coble invited her into the parlor.

"The contract I signed when I bought your bond fourteen years ago said you were bonded to our family until your eighteenth birthday. It will be difficult for us until John and Martha are married, but under the circumstances, I can understand your desire to move on with your life. As your present, I have these items for you."

Amy's hands trembled as she touched the box Mr. Coble held out to her. In it she found the contract he had signed for her bond so long ago, a beautiful pendant watch with her initial engraved on the case, a large Bible and ten silver dollars. To Amy it was a fortune and represented the only things she'd ever really owned in her life.

"I don't know what to say," Amy gasped. "The watch and Bible are beautiful and with these silver dollars, I feel as wealthy as anyone in the county."

"I'm glad these things meet with your approval. I know you agreed to stay on until after John's wedding, but Mrs. Gilman is anxious for you to begin working for her. I speak for the entire family when I say we will miss your good cooking as well as the way you keep house. I want to wish you luck in the future. As for your position here, it is officially ended. Mr. Gilman will be here to pick you up within the hour. I am certain this will give you enough time to pack your belongings and be ready to leave."

A lump formed in Amy's throat. All her life she'd been reminded she was nothing more than a bondservant, bought and paid for fourteen years earlier. Now she was being told freedom was hers and with it she would lose the only home she could clearly remember.

Mr. Coble gave her no chance to protest as he turned from her and went out to oversee the morning chores taking place in the barn. With Mrs. Coble in the kitchen, Amy went up to her attic room.

Once there, she packed her few meager belongings into the box she found on top of her bed. Her silver dollars, she placed securely in the inner pocket of her winter cloak. The bond papers, she folded and put in a secure place in the middle of the Bible beside the page for the family tree. Lastly, she took the watch from its resting place in the jeweler's box. Opening it, she gazed upon the delicately painted flowers on its face. It stood in direct contrast to her large boned features. The chain holding it was sturdy and long enough that she didn't have to clasp it. Instead she could easily slip it over her head. With the watch resting in the hollow between her breasts, she looked into the small darkened mirror, which once belonged to Katie. The reflection was not one of a beautiful woman, like the Coble girls, but one of a sturdy woman, the descendant of a half-breed mother and a father she neither knew or remembered.

A light tapping on the door startled her. Would it be John, coming to demand she allow him to take his pleasure with her? Taking a deep breath, she opened the door ready to do battle for the one thing she considered her own, her virtue.

Instead of seeing John standing outside her door, she was surprised to see Mrs. Coble. "I have a small parting gift for you," she said as she stepped into the room.

Rather than concentrate on her former employer's face, Amy couldn't take her eyes from the elegant gown she carried. "This—this is for me?" she questioned as she ran her hands over the fine fabric of the gown.

"I have made a gown such as this for each of my daughters as a gift for their eighteenth birthday. I also had a portrait of them made. My plan was the same for you, but of course you are leaving my home.

31

When I talked with Mrs. Gilman about your employment, I told her I wanted to make an appointment with the photographer in town for you to have such a portrait made. She agreed with me and so as soon as I have the appointment made, I will come and pick you up. I would like to have you wear this dress as well as the watch my husband has given you."

Amy thought of the beautiful portraits of the Coble girls gracing the walls of the parlor. To have her own picture hanging beside them was more than she could have ever hoped for.

"I would be honored. I have thought of you and Mr. Coble as my parents, since I never knew my father and I have no memory of my mother. All I know is what my brother, Ralph, told me when he came to my graduation from the eighth grade."

Tears formed in Mrs. Coble's eyes. "I too have thought of you as a daughter and have been proud of the skills you perfected in my home. I will miss you, but like my own daughters, it is time for you to move on and begin your life. I only pray you will not forget us and keep me informed of your achievements in life."

In a move that came as a surprise, Mrs. Coble, pulled Amy into a tight embrace, crushing the dress between them. For the first time in fourteen years, Amy luxuriated in the love of another human being. It was something she knew she would never forget.

* * * *

The Gilman farm sat ten miles to the east of where Amy spent many hours. This was where Amy Coble would be working, for room and board, and also for a wage. Never before had she been paid for the work she did. In this household she would have something she never dreamed of, a way of supporting herself.

She debated about correcting Mr. and Mrs. Gilman regarding her name, but decided against it. Ralph had called her Annabelle Totten, but in reality, she'd been Amy Coble for far more years than she'd answered to her given name.

Her duties in the Gilman household were relatively light. Mrs. Gilman enjoyed cooking and made the evening meal for the family, leaving breakfast and dinner for Amy to prepare. Until recently, the Gilman's employed a woman to keep house and do the laundry. Unfortunately, she'd become ill and was no longer able to come to work. Now this job would fall to Amy. Once the noon meal on Saturday was served and the kitchen cleaned, Amy would not be needed until Monday morning. The family encouraged her to attend church services with them, but it was not mandatory to her employment.

When she was taken to her room the sheer size of it came as a surprise. The room boasted a large double bed, a chest of drawers, a dresser, a large closet, a washstand and basin and a freestanding mirror. The amount of space reserved for her clothing would remain empty until such time as she could save enough money to purchase new dresses from the store in town.

Mrs. Gilman left her alone in the room so she could get settled. After hanging her new dress as well as the one for church in the closet, she put her undergarments in the drawers of the dresser. In one of the other empty drawers, she placed her new Bible as well as the box, which originally held the pendant watch. She knew this would be nothing she would wear on an every day basis. Instead it would be reserved for when she went to church and when she had her picture taken as Mrs. Coble requested. She also knew it would need to be wound daily, giving her a chance to enjoy the beauty of the only piece of jewelry she'd ever owned.

* * * *

Mrs. Gilman insisted Amy should call her Ellen and Mr. Gilman wanted her to use his first name of George as well. Amy found the work at the Gilman farm to be relatively easy. It soon became apparent to Amy she had much more free time than she'd ever enjoyed in the past. Many evenings she joined Ellen in the kitchen and offered her help in cleaning up after supper.

"You're a hard girl to understand, Amy," Ellen declared after the first week. "I would think you'd want to enjoy your free time rather than helping me in the kitchen."

"What else do I have to do? Ever since I was four years old until I came to you, I worked from the time I got up in the morning until I went to bed at night."

"What about school?" Ellen inquired.

"I went to the school just down the road from the Coble house. I went through all eight grades, but there was little time for study. I did receive the award for perfect penmanship."

"You called it the Coble house, not home," George said from behind her.

Amy was embarrassed to realize he overheard her conversation with Ellen. "The house belonged to Mr. Coble. I wasn't one of his children. Like here, I was a hired girl."

"Did he pay you a wage?"

Amy hung her head. "He bought my bond when I became a ward of the county. I was three years old when my mother died of pneumonia. It took several months, so the county finally decided to sell my bond. I came to live with the family when I was four."

George frowned and shook his head as though in dismay. "That's inhumane. Are you telling me he owned you?"

Amy could only nod. "When I turned eighteen, just before I came here, he gave me a Bible along with the papers that bonded me to him for fourteen years. For the first nine years I worked with Katie, the other hired girl, learning the mysteries of housekeeping. When she left to get married, I took over all of the household chores."

"Do you have any other family?"

"I have a brother. His name is Ralph Totten. Mr. Peters bought his bond."

"Are you in touch with him?"

"I saw him five years ago when I graduated from grade school. He said Mr. Peters was very kind to him. I'm hoping to find the Peters' farm and go and visit him when the weather is better."

George and Ellen exchanged worried glances. "Mr. Peters is dead," George said. "We bought this farm from his daughters four years ago, just after we were married."

Amy mentally calculated the ages of the Gilman children. The older girls were at least ten and twelve and the baby was just walking.

"It's all right, Amy," Ellen said, putting her hand on Amy's shoulder. "I know it's confusing. I worked for George's parents when his first wife died and he moved back home with the children. I make no secret of the fact I fell in love with first the children, and then George. We were married four years ago and heard of this farm being for sale. We decided it was for the best if we left Rock County and moved someplace where the children could adjust better to us being a family."

"Do you know what happened to the people who worked for Mr. Peters?" Amy asked.

"When we got here, everyone was gone," Ellen said. "When we needed a hired man, we asked one of the daughters and she told me the men who worked for her father moved on once he died. She said her mother passed on the year before and just after her father died, she lost her only brother. Since the girls weren't interested in running the farm, the men scattered taking on other jobs. I'm so sorry I don't have better news for you, but we have no idea even where to start looking for your brother."

Amy wiped away her tears. "It's all right. I've spent my entire life without family. It won't hurt me to continue on in the same way."

Several days later, Mrs. Coble came to pick Amy up for the appointment she'd made with the photographer. "I'm so excited," she said as soon as Amy joined the woman who had been part of her life for so long. "We received a letter for you from Madison. Of course we didn't open it, but it was addressed to Miss Annabelle Totten in care of Mr. Joseph Coble. Who would know your given name other than us?"

Amy made no comment, but slipped the letter into her purse. She was certain it came from Ralph and she would once again be reunited with the brother she hadn't seen since the day she graduated from the eighth grade.

The sitting for the portrait took much longer than Amy thought it would, but in the end everyone seemed happy with the way the day went. The photographer assured Mrs. Coble he would have the portrait framed and ready to be picked up in a month.

It made no difference to Amy when the portrait would be ready. She knew if she didn't return to the Coble home she would never see it. This was something Mrs. Coble wanted and nothing more. Although the woman tried to be fair, Amy knew she had no idea whatsoever what Amy's true position within her household had been.

That evening, Amy sat in her room and by the light of the lamp on her nightstand, she prepared to read the letter. Looking at the address on the outside of the envelope, she decided a more ladylike hand had written it. Was it possible Ralph had married and asked his wife to write the letter? Although she had no doubt he was educated she knew most men didn't take the time to write letters and when they did, their handwriting left much to be desired.

After opening the envelope, she pulled out the letter and carefully opened the folded sheets.

> My Dear Annabelle,
>
> I have kept track and know you have reached your eighteenth birthday and your bond to Mr. Coble has ended. I am your sister, Harriett Oswald, and I live in Madison.
>
> I am sure you do not know of our mother's history, but before she married your father, she was married to our father, Charles Mercer. After his death, she knew she couldn't keep the farm going on her own and that is why she married Henry Totten.
>
> Upon his death and then her death, you and your brother, Ralph, became orphans. Please don't judge us too harshly, but my sisters, Letty Ostrum and Ella Leman, and myself had no means to take you into our homes. Therefore, you became a ward of the county. What they did was done to keep you from being sent to an orphan asylum.
>
> I wanted to stay in touch with you, but Mr. Coble said it would do you no good to be in contact with us. I did not agree with his decision, but at the time it would

have done me no good to argue with him.

I hope you will forgive what we had no control over. I will give you my address and hope you will see fit to correspond with me so we can create a family relationship again.

Your loving sister,
Harriett

Amy refolded the letter and thought about the address on the top corner. When she'd first taken the envelope from Mrs. Coble, she'd paid no attention to it, but now it jumped out at her.

The fact she had family living in Madison made little difference to her. From what she'd learned in school, Madison wasn't that far away from where she lived, but it might as well be on the moon. There was no way she could ever afford the train fare to get there and once she did, she had no idea how to find the address she now held in her hand.

Instead of dwelling on what seemed entirely impossible, Amy took a sheet of paper from the desk Ellen and George provided for her and wrote a letter to be posted the next time George went to town.

Dear Harriett,

Thank you for your letter. You are right, I do not know any of the history of my mother or any of my family for that matter. I am now known by the name Amy Coble and have been since the day I went to live with the Coble family.

Since I have lived my entire life without knowing of you, your letter was a welcome addition to my knowledge of my family. I am sorry Mr. Coble forbade you to contact me, but those days are past. I doubt, however, that we will ever meet, for Madison is a long way from where I now live. The cost of making such a trip is far beyond my means. I will stay in touch with you through letters and hope your life is as you planned it.

In the meantime, I am working for George and Ellen Gilman as a hired girl. The work is not hard and I am being paid a fair wage. It is so unlike the home I had with Mr. and Mrs. Coble. I do go to church and upon my eighteenth birthday, Mr. Coble gave me my own Bible along with a fine watch and ten silver dollars. In other words, I am happy with my life and someday hope to find a good man to marry and have a family of my own.

I encourage you to keep in touch with me and I will do my best to answer your letters in a timely manner.

Your sister,
Amy Belle Coble

Chapter Five

For the next three years, Amy corresponded occasionally with her sister in Madison and worked contentedly for the Gilman family. In the spring of 1910 a new hired man came to the farm. His name was Ruben Derr. The gangly man with a hawk nose and brown hair that was thinning on top and reached his shoulders intrigued her in a way no other man touched her emotions in her entire life.

Ruben had been born in Illinois, but moved to Iowa with his family at a young age. Now at the age of thirty, he'd been on his own working on various farms around the area. To Amy's delight, his friend, Ralph Totten, worked with him on a farm just two years earlier.

Since their days off corresponded with each other, Ruben and Amy began spending much of their free time together. On one mild September Sunday, George allowed them to use the buggy and drive over to the farm where Ralph worked as a hired hand. When they left the farm, Amy had no idea where they were headed.

"Are we going somewhere special?" she asked, eyeing the picnic basket Ellen prompted her to pack sitting at her feet.

"Very special," Ruben replied.

After about an hour's ride, a very neat farm with a red barn and white house appeared on their right. Instead of turning into the lane leading to the house, Ruben turned the team in the opposite direction. At the end of the dirt track, Amy squealed with delight at the sight of a slow moving stream in front of them.

"I thought this would be a nice place for us to have our picnic,"

Ruben announced. While Ruben unhitched the team and allowed them to graze, Amy spread the blanket on the grass next to the stream.

"It's good to see you again, Annabelle," someone said from behind her.

She turned to face the man behind the voice and stared into the eyes of her brother Ralph. Although he looked older than he had when he came to her graduation from grade school, she recognized him immediately.

"Ralph! I can't believe you're really here."

"I could hardly believe it when Ruben told me he'd met this beautiful girl named Amy Coble. I immediately told him I thought he was talking about my sister and wanted to be able to meet her. He arranged this picnic. If it hadn't been for Ruben, I would have never tracked you down. I went to the Coble farm after your eighteenth birthday but the son wouldn't tell me where you were working. After that, I moved from farm to farm, you know, wherever I was needed."

Amy didn't care about any of that. All she knew was the irony of the situation was that now she was living and working in the house where he grew up.

"You must know I'm working and living at the old Peters' place and working for Ellen and George Gilman. They told me Mr. and Mrs. Peters both died and their daughters put the farm up for sale. From what I can see, you had a nice home to grow up in."

A look of sorrow crossed Ralph's face and radiated from his eyes. "They were good people," he finally replied. "I sure didn't want to leave there, but I had no other choice. I went to see Mr. Coble right after I learned I would be needing to find a different place to work. At the time he refused to let me see you even to say good-bye. I told him he was being unfair, but he said that didn't matter. He'd been the one to buy your bond and he insisted you live by his rules."

Amy hugged him tightly before turning her attention to Ruben. He'd engineered this surprise reunion and she loved him for it. With Ralph working so close to the Gilman farm, Amy knew they wouldn't lose touch with each other again.

* * * *

By the beginning of November, Amy realized she was pregnant. While she lived with Mr. and Mrs. Coble, she went to church and read her Bible. Nothing she'd learned there prepared her for a baby without being married.

Although Amy wanted to keep her condition a secret, she knew once she started to show everyone would know what she'd been doing. The thought of the coming baby frightened and excited her. For the first time in her life, she would have something that belonged to her and her alone. She knew she'd have to tell Ruben about the child and prayed he would be excited about the coming of a baby.

After telling Ruben about the situation, they went to talk with Ellen and George. They immediately insisted a wedding should be planned. The prospect of finally being a wife was an exciting one. At the same time, she debated her love for the older man who breezed into her life, took her virginity and soon would become her husband and father to her unborn child.

Time went quickly and soon it was December. Not only did it signify the holiday of Christmas, but also her quickly approaching wedding. Although they would both move into Amy's room in the house, George insisted for a wedding present, he would assist Ruben in finding a farm he could work as a tenant. To Amy's surprise, Mr. and Mrs. Coble not only came to the small wedding but also gave them a dining table with matching chairs and a sideboard.

"I have always thought of you as a daughter," Mrs. Coble said once the marriage vows were spoken. "Will you allow me to act as a grandmother to your child?"

Mrs. Coble's request took Amy by surprise. All her life she'd longed for a mother's love and now when she was about to become a mother herself, Mrs. Coble was offering her what she wanted more than anything else.

As soon as the wedding dinner ended, Ruben changed his clothes and went out to the barn to do the evening milking. Amy knew the next morning she would be expected to make the bread and prepare the morning meal. The only change in her life would be the etched gold band on the third finger of her left hand and the dining furniture waiting for a permanent home in the future.

The next few months passed quickly and soon it was the first of March, the time when tenant farmers moved from one farm to another. The place George and Ruben found for them to live was about three miles east of the Gilman farm in Green County.

As one set of renters moved out, George, Ruben and Ralph worked at moving in the furniture they'd been accumulating from either the peddler who often came to the farms or as gifts from people who wanted to get rid of extra pieces they kept stored in outbuildings for such an occasion. The only thing Amy knew was actually hers was the new dining set from Mr. and Mrs. Coble.

Before it was time for evening chores, Ruben returned to the farm and picked up Amy in the buckboard. Snow fell continually all day, making the drive back to their new home longer than it would have normally been. All through the trip, Amy wondered what her new home would look like.

Finally, they pulled into the dooryard of the two story white farmhouse with a red barn silhouetted in the fading late winter sunlight. After stopping the wagon at the house, he took her inside and showed her around. He also told her he was going out to milk and since there was food in the pantry, he expected his supper waiting for him when he returned.

She looked around the house. Even knowing Ruben and the other men tried to make it a home, she was disappointed. Other than the dining room table, all of the furnishings were ones left by the previous tenants. With the birth of her baby only three months away, she knew she shouldn't be moving the furniture, but she vowed that once her child was born, she would move things into positions that were much more to her liking. If she could persuade Ruben to spend the money, she would go into town and buy material to make new curtains. For now, she knew her life would continue as it always had, keeping house, cooking meals, and learning to love the stranger she now called her husband.

Over the next three months, Ralph became a frequent visitor at the Derr farm. For the first time since she was four years old her name belonged to her and she was officially Amy Belle Derr. Even to Ralph it no longer mattered when she didn't answer to Annabelle.

By June, Amy was large and getting around her home seemed nearly impossible. Late in the afternoon on the twenty-first of the month, she felt the first twinges of labor pains and sent Ruben to bring Ellen back to assist with the birth.

The hour it took for Ralph to return was the longest hour of her life. The labor pains she'd only heard described were worse than anything she ever expected. Before Ellen could arrive Amy's water broke doubling her over in pain. As soon as the worst of it passed, she made her way to the spare bedroom with its bed covered with a canvas to protect the mattress covering the ropes supporting it.

Darkness had fallen when Ellen finally arrived. She immediately reassured Amy she'd sent Ruben to town for the doctor and George left their milking for the hired man so he could take care of Ruben's cows. The only reply Amy could make was to grit her teeth against the pain and nod.

At ten the following morning, the cries of a newborn filled the farmhouse. Freddie Ruben Derr had finally entered the world as a heavyweight. Ellen estimated his birth weight as being well over eleven pounds. Considering the birth had been a dry one, Amy was completely drained.

Long after Freddie was cleaned up and placed in his father's arms, the doctor finally left Amy's room. "It was a hard birth," he told Ruben. "It's doubtful Amy will ever have any more children. It's a blessing to have a healthy son to carry on your name and I promise your wife will recover from this ordeal completely."

Ruben shrugged his shoulders. "I'm the youngest of seven children. I have plenty of brothers to carry on my family name. I'm just relieved to know Amy and our son are all right."

* * * *

For ten days after Freddie's birth, Amy reluctantly allowed Ellen and Mrs. Coble to care for her and the baby, to say nothing of taking over Amy's household duties. Never in her life had she laid abed and been waited on hand and foot. Even though she wanted to protest, Amy knew she didn't have the strength to even take care of her newborn son.

Worse than the forced confinement was the fact the doctor told her she would never have more children. All her life, she'd envisioned herself as the mother of a large family and now that dream was completely shattered.

Freddie was a big healthy baby. Every few hours someone brought him to her to nurse. Luckily, her body was able to produce enough milk to satisfy his healthy appetite.

When at last she was able to do for herself, she continued to take things easy. Ruben surprisingly understood. While she prepared meals, he insisted on cleaning up afterwards. It seemed as though in addition to the fieldwork and barn chores, he seemed pleased to be able to help Amy in the house.

By August, she again regained her strength and enjoyed all of the baby firsts Freddy displayed daily. While Freddie slept, Amy took the opportunity to make contact with her oldest sister.

My Dear Harriett,

I'm sorry it's been so long since I last wrote. On June twenty-second, I gave birth to Freddie. Unfortunately, the doctor says because of the difficulty of the birth it is possible I will not be able to have more children. I've always wanted a large family, but now know I must be content with only my son.

After being in bed for ten days, I am slowly regaining my strength. It is a delight to watch as Freddie goes from helpless baby to a happy child. Each day he learns something new. He reaches for bright colored objects and has found his voice. Considering I will never again have another baby, I am enjoying every minute of his childhood.

At this point in my life, I wish I could meet you and talk face to face, but Madison is a million miles away from the farm. I do look forward to your letters.

Your loving sister,
Amy

Chapter Six

From the moment of his birth, Freddie continued to be a healthy active child. As a toddler, Amy was hard put to keep up with him. By the age of three he spent every waking minute trailing Ruben around the farm, be it in the fields or the barn.

He'd just turned five when Ruben bought him his own pony. Being able to ride all over the farm gave him more freedom than ever and Amy many anxious moments.

It was a particularly warm October afternoon when Freddie came into the house crying. A fall from his pony left him with a broken arm. While Ruben hitched the team to the wagon for the trip to town to go to the doctor's office to have it set, Amy comforted her sobbing son.

"My pony was bad. Pa should shoot him. He hurt me."

Amy ignored his ranting, knowing when he was no longer in pain he would be anxious to once again be riding his pony. Luckily by the time his arm healed, winter would hit the Wisconsin countryside with a vengeance and pony riding would have to wait until the weather again warmed.

By spring, Freddie was more than ready to get out of the house and again ride his pony. With him outside playing, Amy reflected on herself at the same age. As soon as she celebrated her sixth birthday, she remembered looking forward to going to school. In comparison, Freddie showed no excitement about the possibility of going to the one room school less than a mile from the farm where they lived.

She ached at Freddie's reluctance to get an education, but decided even though he favored her in looks, where education was concerned he took after his father.

Ruben often told her of his forced schooling and how he'd learned enough to do arithmetic, read and write before leaving school at the age of twelve in order to help his father on the farm.

"Is that what you want for Freddie?" she asked one night after their son was in bed.

"I don't see the need for schooling. Freddie will be a farmer, like me. I agree, he does need to know how to read and write and do his sums. Beyond that, his going to school is a waste of time. Thank goodness he'll still be able to enjoy his summers."

Although Freddie dragged his feet when it was time to go to school, he enjoyed being with the other children at the school. By the time September came and his second grade year loomed, he seemed anxious to return.

One day, when Freddie was in school, Amy received a letter from Harriett.

> Dear Amy,
>
> It is with a heavy heart that I write this letter to you. My youngest daughter Catherine has gotten herself in trouble. I don't know how I will be able to face my friends when they learn she is going to have a baby without the benefit of marriage.
>
> I know it is a lot to ask, but is it at all possible for Catherine to come and stay with you and Ruben until her child is born? She does not want the baby, but perhaps you could find it in your hearts to either take the child or find a loving family for it.
>
> I look forward to your reply.
> > Your sister,
> > Harriett

Amy was still pondering the letter when Ruben came in for the noon meal. "I had a letter from Harriett today," she said as they sat across the table from each other.

Ruben rolled his eyes. In the past he'd been vocal about the fact Amy heard nothing from her older sisters until after her eighteenth birthday. He told her Ralph had confided after their mother died, Letty took them into her home only to relinquish their custody to the county and sealing their fate. Even so, other than Ralph, these women were the only family she had in the world.

"Her daughter, Catherine, is going to have a baby, but she isn't married. Harriett wants to know if she can stay with us until the child is born."

"There's more to it than you're saying, Amy. I can hear it in your voice. What else does your sister want?"

Amy paused for a moment to collect her thoughts. "She asked if we could find a family to take the child."

"What you aren't saying is you want the baby to belong to us."

"Oh, Ruben, you know I do." Tears streamed down her cheeks. "I always wanted a big family, but we both know without this baby it will never happen."

Ruben reached across the table and took Amy's hand in his. "I love you, Amy, and if this is what you want, so be it. Before we were married, we talked about a family. On a farm, there can never be too many children. If you want to raise this child as our own, we can do it. To make things easier to explain, I'll look for a larger farm to rent. We've been here for a long time. I think we can make more money on a farm with more acreage."

Although Amy didn't like the idea of moving, she knew they'd spent eight years on this farm and a larger one would bring in more money. By summer when the new baby joined their family, Freddie would be old enough to help with the fieldwork.

After Ruben went back out to the barn, Amy sat down to write a reply to her sister.

Dear Harriett,
    I am terribly sorry for your troubles. Over the noon meal, Ruben and I talked about this and would welcome

Catherine into our home. We will also keep the child and raise it even giving it a legal name. Since it seems a though we cannot have any more children, this child will be most welcome in our family.

Please let me know when we can expect Catherine. In the meantime, I will begin preparing a room for her.

Your sister,
Amy

Two weeks later Amy met her eldest sister for the first time. By noon Harriett and her husband, Aaron, arrive at the farm in their motorcar. With them was a very sullen sixteen-year-old Catherine.

"You don't know how much we appreciate what you're doing for us," Aaron said as soon as they arrived.

Amy sensed her brother-in-law's embarrassment over the condition of his youngest daughter. It made her almost glad to have been an orphan when she and Ruben found themselves in the same situation. She knew she'd been lucky to have someone like Ruben as the father of her child. He'd never questioned his need to marry her and fulfill his responsibility to their son. Now he was even willing to take on another man's child in order to make his wife happy.

While she put dinner on the table, Amy assessed her eldest sister. It was evident Harriett bore more of a resemblance to her father, the mysterious Mr. Mercer, than to their mother. The only feature to even remotely remind Amy of herself was Harriett's brown eyes.

Rather than dressing in a plain housedress like Amy wore, Harriett's navy blue suit with its white ruffled blouse were evidence of the wealth of her husband.

By two, Harriett and Ted left for the return trip to Madison with the promise to send money on a monthly basis to pay for the needs of Catherine and later her child.

Amy was amazed by how quickly Catherine adapted to life on the farm. She helped Amy with the housework and as she did, she confided the details of her ill-fated love life.

According to Catherine, she'd been seduced by one of their

neighbors who was a married man. When she told him about the baby, he'd denied it being his, leaving her not only with the shame, but also nowhere for her child to go.

Amy ached for the young girl, but secretly rejoiced at the prospect of having a new baby in her house to care for.

On the first of March, the family moved to a farm closer to Argyle and back into Lafayette County. Freddie would be going to a new school, and this time, Amy was able to help with the move. Excited over her new home, she and Catherine worked making new curtains for the windows and settled in to the daily routine of life on the farm. Catherine had also received money to purchase material in order to make some larger clothing. Amy would have offered her some of the things she wore, but she knew they would be way too large since Catherine was much smaller than Amy.

To Amy's delight, the farm was much larger than the one where they had begun their married life. One of the outbuildings contained a good-sized chicken coop with an established flock of chickens. On their first farm they only kept a few chickens for their eggs and they roosted in the barn. Here, Amy would be able to raise chickens for the table as well as eggs for the house with enough to sell in town.

When school let out, Freddie enjoyed helping with the chickens. Even though they pecked at him he gathered the eggs and brought them into the house so his mother could get them ready for market.

Amy realized life on the farm was a completely new experience for Catherine. Having been brought up in the city, she had no idea where the food her mother put on the table every day really came from. Most of the food Amy prepared was something grown on the farm. Of course coffee, sugar and flour were bought in town, but with the canning Amy did in the fall and the jelly and jams she made in the summer, their root cellar was always filled with nutritious fruits and vegetables for the entire winter.

"Aunt Amy, how long do you want me to stay with you and Uncle Ruben?" Catherine asked one morning closer to the time of her delivery.

Amy thought for a moment before answering. She and Ruben had been discussing the matter ever since Catherine's arrival. "We have talked about it. The baby will need to be nursed and of course, I will be unable to do so. It would be best if you stay with us until the child is weaned."

Catherine agreed and fanned herself against the unbearable July heat. With the baby due any day, Amy was glad Freddie was born in June before the heat of summer set in.

It was just after breakfast on August second when Catherine's labor began. Amy worried as she remembered her own delivery with its disastrous aftermath. Would the same thing happen to Catherine, and if it did would they still be able to keep the baby?

Even though Catherine was young, her labor went quickly and by four in the afternoon, Harriett Leila was born with no complications. Amy was delighted at the prospect of having a beautiful daughter to raise and was pleased when Catherine decided to name the child after her mother. Her only prayer was that when the girl became old enough to be weaned, Catherine would be willing to return to her life in Madison and forget the precious child she just delivered.

Day by day Amy's fears became even more pronounced as Catherine's strength returned and she took over the feeding and care of her daughter. As Harriett's first birthday approached, Amy watched Catherine trying to distance herself from the little girl.

When at last Harriett could drink her milk from a cup, Catherine packed her belongings and prepared to leave the farm where she'd lived for almost two years,

"Won't you miss Harriett?" Ruben questioned as they waited for Ted and Harriet to arrive and take their now eighteen-year-old daughter back to Madison and the social life she'd left behind.

"Of course I'll miss her, but I could have never given her the life she deserves. You and Aunt Amy will always be special to me and I will miss you terribly. I'm content knowing you and Aunt Amy will give her a good life and raise her as your own."

Amy breathed a sigh of relief after overhearing the conversation not meant for her ears. As soon as Catherine left the farm, Harriett would become her daughter to raise and love.

Chapter Seven

Catherine left in September, leaving Amy feeling complete with her family. At Christmastime, she received yet another letter from one of her Mercer sisters. This time it was Ella's daughter, Flossie, who was in a family way.

It took more pleading to get Ruben to allow Flossie to come to the farm until yet another child would be born and given to them in August.

"I think your sisters are taking advantage of you. Who will be next, Letty?"

Amy thought for a moment before answering. "I doubt I'll ever hear from Letty. From what Ralph has told me, Letty wanted nothing to do with us when our mother died. I doubt she will ever want to send one of her children to me and allow me to raise her grandchild. Harriet and Ella are different. They have respect for me, which is more than I can say for Letty."

Ruben finally agreed and awaited Flossie's arrival at the farm.

Like Catherine before her, Flossie settled in at the farm and helped with everything from housework to caring for Harriett. On August twelfth she gave birth to a baby boy. Like Catherine, Flossie had a name picked out and insisted she wanted to name her child Ralph Eugene.

The name was, in no way, one Amy would have chosen. With her brother both having the same name, she certainly didn't want a son named Ralph as well. Unfortunately, Flossie had been the one who carried the boy for nine months and given birth to him. Therefore, naming him was her right.

Ralph was a good baby but he nursed longer than Harriett. Amy was certain Flossie didn't want to leave her son, even if she knew it was for the best.

Almost three years since her arrival at the farm, Flossie prepared to leave. Before going back to her parents' home, she insisted on going into town. While there, she visited a photographer and had a portrait taken to be left on Ralph's dresser.

At last Flossie returned to her family and Amy became Ralph's mother in every sense of the word. For a few days, Ralph cried for Flossie. Soon he attached himself to Harriett and followed her around, imitating her every move. Being so close in age, their bond was expected. Unfortunately, Freddie, now age twelve considered himself far too old to be bothered with his younger brother and sister.

There was also a down side to Ralph's attachment to Harriett. With Flossie staying at the farm for a longer period of time than Catherine, she had been the center for Ralph's world for over two years. As a result, Amy found it hard to bond with this, her third child.

The year Harriett turned six, she looked as forward to going to school as Freddie did to having completed the mandatory eight grades. Now he was able to stay on the farm and help Ruben. His work schedule included cleaning the barns, helping in the field and doing the night milking with his father. As for the morning milking, he showed no desire to get out of bed early enough to join his father in the barn for morning chores.

Once Harriett was in school, Amy took the opportunity to get to know her youngest son better. He had a mind of his own and proved to be a ball of energy. His black hair and piercing brown eyes bespoke his connection to his great grandmother, Amy's mother. The way he could sneak up behind her without making a sound also branded him as being more Indian than white.

While Ralph stayed by Amy's side during the long days of winter, she knew he longed for Harriett to return home from school and share what she learned and could teach him.

This boy, Amy thought, *will not be content to be a farmer. He has a thirst for education. I only pray Ruben will understand this need and nurture it.*

* * * *

"I don't understand that boy," Ruben said as he watched Ralph and Harriett playing in the front yard. "When Freddie was his age, he wasn't playing silly games with a little girl. He was out with me whenever he could be and riding his pony."

Ruben's statement saddened Amy. "When Freddy was Ralph's age, he had no one to play with. You were his only playmate and you gave into his every whim. Have you bought a pony for Ralph?"

"You know I haven't. Money is tight and he's shown no interest in learning to be a farmer or a man for that matter. Tomorrow morning, he will start helping me with the milking. Maybe hard work will wipe that smile from his face. It's not natural for a man to smile as much as that boy does. Another thing, I want that damnable picture of Flossie out of his room."

Amy thought of protesting, but what good would it do her? She was the one who begged him to raise the children who, in reality, were his grandniece and grandnephew.

Early the next morning, she heard Ruben go into Ralph's room to wake him. It broke her heart to think of a five-year-old boy doing morning chores while Freddie lay in bed asleep in the next room. Against her better judgment, she lit the lamp and went into Ralph's room to remove the picture of Flossie from the dresser.

By the time breakfast was ready, Freddie and Harriett were both up and dressed for the day. They had just sat down at the table when Ruben and Ralph came in from the barn. Without a word of protest, Ralph watched as his father poured warm water from the kettle on the stove to a bowl by the sink and waited his turn to wash up.

"How did the milking go this morning?" Amy asked as they seated themselves at the table.

"Pa showed me how to milk a cow, Ma," Ralph said, excitement sounding in his voice. "He said if I help with the milking in the mornings, I can walk to school with Harriet when it's time for her to start going again."

Amy was confused. "But you're too young to go to school."

"I know, but I told Pa Harriett shouldn't be walking to school alone. I can go with her and then come home. He said if I do my chores I could do whatever I want."

Amy cast a questioning glance at Ruben. His nod of acknowledgment almost broke her heart. She hadn't thought much of Harriett going to school by herself, but with Freddie finishing the eighth grade last spring, it would leave her alone to walk the mile to school. Ralph wanting to walk with his sister certainly didn't come as a surprise, since he was very protective of her.

"I told Ralph how everyone needs to work on a farm. I showed him what to do and he took to it like a duck to water. He milked two cows by himself this morning." The tone of Ruben's voice was one of pride for his youngest son for the first time in Ralph's life.

"Only two cows?" Freddie scoffed. "I can milk six cows when I help with the milking at night. I don't think two cows is anything to be proud of."

Amy studied Ralph's expressive eyes. It was evident Freddie was taunting the boy, but he took it as a challenge. She knew it wouldn't be long before Ralph matched his older brother's expertise and became proficient at milking.

"You have to remember," Ruben admonished, "your brother is much younger than you are. Give him time and he might even be a better farmer than you."

A frown of disgust and anger crossed Freddie's face. Amy realized Ruben's was meant as a challenge, but Freddie had taken it as a slap in the face. Always a sullen child, Amy worried about his competitiveness with a brother ten years his junior.

The next morning Ruben got up and went directly out to milk. Amy smiled to think taking Ralph out to the barn yesterday had been meant as a lesson about responsibility and nothing more.

Getting out of bed, she dressed for the day before going downstairs to start fixing breakfast. To her surprise, Ralph's door stood open, his bed made up in a childish way. Amy knew he'd been in bed the night before so his absence this morning baffled her.

Unable to find Ralph in any other room of the house, she began to panic. Was it possible Ruben's insistence that Ralph go out to the barn and Freddie's challenge prompted her youngest child to run away from home?

She was still questioning Ralph's absence when Freddie and Harriet came down to breakfast. They were just sitting down at the table when the door opened. Amy turned to ask Ruben what he thought about Ralph's disappearance. Before she could begin, she saw Ralph dressed in barn clothes.

"Ralph was waiting for me when I came down this morning," Ruben declared. "I was surprised when I didn't have to wake him."

Amy breathed a sigh of relief. Secretly, she wondered if Ruben insisting Ralph help with chores when Freddie wanted nothing to do with something that got him out of bed would be upsetting to her youngest son. With school starting in a week, Amy knew Ralph was doing the chores in exchange for something he wanted to do more than anything else in the world.

* * * *

On the first day of school, Ralph rushed into the house ahead of Ruben. He quickly washed and ran up to his room. Amy watched him, realizing how excited he was about Harriett's first day at school.

"If I live to be a hundred, I'll never understand that boy," Ruben declared when he came in from the barn. "He worked like a demon this morning and as soon as we let the cows out to go to the pasture, he bolted for the house. Where did he get off to now?"

"He went up to his room," Amy replied.

"Why would he go up there?"

Amy shook her head in amazement. Ever since Ralph started helping with the milking all he'd talked about was walking Harriett to school. How could Ruben not realize the long awaited day finally arrived?

"It's the first day of school, Pa," Harriett answered. "Ralph knows

I don't want to walk to school alone. He promised me I wouldn't have to go by myself."

"Don't see what you have to be scared of," Freddie teased. "The problem is you're nothing but a silly girl. I walked to school alone before you started going last year and I wasn't scared."

Harriett's face screwed into a frown. Amy feared she was going to cry as she often did when Freddie teased her. As Amy recalled, she walked Freddie to school for the first three years because of his fear to walk alone. Added to that, if Freddie hadn't had to repeat the fourth grade because he was so far behind because of a move the previous spring he wouldn't have been in the eighth grade when Harriett started school. Thank goodness he was always small for his age and none of his schoolmates questioned why he was older than they were.

Before Amy could say anything to defuse the situation, Ralph came back into the kitchen. "It's okay, Harriett. I promised to walk you to school so there's no need to worry."

Amy smiled at Ralph's appearance. His usually unruly shock of black hair was neatly combed. He'd also put on a clean shirt and pants. Even his play shoes had been freshly shined, making her wonder how late he'd stayed up the night before to get ready for today.

"Who's going to help me with the barn chores?" Ruben inquired.

Ralph was crestfallen while Freddie looked out the window in disinterest. Amy was sure Freddie hoped Ruben wouldn't consider asking him to do the morning barn chores Ralph had taken over since his fifth birthday in August.

"You promised, Pa," Ralph pleaded. "I'll help with the night milking if I can do this for Harriett."

It took a moment for Ruben to consider what Ralph just said and voice his opinion. At long last he agreed Ralph could walk Harriett to school.

Being still early, Amy insisted everyone needed to have a good meal to start the day.

As soon as they finished eating breakfast, Ralph made certain Harriett had her slate and lunch pail. Once she was ready to leave, Ralph took her hand and together they walked out the door.

"Can't see why he's so excited to take Harriett to school," Freddie commented. "I'm happy it ain't me going to that school. The best day of my life was when I knew I didn't have to go there anymore. Ralph doesn't know anything about school. Once he has to go all the time, he'll change his tune."

Amy ached at what her son just said. When she was his age, she craved the educational opportunities the other Coble children enjoyed. Instead she attended school on a daily basis, but never had the luxury of doing homework like the rest of the family. Had she been able to study, Amy knew she would have been an outstanding student. She prayed Harriett and Ralph possessed the eager minds Freddie lacked.

Although Freddie protested, saying morning chores were Ralph's job, Ruben insisted his son accompany him to the barn. As much as Amy hated to admit it, Freddie was lazy. She doubted he would ever amount to anything.

Throughout the morning, Amy did her daily chores, but kept one eye on the dooryard watching for Ralph to return from school. When noon came and he still wasn't home, she seemed to be the only one concerned by his absence.

"Don't know why you're so upset, Amy?" Ruben commented. "You know how that boy is. He's probably down by the creek or watching the squirrels hiding their nuts for the winter. He's a dreamer and when he gets in that mood, he loses all track of time."

By mid afternoon, Amy saw Harriett and Ralph coming into the yard. As soon as they entered the house, she noticed the gleam in Ralph's eyes. "Where have you been all day?" she asked, before Ralph could go up to his room to change into his barn clothes.

"I waited for Harriett. When she came out for recess and lunch, I played with the other kids."

"Weren't you lonely waiting outside all by yourself?"

Ralph shook his head. "At recess, the teacher said if I wanted to stay, I could sit by her desk."

Amy smiled at the excitement in Ralph's voice.

"The teacher even gave Ralph a slate so he could practice his letters," Harriett explained. "She even said if it was all right with you he could come back tomorrow."

Amy considered what Harriett just said. Last year, Ralph waited anxiously for Harriett to get home so she could show him what she'd learned. It was entirely possible he had the same knowledge as his sister and could easily do the second grade work. "We'll talk to your pa about it tonight. I don't see any harm in it, but I worry it will be too much for you with your morning chores."

"I won't have any problems," Ralph promised. "I have to get my clothes changed so I can go out and help Pa like I said I would."

It saddened Amy to see her youngest son turn down the plate of cookies she put on the table earlier in order to work even harder to gain his father's approval. She'd always had an after school snack ready for the children when they came home and as she recalled, Freddie was eager to eat more than his share leaving little or nothing for his younger brother and sister.

With his clothes changed, Ralph came back downstairs, grabbed a cookie and went out to the barn. It didn't take long for Freddie to come back into the house.

"Aren't you helping your father?" Amy inquired.

"I helped with the morning chores, the ones Ralph was supposed to do. I didn't think he'd come out to help with the night chores, but he surprised me. Pa certainly didn't need both of us out there. Besides I've done enough work for one day."

He grabbed the remainder of the cookies on the plate and went back outside to sit in the swing and eat them. From the open kitchen window, Amy could hear Freddie taunting Harriett because he had the rest of the cookies and she couldn't have any. She looked up to see the tussle between her oldest son and her only daughter. As she watched the scene unfolding, Ralph came out of nowhere and challenged his older brother. She equated her youngest son with one of the little roosters who always wanted to challenge the other chickens for the spot of top rooster in the henhouse.

"Share those cookies with Harriett," Ralph demanded. "She's littler than you are. You're her big brother and should be looking out for her, not teasing her."

"And what does that make you? The way I see it, you're like a pesky little mosquito buzzing around my ear, so why don't you fly away. I thought you were going to be doing the night chores with Pa. The way I see it, I did your morning chores, so you'd best get to work."

To Amy's astonishment Ralph began to pummel Freddie with his small fists, landing blows one after another. In the end, Ralph returned to the barn and Freddie reluctantly shared his cookies with Harriett.

The way this first confrontation between Ralph and Freddie played out, Amy knew her younger, adopted son would always be superior to his older brother. Ralph's thirst for knowledge and drive to be the best far surpassed Freddie's negative attitude and natural laziness.

Once the children were in bed, Amy pleaded Ralph's case to Ruben. "Ralph has a thirst for education. I recognize it because it's the same thirst I had at his age. If he has this chance to go to school, then I think we should allow him to do so."

"I don't see what good school will do him. Freddie went through all eight grades and as you can see it's done him no good. I thought it might make him a better farmer, but he has no interest in work whatsoever."

"That's my point. In addition to going to school, Ralph is still anxious to go out to the barn and help you with the chores. I can't say I approve of him doing the morning and evening milking while Freddie does little than the day chores. Of course, if his taking on more of the work gets him an education, I'll help him all I can with his studies."

The argument went on long into the night, but at last Ruben agreed to Ralph going to school rather than waiting another year until he was old enough to actually attend classes.

Chapter Eight

Life for Amy and her family fell into a predictable routine. Ralph was up and out in the barn before Ruben each morning. Once the milking was done, he rushed to the house to get cleaned up so he could go to school.

Freddie would get up in time for breakfast and grumble about having to do the chores he felt were Ralph's responsibility. Once the daily chores were done, Freddie either spent the evening in his room or rode to town on his horse. He always returned home in time for supper, but never offered to go out to help with the evening milking.

Harriett, although not enamored with school, enjoyed having Ralph walk her to and from every day and eventually made friends. Unfortunately, every two to three years, Ruben decided to move to a different farm, leaving Ralph and Harriett to make new friends in a new school.

The constant moving was hard on Amy. Even though she'd been a servant in the Coble household, her home life had been a stable one. With Mr. Coble owning his farm, she knew all of the children she went to school with and eventually got to know ones who moved into the district the first of every March. She hardly remembered moving to the Coble home, but once she turned eighteen and went out on her own she moved almost constantly. Afraid she'd become like her brother, Ralph, she was thrilled when Ruben told her they would be tenant farmers. What he hadn't told her was his urge to move on to larger farms often.

It was a beautiful late spring day, shortly after their latest move. She enjoyed the beauty of her new home and the thought of school being dismissed for the summer. Having Harriett and Ralph home for the summer would be wonderful. Harriett, at the age of eleven, was now able to help around the house. She'd even expressed an interest in learning how to cook and can the vegetables from the garden.

Absently, Amy set a plate of cookies on the table in anticipation of the children's return from school. Still lost in her thoughts, she heard Ralph rush through the door. "Ma! Ma! Harriett's sick. I left her at the end of the lane cuz she's too tired to walk any more. She says her head hurts and she's puking."

"What's going on?" Ruben demanded when he came into the kitchen just as Ralph finished his plea for help. "Where's Harriett?"

Amy quickly related the story Ralph told her. Once she finished, Ruben turned toward the door to go in search of their daughter.

"I'll go with you, Pa," Ralph said running to keep up with Ruben's larger strides. "I know where she is. I tried to make her comfortable but I couldn't carry her home."

Without further conversation, Ruben allowed Ralph to take the lead. Amy's heart pounded in anticipation of what they would find. Harriett couldn't be sick. Just this morning she was excited about the last day of school and the beginning of summer vacation.

Tears sprung to Amy's eyes as she saw her daughter curled into a ball, cradling her head with her arms and resting on one of the feed sacks the children took to school this morning and covered with Ralph's coat.

Ruben immediately scooped her into his arms and instructed Ralph to ride one of the horses into town to get the doctor. Amy ran ahead of Ruben in order to make up the daybed in the parlor. She knew she needed to have Harriett close by so she could care for her properly.

"She's burning up with fever," Ruben declared when he came into the room. "I'm glad I sent Ralph into town for the doctor. This ain't good. She's so sick, I'm afraid we're going to lose her."

Amy tucked the covers tightly around Harriett's limp body and began bathing her fevered forehead with cool water.

"I don't smell no supper cooking," Freddie called when he came in from outside.

Amy had no idea where he'd been during all the excitement of Ralph's arrival from school and resented his inconsiderate outburst. Before she could admonish her older son, Ruben took Freddie back outside.

It seemed as though several hours passed before Amy heard the doctor's car come to a stop in the gravel driveway. While he examined Harriett, Amy made a pot of coffee. It wasn't that she really wanted the coffee, but it was an automatic response to stress. Even without supper started, all she could do was worry about her daughter's health.

"Where are Freddie and Ralph?" she asked once the coffee was poured and she sat at the table with Ruben.

"I sent them out to milk."

"To milk? Ralph is so little. Can the two of them handle it without you?"

Ruben smiled for the first time since Ralph came home from school alone. "You underestimate Ralph. He's been milking with me for the past four years. If you want to worry about someone, worry about Freddie. There's no way he can keep up with his younger brother. I made a mistake with Freddie. I let that boy get out of doing the chores around here. I doubt he'll ever amount to much. Ralph is different. He has the same spark I did when I was his age. He'll go far."

Amy didn't know if she agreed, but she nodded her head. From what she recalled about her brother, Ralph, he'd been a hard worker in his youth, but now he seemed to drift from job to job without being able to find a purpose in life. She silently prayed her youngest son would not burn out on hard work and follow in her brother's footsteps.

"I'm afraid I don't have good news for you, Mr. and Mrs. Derr," the doctor said as he entered the kitchen.

Amy knew she should get up and pour him a cup of coffee, but she sat rooted to the spot, her stomach in knots.

"What kind of bad news?" Ruben finally asked once the doctor seated himself at the table.

"I'm afraid Harriett has Infantile Paralysis."

Amy tried to remember if she'd ever heard the name of the disease before and decided she hadn't. From the way the doctor spoke the words she knew things were serious. "Is Harriett dying?" she finally managed to ask.

"Be assured, Mrs. Derr, Harriett isn't dying. She has a mild case and with lots of rest as well as the medication I'm leaving for her, she'll be as good as new. The problem is the entire farm will be under quarantine for the next two weeks."

"Quarantine?" Ruben echoed. "What about the milk?"

"I'm afraid you'll have to dump it. I have to report this to the milk inspector. When I say two weeks, that's an approximation. Everything depends on how well Harriett responds to the treatment."

"But what about school?" Amy questioned.

"Fortunately, school let out for the summer today. That's one thing you won't have to worry about."

Amy nodded her head. How could she have forgotten today was the last day of school?

"Is this contagious?" Ruben inquired.

"There's a lot we don't know about this disease. I've only seen three cases of it and I haven't contracted it, but people fear it. I doubt any of you will come down with it. All of this is precautionary but at the same time necessary."

Once the doctor left, Freddie and Ralph came in from the barn. "The chores are done, Pa," Ralph declared.

Amy couldn't miss the look of disgust on Freddie's face when no supper was cooking on the stove. To her relief, Ruben took over the explanation of what was wrong with Harriett and why they were all quarantined.

"I don't understand why we all have to be quarantined," Freddie protested. "I wanted to go into town tonight and see my friends."

"Well, you won't be going," Ruben shouted. "No one will be leaving this farm until Harriett is better. For now, it's best if you boys go out and bring in some milk for your mother before you dump the rest of it."

"Dump it?" Ralph repeated his father's words as an astonished question. "Can't we send it with the milk man in the morning?"

Ruben's patience in explaining the situation was a godsend. While they discussed what would be happening on the farm, Amy returned to the parlor to check on Harriett. When she came back she saw Ruben had brought leftover roast beef from the springhouse and was making sandwiches from the fresh bread she'd baked hours earlier.

All during the time Harriett lay in the parlor, Ralph refused to sleep in his own room. Instead, he insisted on bringing down his blanket and pillow in order to sleep next to his sister. When Ruben questioned Ralph about it, he said he didn't want Harriett to wake up alone and afraid.

Amy understood Ralph's concern. Ever since she'd been a small child, Harriett was so afraid to be alone she often slept with a lamp burning dimly in her room.

As the doctor predicted, Harriett recovered within the two-week quarantine period. Unfortunately, she remained weakened by the illness that struck so quickly and without warning.

Even though they needed to dump their milk for the two weeks of Harriett's quarantine, there was fieldwork to be done. Although nineteen-year-old Freddie complained bitterly about planting corn and making hay, Ralph never said a word about the grueling schedule summer on the farm demanded.

Whenever Ralph came in from the field, be it either for a meal or to do the milking, he never failed to spend a few quality moments with his sister. At first Ruben complained bitterly about Ralph dawdling, but finally gave into his desire to make Harriett happy considering he easily outworked his older brother.

Soon summer ended and school again resumed. After a summer of rest, Harriett was anxious to get back to school and the friends she'd made before her illness. Ralph, on the other hand, didn't seem to have made the same number of friends as his sister.

After a summer of hard work and concern over Harriett's health, he became more mischievous than ever. Even though Ralph's grades didn't suffer, his behavior did. More than once, he'd bring home a note from the teacher praising his grades while saying he'd once again, lost his recess and lunch hour privileges for some infraction or bad behavior.

Chapter Nine

In the spring of 1933, Harriett graduated from the eighth grade and was relieved to finally be done with school.

Throughout the fall, Freddie helped with getting in the crops, but at night he often went into town, leaving the night chores for twelve-year-old Ralph.

By Christmas, Freddie announced he'd met a young woman at one of the dances he'd attended in town. Marion Walmer was barely eighteen and a very delicate young woman.

Freddie's love for Marion was so intense they planned to be married on February 20, 1934. Amy was concerned about the union. Freddie had never worked anywhere but on the farm with Ruben, but if the truth were known, he did little to be called work. She prayed being married to Marion would turn Freddie into a responsible farmer.

The wedding was a small affair, held in the parlor of Mr. and Mrs. Walmer's home. As a wedding present, Amy and Ruben scraped together every spare penny they could find and not only helped Freddie to get a farm to rent but also supplied him with the equipment he would need to run it properly.

Amy was pleased to know the farm sat just down the road from their place. As was normal for the mobile farm families of the area, Freddie and Marion wouldn't be able to move in until March first, leaving them to live with Amy and Ruben for the first week of their married life.

Amy wished the young couple would be able to move in right

away, because she disliked hearing Freddie's robust lovemaking at night. As much as it bothered her, she said nothing, since Freddie had been helping his father more and she didn't want anything to make him stop doing the hard work of farming. With Marion to provide for, he needed to become a productive farmer.

Through the days Freddie and Marion stayed at the home farm, Marion and Harriett became close friends. Of course, Amy welcomed the added help around the house and in the kitchen. Even though Marion was frail, she proved to be a hard worker and Amy, in those few days, came to love her like another daughter.

On the first of March, they all pitched in to help Freddie and Marion move to their own home. The owner of the farm provided half of the cattle and once again Ruben scraped together enough money to help Freddie buy the other half. Although Amy didn't approve, Ruben assured her he was investing in Freddie's future as a farmer. She certainly didn't understand his reasoning. When they started farming no one helped them. If they financially helped Freddie now, would he expect more help in the years ahead?

In Amy's opinion, the house that went with Freddie's farm left much to be desired. She had no doubt Marion would turn it into a comfortable home, but the dirt and grime they found would be a challenge. The cupboards were filled with mouse and rat droppings. Everything else needed a thorough cleaning. Between Amy, Harriett and Marion's mother, they spent an entire day getting the house habitable again.

It came, as no surprise when Mrs. Walmer told them Marion had been a sickly child. She often suggested the thought of establishing a home in an old farmhouse was overwhelming to her frail daughter.

Marion's family provided the young couple with furniture. Even so, Amy knew with Freddie and Marion living so close to her home, they would become dependent on Ruben for assistance.

* * * *

By late spring, Ralph graduated from grade school with not only good grades, but also the award for good penmanship.

"I wanted to speak with you, Mr. and Mrs. Derr," Ralph's teacher said to them after the graduation ceremony at the courthouse. "Ralph has a brilliant mind, even though he has a mischievous nature. Will he be going to high school?"

Amy held her breath. More than once Ralph told her he wanted to go not only to high school, but also to college. She thought of saying something to Ruben about it. Unfortunately, the timing never seemed to be right to make such an announcement.

"I don't know what the boy told you but his brother didn't go to high school and neither did his sister. As far as I'm concerned he has all the schooling he needs to be a farmer."

"But Pa, I want to go to high school. I want to be a doctor."

"What you want don't matter. If you don't want to do what I say, you can get out on your own."

"Look, Ruben," Bob Parker, their closest neighbor aside from Freddie said. "Ralph can work for me and go to school with my kids."

"Over my dead body!" Ruben shouted. "Come on, Amy, we're going home."

To Amy's horror, Ruben turned his anger against Ralph. "And you, don't think you're coming home tonight. You need time to think about what you plan to do with your life. One thing is certain, you won't be going to high school. I'm sure I'd have to sign papers for you to go and there's no way in hell that will happen. Do you understand me?"

"I understand you perfectly," Ralph replied. "You don't have to worry, Pa. I won't be back tonight and tomorrow I'll come for my clothes."

Amy's heart broke as her youngest son stood toe to toe with Ruben, anger flashing from his brown eyes.

It was Ruben who turned away from Ralph and motioned for Amy to follow him back to the car. With one backward glance, she saw Ralph, not as her youngest son, but as an angry young man about to embark on an uncertain future.

"Please, Ruben," Amy pleaded. "What harm would it do for Ralph to go to high school?"

"Why should that little bastard go to school when neither Freddie nor Harriet went?"

"Because he has the desire to learn. Freddie lived for the day when he finished school and Harriett wasn't strong enough to go on any further. I remember what it was like to want to get more education and to have to be content with what little I was allowed to have."

"That was you and you know good and well why you didn't get more schooling. I feel a bit like Joseph Coble must have felt. I don't want that little bastard getting something my own son didn't have."

Amy didn't reply. For the first time she saw Ruben in a new light. Although he'd been excited about taking Harriett into his life as a beloved daughter, he saw Ralph as an indentured servant. Ruben loved Harriett unconditionally, but to him, Ralph was little more than a hired man.

Freddie and Marion were waiting for them when they got home, giving Amy no time to plead Ralph's case.

"We have an announcement to make," Freddie said as soon as they got out of the car. "You're going to be grandparents. It will be like a Christmas present, since the baby is coming in December."

Amy's heart swelled with excitement. It had been almost thirteen years since she'd held a baby in her arms. All her life she'd longed for a large family. When God decided to withhold those children from her, she'd willingly taken the bastard children of her nieces as her own. For the first time, in too many years, the family would begin growing. Freddie and Marion would have a large family to fulfill Amy's desires, as would Harriett. That would have to be enough for her.

"Where is Ralph?" Marion inquired, looking around the dooryard.

"He's cut his ties with this family," Ruben declared. "Whatever he does and wherever he goes is up to him. He's no longer a part of our lives."

Harriett's eyes were filled with questions but Amy knew the tone of Ruben's voice caused her daughter to leave them unspoken.

The conversation soon turned from Ralph's absence to the new baby expected to arrival in December. Harriett was particularly excited about the coming of the new addition to the family.

In the late afternoon, Freddie went home to milk and Ruben went out to the barn to do the same. Amy wondered how her husband would do milking alone for the first time in almost eight years.

"What happened with Ralph?" Marion asked, once the men were gone.

"This has been building for a long time," Amy confessed. "Ruben and Ralph have been ready to clash for several months. It all came to a head when the teacher asked if Ralph was going on to high school. When Ruben said no, Ralph rebelled. Ruben told him it was high time he made his own way and Ralph stood his ground. In the end we came home alone and I have no idea where Ralph went. He did say he would be coming back tomorrow to get his clothes."

"Hopefully, he'll keep in touch with Freddie and me so at least someone in the family will know where he's at," Marion said. "I can't imagine anyone his age going out on his own. He's only twelve. I mean Freddie was twenty-two when he moved from here to his own farm. No matter what Harriett wants, Freddie says that Ted can't even begin courting her until next year when she's fifteen."

"What you're forgetting is that Ralph isn't Freddie and he certainly isn't Harriett. The way Ruben sees it, he quit school when he was twelve to help his father with the farming and he feels Ralph should do the same. He's been working in the barn since he was five. Back then he did it so he could walk Harriett to school. He's always been very self-sufficient and no matter what, he does things his own way. The teacher says he has a brilliant mind and that's something of which I have no doubt. If he weren't smart, he wouldn't have finished school so early. He's always been the youngest one in his class no matter where we've moved."

After he finished milking, Freddie returned for supper. When he came back and Ruben came in, all talk of Ralph and why he wouldn't be sharing supper with them ceased. It was late when Freddie and Marion finally returned home, saying they'd be back for Sunday dinner.

Amy spent a sleepless night not knowing where Ralph went once they drove away from the courthouse. As she feigned sleep, she obsessed over her youngest son.

The next morning, Ruben was up early and insisted they all needed to go to church. The unusual request by Ruben came as a surprise and at the same time it shouldn't have been unexpected. In no way did Ruben want to be at home when Ralph came to pick up his belongings.

Harriett was thrilled to be going to church since she'd recently met a young man there. Ted Baumgartner took an immediate interest in Harriett and had even gone so far as to ask Ruben if he could court her. Being older than Harriett, Ruben insisted Ted wait until Harriett's fifteenth birthday before he paid serious court to her.

After church, Sarah Parker sought Amy out. "What happened at the graduation between Ruben and Ralph?"

Amy took a deep breath. How could she explain what she didn't understand herself? "It's a long story I'm just worried sick because Ralph didn't come home last night."

"That's because he stayed with us. He didn't want to, but Bob insisted there was nothing he could do until Monday morning. I don't mean to interfere with your family, but I couldn't stand to see that boy with nowhere to go. Bob said he'd ask around to see if anyone needed help. I would like to have him work for us, but Bob said he didn't want to anger Ruben further."

Amy wanted to continue the conversation with Sarah, but Ruben motioned he was ready to leave. Even though Amy was exhausted from a night without sleep, she knew she needed to fix a good Sunday meal. With Freddie and Marion coming for dinner, it would be expected. Fortunately, she had a roasting chicken ready to go in the oven as soon as she got home.

By the time Amy got to the car, Harriett was protesting the need to go home so soon and take her away from Ted's company. Ruben's insistence she do what he said silenced her protests as she got into the back seat of the car.

* * * *

As summer turned into fall, Amy heard Ralph easily found work. With the economy in such bad shape, she knew most farmers couldn't afford to hire someone on a full time basis. Most farmers hired extra help for major things like planting, haying, cultivating, thrashing and corn picking. Her concerns about where Ralph would find employment and a home increased as she thought about the coming winter.

Worries over Ralph soon went to the back of Amy's mind as Marion's pregnancy progressed. Amy and Harriett often went over to Freddie and Marion's farm to help out with the household chores Marion now found herself too weak to accomplish.

Keeping up with two households soon took its toll on Amy, but she dared not complain. Freddie expected the help and Ruben supported him in every way.

Christmas was hard as Amy missed Ralph terribly. It had been well over six months since she last saw her youngest son. Although it didn't seem to bother Ruben, she knew Harriett missed Ralph as much as she did.

Beverly Leila Derr was born on December 28, 1934 bringing Ralph to Freddie's farm to see his first niece. If Amy hadn't known his age to be thirteen, she would have thought him much older. After a summer of hard work, he had become much more muscular and filled out than when he'd left home in May.

It surprised her to see Ralph had his own car. Although he was much too young to drive, he proudly produced a valid driver's license. Amy did notice it said he was three years older than his actual age.

When Amy asked Ralph where he was working, he gave her the name of a young couple who hired him to do the milking throughout the winter. It came as a relief to know Ralph would have stable employment until the following spring when fieldwork would give him several more opportunities.

Chapter Ten

After Harriett's fifteenth birthday, Ted became a frequent visitor at the farm. While Ralph continued to drift from job to job and Freddie needed more and more help running his place, Ted purchased a farm closer to Evansville, in Rock County.

Just after the first of the year of 1935, Ted asked Ruben for permission to marry Harriett as soon after her sixteenth birthday as possible. Ruben gave his consent, leaving Amy and Harriett to begin planning the August 24th wedding.

Although Harriett wanted the ceremony to be held in the yard of her new home, Amy convinced her to be married on the home farm.

While Harriett worked on a special dress for her wedding and Amy planned the food, she soon heard Ruben and Freddie were also making plans. By mid February, they announced they'd found farms around Evansville so they could remain close to Harriett and Ted.

Harriett was thrilled, but Amy had reservations. Living close to Freddie had kept him dependent on Ruben. Would the same be true with Harriett and Ted? She hoped not, but knew she had little say in the matter.

"You'll see," Ruben said on the night before the move. "The new house is much better than this one and you'll be close to Evansville. It will be perfect living so close to both of the kids. Between the three of us we can exchange work and not have to hire extra help."

His mention of extra help reminded Amy of Ralph. If it weren't for Ruben's temper, their youngest son would be helping with the work. If that were the case, it would eliminate the need for this move to yet another farm.

As she thought about the new farm where they'd be moving, she knew being closer to Evansville wouldn't be important to her. She rarely went into town without Ruben and didn't even know how to drive the truck Ruben purchased a few years before.

The next morning started early with Ted coming over to help move the two households while Ruben and Freddie prepared to move the equipment and livestock. Amy dreaded moving to a new location. After the mess she'd found at Freddie and Marion's home a year ago, she didn't think she was up to settling two households, to say nothing of cleaning them until they were habitable.

With the last of their belongings loaded, Amy, Harriett and Marion, along with the baby drove to the farm where Freddie and Marion would be living. Once they arrived, Amy was pleasantly surprised by the condition of the house. When Marion's mother came down from the upstairs bedrooms, Amy knew she'd been there cleaning most of the morning.

"I'm very impressed with your new home, Marion," her mother greeted them. "I came out this morning expecting to find a mess, but whoever lived here before you left the place spotless. After we get you settled, I plan to go over to help Amy and Harriett move into their new home."

Amy appreciated Mrs. Walmer's offer, but at the same time it made her feel uneasy. It was no secret the Walmers were considered to be wealthier than any of the other area farmers. Never having enough money to live comfortably, Amy didn't feel at ease in this woman's presence.

At noon the men came in for dinner. If they were surprised to see the house completely settled and a hot meal on the table, they didn't show it.

Among the men Amy was astonished to see Ralph. Although Ruben seemed less than thrilled with Ralph's presence, he remained civil.

"It's good to see you, Ma," Ralph said has he hugged first Amy and then Harriett.

"How did you know where to find us?" Harriett inquired.

"I heard about the move in town. So I thought I'd come over to see if I could be of help."

Amy marveled at how happy go lucky Ralph seemed. The smile Ruben so hated filled Ralph's face and Amy's heart. In all her life she'd never found anything to smile about. Freddie and Ruben were both like her but Harriett and Ralph shared the same smile. Harriett had learned how to hide her emotions, but for Ralph it was only natural. No amount of humiliation from his father or brother could wipe it from his face.

"You look good, Ralph," Amy observed.

"So do you, Ma."

"Where are you working?"

"At the same place, but come spring, my boss is selling out. I'm looking for something else, but so far I haven't found anything. You don't have to worry about me. I'll be okay."

"I'm sure you will," Harriett said, showing Ralph into the dining room to find a seat at the table.

Amy wished she had more time to talk to Ralph but she knew the men were anxious to get back to the work of settling the two farms.

With the remnants of dinner cleaned up, Harriett drove over to the farm where Ruben and Amy would be living. To Amy's relief, the condition of her home rivaled that of Freddie and Marion's house.

With Marion and Beverly staying at their farm, Mrs. Walmer drove over to the new place and worked relentlessly until Amy was satisfied by the condition of her new home. Over the course of the afternoon, Amy's opinion of Freddie's mother-in-law, changed dramatically. It would be the beginning of a wonderful friendship.

* * * *

The following Sunday, Ralph surprised them by coming for dinner. For Amy, it was good to see her entire family around the table. After dinner, Ralph played with Beverly while Ruben, Freddie and Ted discussed the upcoming planting season. Not fitting into either scenario, the women worked at making plans for Harriett's wedding in August.

The division of men and women tugged at Amy's heart. Growing up, she'd never seen such a division in the Coble household, but Ruben had never seen women as equals.

"I have to get back to work," Ralph announced at three o'clock.

"Will you be back for supper?" Harriet questioned.

"I'm afraid not. I'm doing the milking alone. By the time I drive back and do the chores, it will be too late to come back to eat supper."

Ruben, Freddie and Ted walked out to the car with Ralph since it was time for the men to start doing their chores as well.

Amy noticed how tired Marion looked. "Beverly is taking a nap," she said. "Why don't you go in the parlor and take one as well. Harriett and I can clean up the kitchen and get supper ready."

Marion seemed appreciative of the offer. Unfortunately, Harriett didn't agree. "It's not right for you and me to have to fix dinner and clean up too. I think Marion should come out to help us."

"You must be able to see Marion is exhausted. Once you're married and have a child of your own, you'll understand how demanding running a household and catering to a husband and child can be."

"With Freddie I can see what you mean, but Ted isn't like that. My marriage won't be like Marion's. Ted is more considerate than Freddie will ever be. What I don't understand is why Freddie and Ralph are so different?"

Amy bit her tongue rather than blurt out the truth regarding Ralph and Harriett's parentage. "Those two boys have always been as different as day from night. Freddie takes after your father and Ralph is more like my side of the family."

Harriett made no further comment, but Amy knew her daughter had more questions. Over the years there had been little or no contact with Amy's Mercer sisters. The only family Harriett was aware of was Ralph Totten and he certainly carried no traits that could be remotely equated with Ralph.

"Ralph had a lot of guts to show up here today," Ruben said when he came in from milking.

"I thought it was good to see him," Amy replied without looking up at her husband.

"Maybe it was for you, but as far as I'm concerned, he saw what a nice house this is and he wanted to move back home. Well, I made it perfectly clear that he made his bed and he could lie in it."

"I can't believe that."

"You heard him the same as I did. He's going to be out of a job as soon as that old man he's working for sells the place. I'm sure he thinks living here would be much easier for him."

Amy heard the door open and knew either Freddie or Ted had returned for supper. She knew pursuing the argument over Ralph's intentions would be fruitless.

Chapter Eleven

The morning of Harriett's wedding dawned bright and clear. Even the oppressive heat of the past week had subsided after last night's rain. Amy was proud of how lush her garden looked. She'd worked hard weeding the flowerbeds around the house.

Harriett looked beautiful. Her dress accented her slim figure and Amy marveled at how much she resembled her true mother. Gladiolas from Amy's garden made up her bouquet and added just the right touch of color.

While Ted's brother acted as his best man, Marion stood beside Harriett as the matron of honor. For this day, Beverly remained in the care of Marion's mother so she wouldn't be continually underfoot. For the first time since Beverly's birth, Amy thought Marion looked radiant.

The wedding was just about ready to begin when Ralph arrived at the farm. Amy noticed he carried a carefully wrapped gift.

"I'm so glad to see you, Ralph," Harriett gushed. "I wondered if you'd be able to come today."

"I wouldn't miss your wedding for anything in the world," he replied as he kissed her cheek. He put his gift on the table before going out to the garden to witness the ceremony

"What does he want?" Ruben asked when he joined them in the kitchen.

"I sent Ralph an invitation, Pa," Harriett replied.

"How did you know where to find him?"

Amy watched Harriett's expression. The look of shock at her father's question crossed Harriett's face.

"Freddie always knows where to find Ralph. He asks him for help and extra money when things get tight."

Amy was horrified. She had no idea why Freddie would need money from Ralph when she knew Ruben paid many of their bills. Of course, as usual, Amy held her peace. This was her daughter's wedding day. She certainly didn't want her concerns over the relationship between her two sons to spoil it.

The wedding was beautiful. To Amy's delight, Ralph stayed for the reception afterwards and enchanted the guests with stories of working on various farms in the area.

While the men went off to talk about farming as well as the upcoming harvest, Harriett opened the gifts she'd received. Amy was extremely interested to see what Ralph's present contained. She smiled to see Harriett as anxious to open her younger brother's present as Amy was.

Inside the box was a card with a note saying Ralph would be doing Ted's chores for the weekend. Under the card was a beautiful set of embroidered dishtowels. The remainder of the gifts included many other types of linens, but Amy knew none would mean as much to Harriett as the dishtowels did.

After the gifts were opened, the men joined the women for cake and coffee. Amy took the opportunity to talk to Ralph. "The dishtowels were beautiful. Where did you get them?"

Ralph flashed her one of his infamous smiles. "When I told my employer why I wanted to have off this weekend, his wife insisted I needed a perfect wedding gift. She went right to work on making the towels for Harriett."

"Did you tell Ted about what you wrote in Harriett's card?"

"You didn't think I'd write something like that without talking to Ted, did you? Like I said I asked for this weekend off when I knew about the wedding. Since I usually get Saturday off, I made a deal with my boss to work next Saturday to get this entire weekend off."

"I don't see you taking off work to help me," Freddie complained.

Amy knew he meant the comment as a tease, but things like these never came off the way Freddie meant them to.

"As I recall, Pa and I milked your cows when you moved to your first farm. At the time of your wedding you and Marion were living with the folks and didn't need to get away to get to know each other without having to worry about chores. It seems to me you rarely did any of the milking when you lived at home."

Although Ralph's tone said he was teasing, Amy knew his anger was building.

"Well, I think it's a very generous offer," Amy said in an attempt to defuse the situation. "Where will you and Harriett be going, Ted?"

Ted had a mischievous twinkle in his eyes. "I made reservations for us in a hotel in Madison for tonight. I thought we could explore the city tomorrow."

Harriett squealed with delight at Ted's announcement. It pleased Amy to think Ted planned such a wonderful surprise for her daughter.

After the last of the guests left, Marion and her mother helped Amy clean up. "Freddie was very upset about Ralph offering to do Ted's milking tonight and tomorrow night," Marion said.

"I don't see why he should be," her mother responded. "I think it's a wonderful wedding present."

"I do too," Amy agreed. "I do know Ruben doesn't approve of something so frivolous as Harriett and Ted going away overnight, but I think it's a nice way to celebrate their marriage."

If Amy expected to see Ralph while he did Ted's chores, she was mistaken. From what she'd overheard, Ruben and Ralph exchanged angry words, keeping her youngest son from returning to her home,

From Freddie, Amy learned Ralph hadn't stayed in Harriett's house, but returned to his employer's farm after finishing each milking.

* * * *

By 1937, Harriett was expecting the birth of her first child, while Freddie and Marion seemed unable to conceive a second child. Amy blamed it on the fact Beverly was still nursing at her mother's breast. She'd always heard a woman couldn't conceive while she was nursing, giving credence to her assumptions.

"I certainly don't like to see a child of three still sucking on her mother's tit," Ruben said on Sunday evening after the family left. "I thought it was bad when Flossie nursed Ralph until he was almost two."

Amy agreed. She'd been persistent and had Freddie weaned shortly after his first birthday. It certainly wasn't easy, since he wanted to suckle for security long after she refused to nurse him.

On July 21, 1937, Harriett gave birth to Amy's second granddaughter, Donna Jean. As much as Amy loved Beverly, she longed to again cradle a tiny baby in her arms. As she'd learned with her own children, love could be expanded to encompass each new member to the family.

Chapter Twelve

Two days after Freddie and Marion's fourth wedding anniversary, Freddie brought Beverly over to the farm. "Can Beverly stay with you for a few days?" he asked as soon as he got out of the car.

The expression on Freddie's face frightened Amy. "What's wrong?" she asked as a sobbing Beverly sought comfort in her arms.

"My mommy is sick," Beverly blurted out before Freddie could say anything.

Freddie reached into the back seat of the car to retrieve the suitcase with Beverly's clothes. "I called Marion's folks this morning and they came out to take Marion to the hospital. I have go to the hospital to see her. Marion's mother said she thought it was her heart, but it can't be anything like that, it just can't be."

"You go on," Ruben advised him. "Your mother will take care of Beverly and when I get done milking, I'll go over to Harriett's and get Ted to come over and help me do your chores."

Amy took Beverly into the house after Freddie pulled out of the driveway. It was still early afternoon and she knew Ruben would go over to inform Ted of what was going on. She was relieved to know Ralph was working in the area and had made an uneasy peace with his father. It was entirely possible Freddie would stop at the farm where Ralph was working to rally the entire family at this time of crisis.

Within less than a week, Ralph came to the farm to inform Amy and Ruben of Marion's passing. Amy had always known of Marion's sickly nature, but never thought her daughter-in-law would die at such a young age.

Beverly continued to stay with Amy while Freddie planned Marion's funeral. When it came time for him to decide where she should be buried, Ruben offered to purchase six gravesites in the Evansville cemetery. Amy didn't think they could afford the expense, but neither could Freddie.

On the morning Marion was to be laid to rest, one of the neighbors came to care for both Beverly and Harriett's daughter, Donna Jean. So the family could mourn their loss.

To Amy's amazement, Ralph stood next to Freddie lending his strength of youth to his older brother. She was horrified to realize Freddie was drunk. She knew everyone had to be aware of Freddie's condition and it embarrassed her.

She glanced across the aisle of the church at Mr. and Mrs. Walmer. She'd seen them just days earlier when Mrs. Walmer invited them to dinner to celebrate Freddie and Marion's anniversary. It was hard to believe they were the same people she'd eaten dinner with, as they seemed to have aged almost overnight. Seeing them in this shape, Amy was certain they would not be able to help out with Beverly's care.

"What are you going to do now, Ralph?" Harriett asked, once they sat in Amy's dining room.

"I've quit my job and moved over to Freddie's place so I can help him with Beverly," Ralph said when Freddie sat with his head in his hands sobbing softly. "I talked it over with the people I'm working for and they agreed with me. With winter there's not much for me to do there and paying me has become a hardship. If Ma can keep Beverly for a few more days, it will give me time to get settled in."

Throughout the summer, Ralph took over much of Freddie's farm work as well as Beverly's care. At the same time, Freddie lost himself in the numerous whiskey bottles whose contents numbed his mind and kept him unaware of what was happening both on the farm and with his daughter.

By fall, Freddie seemed to have accepted Marion's death and his responsibility both to his farm and his daughter. Even so, Ralph stayed on, doing the majority of the work, if for no other reason than to give

Beverly a stable home life.

On October 2, 1938 the family met at Ruben and Amy's home for Sunday dinner. To Amy's relief, although Freddie had been drinking, Amy wouldn't call him drunk. Without Freddie's drunkenness, the main topic of conversation was Ralph's new car.

"How could you afford that car?" Ruben asked.

"I've been saving for it for a long time," Ralph replied. "I got a good deal on it and with my trade in they didn't need that much money."

"I think it's great," Harriett said. "Can I drive it?"

Amy knew Ralph couldn't say no to Harriett. He'd always catered to her every whim and today would be no different.

"Sure you can."

Harriett was overjoyed. "You know, I wish I'd have an accident."

"Why would you say such a thing?" Freddie inquired.

"You and Ralph have both had accidents and you're good drivers. I think I'd be a better driver if I had an accident."

"Oh, honey," Amy lamented. "Don't wish for such a thing. Freddie and Ralph have more experience driving than you do. That's why they're better drivers. I don't see why you want to drive anyway."

"I keep telling her the same thing," Ted commented. "She says it gives her more independence. It's all the fault of this modern society we live in."

Everyone laughed, but Amy couldn't shed the feeling of dread at Harriett's comment.

After dinner, Amy and Harriett cleaned up the kitchen. Even though they worked together, Amy knew Harriett's mind was on getting to drive Ralph's new car rather than doing the necessary clean up.

Since it was such a beautiful October day, the men were all sitting in the yard watching Beverly and Donna Jean playing on the lawn.

"Are you ready to go for your ride?" Ralph asked.

Harriett's eyes sparkled. "Are you kidding? Of course I'm ready to drive your new car. Can I go into Evansville and get us some ice cream?"

Ralph laughed at her enthusiasm. After giving her his keys, he reached into his back pocket and pulled out his billfold to give her the money for ice cream.

"Can we go with you, Aunt Harriett?" Beverly begged, holding tightly to Donna Jean's hand.

"Of course you can," Harriett replied. "It will be a great adventure."

Amy watched apprehensively as Harriett slid behind the wheel and the little girls got into the passenger seat. Once they were seated, Harriett pulled out onto the gravel road and headed toward Evansville.

With the farm just two miles out of town, Amy silently counted the minutes her daughter had been gone. Finally, Freddie pointed toward the road. "Here they come!" he shouted.

He no more than spoke the words when the shrill whistle of an oncoming train rent the air. Amy was horrified to see the tracks that bordered her side yard filled with the freight train.

Everything seemed to move in slow motion as the two little girls waved toward the family gathered in the yard. To everyone's horror, Harriet crossed the tracks at the same time as the train applied the brakes to avoid smashing into the car.

By the time the train finally came to a halt, the car had been pushed almost a mile down the tracks. Amy knew in that one brief moment her life changed forever. It was apparent not one of the people in the car could have survived. In the blink of an eye the three most important women in her life were gone. Until her dying day, Amy had no idea why Harriett didn't see the train.

The next few days were a blur. The railroad agreed to pay for all three funerals, give Freddie and Ted cash settlements and replaced Ralph's car. Under the circumstances the railway said they thought it was the proper thing to do. Even though the accident had been, technically, Harriett's fault, they also felt responsible for the family's loss. Newspaper reporters interviewed all of them over and over again. They came from Janesville as well as Madison. No matter how many articles they wrote, it would never bring back Harriett, Beverly and Donna Jean.

While Ruben, Freddie and Ted mourned their losses, they also verbally blamed Ralph for the accident.

"It's all your fault," Ruben spat on the morning after the accident. If you hadn't bought that damnable car and allowed Harriett to take it to Evansville, the accident wouldn't have happened."

Freddie and Ted were quick to add their voice to the biting words. Although Amy wanted to have someone to blame, she didn't want to see her younger child accused of being the cause of the accident.

As a defense mechanism, Ralph avoided the family. He took over not only Freddie's chores but also the ones that needed to be done for Ruben and Ted.

Amy often found Freddie and Ted sitting around her dining room table trying to decide what to do about the funerals and burials. Since Ruben and Amy purchased the six cemetery plots at the time of Marion's death, they offered them to Freddie and Ted. Freddie immediately said he wanted Beverly buried beside her mother, but Ted insisted on buying a separate plot for Harriett and Donna Jean.

Ted's rejection of their generous offer came as a blow to Ruben and caused a rift that would soon drive a wedge between Amy and Ruben and their son-in-law.

The night of the visitation, neighbors offered to do the chores so the family could all be at the funeral home. Amy hesitated to walk into the flower filled room. Two caskets, one opened and one closed stood at the front of the room. Amy knew the smaller one contained Beverly's remains, making her wonder where Donna Jean was. Upon looking into the open casket, Harriet's face looked so serene she looked as though she might just be sleeping. It seemed as though she could sit up and talk to them, when in reality she had been taken from them forever. Tucked into the casket at Harriett's side was a pink blanket that held Donna Jean's remains.

Ralph seemed to suffer in silence, unlike Freddie who sobbed loudly. Ted broke down often and Ruben spoke with family and friends while tears rolled down his cheeks. For Amy, the nightmare continued and she saw no end to the line of mourners who came to pay their respects. It became hard to tell the actual family and friends from the curiosity seekers.

By the time they returned home, Amy was completely exhausted and wondered how she would ever be able to endure the next day's funeral. She decided the visitation had been easier on Mrs. Walmer. Eight months earlier she'd gone through the loss of her daughter and was steeled against the loss of her granddaughter. With the closed casket, she hadn't had to look on Beverly's sweet face and endure the horror of death, nor did she have to look at a pink blanket and know it contained a child she had loved with all her heart just days earlier.

Mrs. Walmer had something else that Amy knew she'd never have. She had other children and grandchildren to love. Amy had nothing. Ralph had become a virtual stranger and Freddie spent his days and nights lost in a bottle.

The next day, the Methodist Church in Evansville was packed to overflowing. While Amy's family sat on one side of the church, his family on the other side of the aisle surrounded Ted. The man she loved like another son for the past four years acted as though he wanted nothing to do with any of them.

Amy, Ruben and Ralph sat on one side of Freddie with Mr. and Mrs. Walmer on the other. Throughout the church, men and women alike sobbed, as the service seemed to drag on forever.

For the second time in the year of 1938, a line of cars drove from the church, out Highway 14 and up Cemetery Street to the final resting place for the girls of Amy's family.

At the cemetery, Amy was torn. She needed to be with Freddie as they laid Beverly to rest, but at the same time, she felt compelled to be with Ted to hear the final words spoken over the bodies of Harriett and Donna Jean.

The minister did the graveside service for Beverly first. As Amy listened, she saw a little boy come up to Freddie's side. She immediately recognized him as the son of one of Marion's cousins. To Amy's surprise, she heard Freddie speaking in hushed tones to the little boy.

"Would you like to come and live with me?" Freddie asked. "I don't have a little girl to love anymore. I could love you like I did

Beverly."

Before Amy could hear any response from the child's parents, the group moved to the gravesite for Harriett and Donna Jean. As the crowd gathered around the flower-draped casket, only Freddie stayed behind.

It was Ralph who turned back to guide his older brother away from the small casket containing his daughter's remains. When Freddie rejoined the family for the second graveside service of the day, it was Ralph who helped him stand and not buckle at the knees.

As the service began, Amy gratefully sat down on one of the chairs provided by the funeral home next to Ted and his mother. Behind her, Ruben sank to his knees and cried bitterly. Amy had shed her tears in private and refused to allow the curious public to see her devastation.

Chapter Thirteen

By January of 1939, the three farms where Amy's family had lived were all gone. Ted sold his farm as well as all his equipment and moved out of the area. Freddie lost all interest in farming and Ruben could no longer live in the house next to the tracks where Harriett and the girls had lost their lives.

For a while, Freddie moved to the home farm, but when Ruben sold out they all moved to a large rooming house on Madison Street in Evansville. For the first time in her married life, Amy was able to live in a house she and Ruben actually owned. The upstairs bedrooms were rented to several single men and the lower apartment was also rented. Amy knew the money from these men would help with expenses until Ruben could find a job to support them. Ralph went his own way. Rather than go back to farming, he landed a job on the city delivery and rented a room on the other side of Evansville. Even though they lived in the same town, Amy rarely saw her youngest son.

On February 27, 1939, Freddie came home and announced he'd gotten married. Amy could smell the alcohol on his breath as he introduced Leona Hosely Derr to his parents.

Over the years, Amy had heard stories about the Hosely family. Unlike the Walmers, Mr. Hosely was a man with a severe drinking habit and a temper to match. Several years earlier, she heard old man Hosely came home from a night of drinking and raped his wife and all his daughters. Once the authorities got wind of it they insisted all the

90

girls be sterilized.

It broke Amy's heart to think that with Leona as his wife, Freddie would never have another little girl to love. Maybe it was for the best since she never wanted the pain of loving a child only to have God take her away from them.

After the wedding, Freddie decided he wanted a place of his own again. With the settlement from the railroad, he bought half a herd of cattle and some equipment to move to a farm owned by Plenty Tolls and work it on halves the way he had before Marion died and Beverly was killed.

Freddie moving out of the house came as a relief, as his new wife far from impressed Amy. She knew it would be difficult to be civil to Leona during Sunday dinners to say nothing of doing it on an everyday basis.

With spring came new opportunities for both Ruben and Amy. Ruben landed a job working for the city. In the spring, summer and fall he would be working for the city keeping the park clean. During the winter, he would run the warming house on Lake Leota for the kids who came to skate.

Amy also found employment cleaning offices and private homes. Her favorite customers were Dr. and Mrs. Gray and Maude Lewis. She started by cleaning Dr. Gray's office and soon found a job cleaning for his wife as well. Within a month she was introduced to Maude Lewis and picked up yet another job.

Maude was confined to a wheelchair. As a young wife, she and her husband had been in a serious accident, leaving Maude an invalid. Amy enjoyed cleaning Tower House, as Maude called her home, since Maude had so many interesting stories to tell. Her father once owned the house and was a well-known photographer in town. Her many knick-knacks gave Amy a lot of dusting to do as she listened to Maude's stories while she worked.

In late August, Ralph stopped by for Sunday dinner. Amy hadn't had him at her table since the Sunday in October when their lives had been shattered.

"I'm glad to see you, son," Amy said when he came to the house.

Ralph entered and looked around the living room. "This sure is different from your last place. It looks like you got a nice house here."

Amy realized Ralph was making small talk, but didn't want to broach the subject of why he hadn't been coming for Sunday dinner.

When Freddie and Leona arrived, he didn't seem at all shy about questioning his brother. "So what brings you here?"

"I'm tired of living in town. I signed on at a farm in LaPrairie Township."

"LaPrairie?" Ruben echoed. "How in the hell did you get a way down there?"

"Well, I met this girl and she said her dad needed someone to milk and run the farm while he takes care of his dead stock business."

"Does this mysterious girl have a name?" Freddie teased.

"Of course she does, she's Norma Howard."

"Are you telling us you're going to be working for George Howard?" Ruben asked. "I heard he was working with Woody Traxler picking up dead animals. I think this time you might have fallen into a pile of shit and came out smelling like a rose. From what I've heard, those old boys are both loaded. Of course, everyone knows the Howards practically own LaPrairie Township."

"So," Freddie began, nudging Ralph with his elbow and winking broadly. "Is this girl special. Are you going to marry her? With all that money, you'd be a fool not to get hooked up with her. I'll give you a word of advice, though. Be careful marrying above yourself. I did that with Marion and came to regret it."

Amy listened intently to the conversation between Freddie and Ralph. She wondered if Freddie was right. Did this woman Ralph talked about become someone special in his life? She'd never considered the possibility of Ralph falling in love and getting married. He was too young, too rebellious for her to believe he was ready to settle down.

If he were to marry, would there be children? She had no doubt Ralph would give her grandchildren, but could she accept them? Freddie was her true son and Beverly her beloved granddaughter. Harriett had won her heart the minute she was born. Even though she wasn't Amy's natural daughter she loved her without question and Donna Jean had been the light of her life.

As much as she wanted her grandchildren back, she knew she could never accept any others to take their place. Ralph had never been hers, not really. Maybe if Flossie hadn't stayed at the farm so long after his birth she would have bonded with him, but that hadn't happened. She'd raised her youngest son, but in reality she'd never understood him.

Part Two

Little Boy Lost
Lafayette County Wisconsin
1926

Ralph

Chapter Fourteen

August 1926

"Now, make your letters the same way I did," Harriett instructed.

Ralph looked at the letters his seven-year-old sister wrote on the slate. "R-A-L-P-H," he read aloud pointing to each letter as he gave it a name. "That spells Ralph, my name."

"Very good," Harriett said in her best schoolteacher voice. At least Ralph thought she said it like a teacher.

Carefully he copied the letters Harriett wrote on the slate she used for schoolwork. Ever since she started school last fall, she'd been teaching him everything she learned when she came home at night. The knowledge he gained from his sister excited him.

"I did it," he proclaimed. "I wrote my name."

Harriett scrutinized the letters that closely resembled the ones she'd written earlier. "That's perfect. Now can you write your last name?"

Without Harriett's letters to copy, he closed his eyes mentally visualizing how to write his last name. A smile crossed his lips when he proudly wrote D-E-R-R.

"You did it all by yourself," Harriett said as she hugged him tightly. "I'm so proud of you."

"What's there to be proud of?" Freddie, their fifteen-year-old brother, asked as he joined them at the table. "Any fool can write his

97

Sherry Derr Wille

name."

Ralph bit the inside of his cheek until he could taste blood. Freddie teased him unmercifully, but he was too young to do anything about it. He'd learned not to get into a fight he couldn't win. Tomorrow he would have his fifth birthday, but no matter how many birthdays he had, Freddie would always be ten years older, with ten years more experience in life.

"Don't tease your brother," his mother admonished. "For his age, he's very intelligent. When he goes to school next year, he'll be way ahead of the other children in his class."

"Why can't I go to school when Harriett does?" Ralph inquired.

"'Cause you're too little, squirt, that's why," Freddie said.

"I wish Ralph could go to school with me. I don't want to walk alone," Harriett lamented.

Ralph didn't say anything more. He knew his sister was afraid to be alone. Ever since he'd been old enough to follow her around, he'd become her self-proclaimed protector.

By bedtime Freddie's teasing was all but forgotten. Across the hallway, a light burned dimly. Ralph knew it was because Harriett was afraid of the dark. As much as he wanted to go to Harriett's room to give her comfort, Ralph got ready for bed. At one time he'd gone to her room at night. When Pa found out, he took him out to the barn and gave him a good whooping with the strap hanging next to the ladder leading to the hayloft.

Dreams of Flossie filled Ralph's subconscious. In them she held him in her arms and told him how much she loved him. He had no idea who Flossie was other than the woman in the picture on his dresser, but in his dreams, she was someone who loved him unconditionally.

"It's time to get up," his father's voice came from the hallway outside Ralph's room, shattering the dream of Flossie. "You're five years old today. It's time you learned to pull your own weight around here."

Ralph rubbed the sleep from his eyes and got up to get dressed. He knew it would do no good to argue with his father.

Outside, the August sky was just starting to turn a delicate pink,

98

indicating the sunrise wouldn't be too far behind. Although he marveled at the beauty of it, Ralph didn't say anything. This was a memory he knew would be best left within the confines of his mind. Maybe he would tell Harriett about it, but no one else. She and she alone would understand what he was talking about.

"If you're going to be a farmer, Ralph, you have to learn how to milk and the milking is done early in the morning and again in the late afternoon.

In the barn his father patiently showed him how to milk a cow. It certainly wasn't anything Ralph hadn't seen before. He and Harriett often played around the barn while Pa did the milking.

The big cows were intimidating. He soon found they were gentle enough to allow him to wash their bags before wrapping his small hands around the teats in order to prompt the cow to drop her milk into the waiting pail.

By the time the milking was finished, Ralph had washed all the cows' bags and milked two of them all by himself.

"You did a good morning's work," his father complimented him as they walked toward the house.

All the while Ralph worked, he thought about his plan to walk Harriett to school.

"I know you don't want me walking Harriett to school. If I help with the morning milking every day would you think it over and maybe change your mind?"

His father gave him a surprised look and nodded. "I'll think on it and talk it over with your ma."

Ralph hurried to his room, anxious to share what he'd done all day with the picture of Flossie on his dresser. He knew it was only a picture, but considering the dreams of her he experienced, he felt as though she was a special person in his life. He could tell the picture anything and once he went to sleep she could come to him and tell him how proud he'd made her.

As soon as he got to his room, he went directly to his dresser. To his disbelief, the picture that gave him so much comfort in the past was gone. The dresser had been dusted and his childish belongings were repositioned so he couldn't even tell where the picture once stood. After searching his entire room, he realized for some reason it had been taken away from him forever.

"They can't stop me from talking to you, Flossie," he whispered. "I don't need a picture on the dresser to have you come to me in my dreams."

* * * *

Ralph didn't think the first day of school would ever come. When it finally arrived he rushed through the milking and ran ahead of his pa into the house. After washing his hands and face, he hurried upstairs to his bedroom.

The night before, he'd taken the time to choose the best of the clothes handed down to him from Freddie and polished his play shoes. For today, he wanted to look his very best.

"If I live to be a hundred, I'll never understand that boy," Ruben declared when he came in from the barn. "He worked like a demon this morning and as soon as we let the cows out to go to the pasture, he bolted for the house. Where did he get off to now?" Ralph heard his father say.

"He went up to his room," his mother replied.

"Why would he go up there?"

"It's the first day of school, Pa," Harriett answered. "Ralph knows I don't want to walk to school alone. He promised me I wouldn't have to go by myself."

"Don't see what you have to be scared of," Freddie teased. "The problem is you're nothing but a silly girl. I walked to school alone before you started going last year and I wasn't scared."

Ralph walked into the kitchen and decided he needed to come to Harriett's rescue. "It's okay Harriett. I promised to walk you to school so there's no need to worry."

"What about the morning chores?" his father asked.

"You promised, Pa," Ralph pleaded. "If I can walk Harriett to school, I'll help with the night milking too."

Finally, his father gave in and said it was a deal. With the situation settled, Ralph was so excited he could hardly eat breakfast, but he forced himself to finish what his mother set before him. If everything worked out as he planned, it would be a long time until supper.

After Harriett finished eating she was finally ready to leave for school. Ralph picked up her lunch bucket as well as the small cloth bag containing the school supplies she would need for the second grade.

"Freddie never carried my things," she confided once they started down the road to school.

Ralph nodded. He knew Freddie only walked Harriett to school last year because Ma made him. Even though Ralph was only five, he realized Freddie wanted to do little other than eating, sleeping and playing. He didn't get up at five to help with the milking and when Pa asked him to help with the morning chores, Freddie was far from happy.

The schoolyard was like a magic land to Ralph. Swings and a teeter-totter beckoned him like a magnet. At home there was a rope swing, but when Harriett or Ralph wanted to play on it, Freddie would make certain he monopolized it until they lost interest.

Harriett met up with her friends, leaving Ralph to hang back. Soon the teacher came out onto the porch and rang the bell to bring the children into the school.

Ralph watched them file in. He knew he should go back home and help with the morning chores, but the lure of the school was stronger than his duties at home.

On the side of the building, he noticed an open window. He knew if he sat below it, he could hear every word the teacher said. After seating himself, he picked up a stick and traced the letters the teacher recited to the first grade class. When she said two plus two equals four, he wrote the numbers in the dirt next to the letters he'd printed earlier. He smiled at how perfect his numbers and letters looked to his young eyes.

Time seemed to fly when at last he heard the teacher announce it was time for recess. Once she did, the children came out to play on the swings and teeter-totter.

"What are you still doing here, Ralph?" Harriett asked once she saw him sitting under the window.

Ralph got to his feet to stand in front of her. "I wanted to be sure I'm here in time to walk you home. I've been sitting under the window listening to the teacher. See, I've been writing my letters and numbers, just like you showed me." Proudly he pointed to what he'd scratched in the dirt under the window.

"Who do we have here?"

Ralph felt his stomach knot at the sound of the teacher's voice so close to him. He knew it wasn't right for him to be here and expected to be punished.

"This is my little brother, Ralph," Harriett said so Ralph didn't have to explain anything to this strange woman.

"Why are you here and not in school?" the teacher questioned kneeling next to Ralph.

To him, the teacher's voice sounded sweet, not as though she wanted to punish him. "I'm not old enough to go to school. I walked Harriett to school and I'm waiting so I can walk her home again."

He watched as the teacher's gaze moved from his face to the letters scratched in the dirt. "Did you write these?"

Ralph nodded. "Harriett showed me how to do it."

"She's done a great job. Would you like to come in and sit by my desk for the rest of the day? It looks like it's going to rain and I certainly wouldn't want you to get wet."

Ralph's mind raced at the possibility of being able to go to school, really go to school and not just sit under the window listening to the teacher instructing the children. "Yes Ma'am, I'd like that."

"Good. Come along with me and I'll get you a chair so you can sit by my side. I'll talk to your parents and if they say you can come to school this year, I'll enroll you in the first grade class."

Ralph was so thrilled about being able to go to school, he gave no thought to what his parents would think about his absence for the day or even what he would eat for the noon meal. Food was far less important than being able to learn the things the other kids were learning from the teacher.

At noon the children went outside to eat their lunches, even though it looked as if it would rain at any minute. Since Ralph knew none of the kids other than Harriett, he went over to the swings to entertain himself.

"I'll share my lunch with you," Harriett said, as she came over to join him.

"Ma packed it for you. I shouldn't eat your food. If I did, Pa would tan my hide good."

"But you have to eat. No one will know if you had half my sandwich."

Reluctantly, Ralph took the half of a cheese sandwich from his sister. He'd been so excited about school even thought he'd eaten breakfast, he realized how hungry he was. As soon as he tasted the sandwich made of a slice of cheese and Ma's fresh bread, his stomach growled in anticipation of getting more.

By mid afternoon, school was released for the day and Ralph proudly escorted Harriett home.

"Where have you been all day?" Ma asked, before Ralph could go up to his room to change into his barn clothes.

"I waited for Harriett. I knew when she came out for recess and lunch I could play with the other kids."

"Weren't you lonely waiting outside all by yourself?"

Ralph shook his head. "At recess, the teacher said if I wanted to stay, I could sit by her desk."

Ralph watched as his mother smiled at what he'd said.

"The teacher even gave Ralph a slate so he could practice his letters," Harriett explained. "She said if it was all right with you he could come back tomorrow."

"We'll talk to your pa about it tonight. I don't see any harm in it, but I worry it will be too much for you with your morning chores."

"I won't have any problems," Ralph promised. "I have to get my clothes changed so I can go out and help Pa like I said I would."

"Why don't you take a cookie before you go upstairs," she said, holding out the plate toward Ralph.

"I don't have time. Pa needs my help." Even though he wanted the cookies on the plate, he knew he would be expected to hold up his end of the bargain and help his father if he wanted to be able to return to school the next morning.

With his clothes changed, Ralph came back downstairs. To pacify his mother, he grabbed a cookie and went out to the barn.

From just outside the barn, Ralph could hear Freddie tormenting Harriett because he had the rest of the cookies and she couldn't have any.

"Share those cookies with Harriett," Ralph demanded. "She's littler than you are. You're her big brother and should be looking out for her, not teasing her."

"And what does that make you? The way I see it, you're like a pesky little mosquito buzzing around my ear, so why don't you fly away. I thought you were going to be doing the night chores with Pa. The way I see it, I did your morning chores, so you'd best get to work."

Ralph could feel his anger threatening to boil over at Freddie's words and the tone of his voice. It took only a minimum of steps for Ralph to stand toe to toe with his brother. He began to pummel Freddie with his small fists, landing blows one after another. In the end, Ralph returned to the barn and Freddie reluctantly shared his cookies with Harriett.

Ralph knew his pa saw what went on between him and Freddie, but he didn't say anything. He also didn't say anything about Ralph going back to school, but Ralph prayed he'd be able to return to the classroom where he sat next to the teacher all day and learned all the things he wanted to know about reading, writing and arithmetic.

The next morning, Ralph returned to school and his days fell into a natural routine. Even though he now helped with milking both in the mornings and at night, he didn't care. He was doing what he loved by going to school.

Chapter Fifteen

Even though Ralph was a good student, the fact they moved every couple of years left him with few close friends. He also struggled with different teachers at each school he attended.

Unlike the first teacher he had, most of them didn't realize his full potential. The year he was ten, they moved once again and he finally made a good friend by the name of Bill Dishrude. Bill was a year older than Ralph, but not having started school at the age of five they were in the same class. Ralph decided their friendship blossomed since they had both moved into the district on the first of March and the other kids didn't want to take the time to get to know them.

After a particularly bad blizzard, Bill and Ralph wanted to play with the kids who had built a snow fort the day before. When they were told they couldn't play with them, Ralph and Bill decided to build a snow fort on the opposite side of the schoolyard. Since the other kids loved to torment them, they spent their recesses and lunch hour being bombarded by snowballs.

Once everyone left school, they made a pile of snowballs and dipped them in water before they left to go home for the day.

The next morning, they were pleased to see their frozen snowballs were just waiting for them to send them flying at the first recess. After the pelting they took yesterday, revenge would be sweet.

With each snowball they lobbed, a kid from the opposing snow fort went down and didn't come back up.

"Just what is going on…" the teacher's words were cut short as one of the ice balls connected with her head.

Ralph never knew which one threw the fated ice ball, but he realized it didn't matter since they both would share the blame.

"Ralph, Bill, get in here immediately!" the teacher shouted as she held her hand to her now bleeding head.

Obediently, they followed their teacher into the school, each dreading what they would receive for punishment for retaliating against their fellow students who had not allowed them to play in their snow fort less than twenty-four hours earlier.

* * * *

"I'm gonna tell Ma what you did," Harriett teased as they walked home from school.

"Not if I tell her first," Ralph retorted as he kicked at a snow-covered rock on the side of the road.

"Pa will whoop you good."

Ralph could feel tears threatening to spill from his eyes. "It won't be the first time."

"I heard you and Bill can't go out for recess or lunch for the rest of the school year."

"It don't matter none. I don't get much studying done at night. I guess I need the extra time to study to keep up."

"Why is it you do the morning milking and have to help at night, too, when Freddie doesn't do any of it?"

Ralph pondered his sister's question. "Freddie has other things to do with his time. Besides I promised Pa I would do the milking with him so I could go to school with you. I don't mind doing the chores, especially since I can milk almost as fast as Pa."

Their conversation ceased as soon as they started down the lane toward home. In order to be the one to tell what had happened in school, Ralph broke into a run.

Once in the house, Ralph went right into the kitchen to tell his mother about getting in trouble before he lost his nerve. He knew it would bring about a more severe punishment than the one the teacher handed down, but he didn't care. He'd had the satisfaction of revenge and shown the kids who shunned him he was a force to be reckoned with. It didn't matter that he was a year younger than the other kids in his class, he could hold his own.

After he'd confessed, his father used the strap he had hanging in the barn on Ralph's bare behind. Although the punishment hurt initially, once it was over the pain was forgotten unlike the ongoing punishment he would endure at school.

From the schoolhouse window, Ralph and Bill watched as the other kids played in their snow fort until it melted into a muddy mess on what would soon be the lush grass on the schoolyard.

By the time spring brought warm breezes, they envied the other kids who could play baseball at recess and noon. The only thing they didn't miss would be the fact they probably wouldn't be chosen for either of the teams until last.

On the final day of school, Ralph and Harriett both took feed sacks to school so they could clean out their desks.

"Can you carry my bag?" Harriett asked as they started to walk home.

Ralph gladly took her bag along with his own. He knew he'd do anything for Harriett. Being close in age, they enjoyed a good relationship in comparison to how they viewed Freddie. He was so much older than either of them his interests in no way matched theirs.

They were ready to head down the lane toward home when Ralph noticed Harriett had lagged behind. "You better hurry up or I'll eat all the cookies," he teased before he saw the expression on his sister's face. "Do you feel all right?"

"No, I don't. My head aches, my throat is sore and I'm so tired I can't go any further." She no more than said the words, than she began to vomit.

Ralph helped her to lie down under the big oak tree at the end of the lane. He put all their school things into one bag and folded the other so she could use it as a pillow. The way she was shaking, he realized she was cold, so he took the coat Ma insisted he take to school this morning to cover her up. Once he touched her, he realized she was burning up with fever. Knowing he'd done all he could for her comfort, he began to run for home.

"Ma! Ma! Harriett's sick. I left her at the end of the lane, cuz she's too tired to walk any more. She says her head hurts and she's puking."

"What's going on?" Ruben demanded when he came into the kitchen just as Ralph finished his plea for help. "Where's Harriett?"

Amy quickly related the story Ralph told her. Once she finished, Ruben turned toward the door to go in search of their daughter.

"I'll go with you, Pa," Ralph said running to keep up with Ruben's larger strides. "I know where she is. I tried to make her comfortable but I couldn't carry her home."

Without further conversation, Ruben allowed Ralph to take the lead. They found Harriett exactly where Ralph left her earlier, her head resting on the makeshift pillow and covered with his coat.

Pa immediately scooped her into his arms and instructed Ralph to ride one of the horses into town to get the doctor.

Knowing his father would get Harriett to the house, he ran on ahead and quickly saddled a horse. Just as Pa and Ma were getting to the house, he was already on his way down the lane and heading toward town. About halfway there, he saw Freddie's car, but didn't take time to stop. He knew he had to get the doctor to come out to the farm as quickly as possible.

It came as a relief to find the doctor's office relatively empty. "I have to have Doc come out to the farm," he blurted out as soon as he entered the office.

Dr. Mason came from the back office. "What farm?" he inquired.

Ralph realized he hadn't taken time to tell the doctor who he was. Taking a deep breath, he explained just who he was, where he lived and what happened with Harriett after school.

Although the doctor offered Ralph a ride out to the farm, he turned it down. He had the horse to consider. By the time he got home, the doctor's car was parked up by the house. He was just about to head out to the barn to start the evening milking, when Pa came out onto the porch with Freddie.

"The doctor is in with Harriett. I'd like the two of you to go out to the barn and get started on the evening chores."

Ralph immediately turned toward the barn, leaving Freddie to stand on the porch until their father went into the house. "I don't see why I have to help with the milking," Freddie grumbled when he caught up with Ralph. "I was planning to go into town tonight."

"You don't have to help. I can do it by myself."

Moments later, Ralph regretted his words. Freddie took him at his word and stood by the ladder leading to the hayloft while Ralph did all the work.

"I'd go into town right now, but I ain't had anything to eat since dinner. I don't see what the fuss is all about. Kids get sick all the time and everything doesn't stop because of it."

"Harriett's more than just sick," Ralph snapped. "She's got more than a cold or the way you throw up in the mornings after you've been in town at night. This is really bad."

"A lot you know."

As soon as the milking was finished, they went back to the house. The doctor's car was gone. Pa sat at the kitchen table, a plate of bread and one of cold roast beef sitting before him.

"Is this all we get for supper?" Freddie asked.

"For tonight it is. Harriett has Infantile Paralysis. Your ma is in with her."

"Then I'm gonna go into town," Freddie said. "I can get something better than this to eat at the tavern."

"No one is going anywhere. We're under quarantine. Other than the doctor no one can come on the farm and no one can leave."

Ralph thought about the milking he'd just completed. "What about the milk?"

"We'll have to dump it, at least for the next two weeks. The doctor says Harriett has a very mild case, but we can't take any chances."

Although Freddie stayed home, he refused to help with any of the chores that needed to be done.

With the farm under quarantine, Ralph's chores seemed to increase. Pa spent more time at the house with Harriett and Freddie grumbled about not being able to go into town to be with his friends at night. Ralph knew what Freddie missed the most was the whiskey he could get in town, but said nothing about it.

With each completed task, Ralph came up to the house to check on Harriett. At night he moved his pillow and blankets down to the parlor so he could sleep on the floor next to Harriett. He understood her fear of being alone and in the dark and felt it was the least he could do to help his sister.

After one of Ralph's morning visits, his mother met him in the kitchen. "Would you go down to the creek and get me some watercress? I think it would be good for all of us to have watercress sandwiches for dinner today."

Even though Ralph knew it was late in the season for watercress, he said he would gladly go. Not only would it get him away from Freddie's grumbling but also he needed a break from the never-ending barn chores.

He'd just filled his feed sack with the tender greens when he saw movement in the grass. Pa warned him about the blue racers down by the creek, but he'd never seen one of the infamous snakes. Fear clutched at his heart as he made a mad dash for his horse. With the bright blue snake on his heels and his bag of watercress clutched in his hand, he jumped on the horse's back and rode for home.

"What's wrong with you, squirt?" Freddie asked, as Ralph reined his horse to a halt at the porch.

"S-Snakes," Ralph stammered. "Down by the creek—blue racers."

"What's this about snakes?" Pa asked, coming out of the house.

"I-I went down to get watercress for Ma and I saw one in the grass. It chased me to my horse."

"Did you get what your ma wanted?"

Ralph held out the sack of greens.

"Your ma will be glad to get these. I know I told you about the snakes and I give you credit for doing what you were told in spite of them."

"Yah," Freddie chimed in, "Ma wanted me to go down there and I said no. You wouldn't catch me within a hundred miles of snakes if I can help it."

Ralph understood Freddie's fear. What he didn't understand was the way his older brother could defy their parents. He would never think of saying no to something the folks asked him to do.

Although the quarantine ended after the first two weeks, Harriett didn't seem to regain the strength she'd had before she got sick. Ralph became even more protective of her once school started. The mischief he and Bill participated in last year was forgotten as his duty to his sister now took precedence.

Chapter Sixteen

"Can you believe we'll be graduating on Saturday, Ralph?" Bill Dishrude asked.

Ralph shook his head no. "Are you still planning to go to high school?"

"I'm not happy about it, but my pa says things are changing in this world and I'll need an education if I don't want to be a farmer like him. How about you?"

"I want to. After what Dr. Mason did for Harriett when she was so sick, I'd like to be a doctor."

Bill looked at Ralph in bewilderment. "That's a lot of studying. I don't think it's anything for me. Besides I've never seen a doctor with hands as big as yours. I think small hands are one of the requirements for getting into medical school."

Ralph looked down at his overly large hands. He'd never given them much thought in the past. Would they keep him from his dream? He hoped not.

On Saturday, Ralph sat through the ceremony and proudly accepted not only the penmanship award, but also recognition for having the highest grades in his class.

Ralph finally left the platform and joined his parents, beaming at his mother's praise for his accomplishments.

"I wanted to speak with you, Mr. and Mrs. Derr," Ralph's teacher said to them after the graduation ceremony at the courthouse. "Ralph has a brilliant mind, even though he has a mischievous nature. Will he be going to high school?"

"I don't know what the boy told you but his brother didn't go to high school and neither did his sister. As far as I'm concerned he has all the schooling he needs to be a farmer" Ralph's pa said

"But Pa," Ralph pleaded. "I want to go to high school. I want to be a doctor."

"What you want don't matter. If you don't want to do what I say you can get out on your own."

"Look, Ruben," Bob Parker, their closest neighbor aside from Freddie said. "Ralph can work for me and go to school with my kids."

"Over my dead body!" Ruben shouted. "Come on, Amy, we're going home.

To Ralph's horror his father's anger turned toward him. "And you, don't think you're coming home tonight. You need time to think about what you plan to do with your life. One thing is certain. You won't be going to high school. I'm sure I'd have to sign papers for you to go and there's no way in hell that will happen. Do you understand me?"

"I understand you perfectly," Ralph replied. "You don't have to worry, Pa. I won't be back tonight and tomorrow I'll come for my clothes."

It was Ruben who turned away from Ralph and motioned for Amy to follow him back to the car.

"Please, Ruben," Amy pleaded. "What harm would it do for Ralph to go to high school?"

"Why should that little bastard go to school when neither Freddie nor Harriet went?"

"Because he has the desire to learn. Freddie lived for the day when he finished school and Harriett wasn't strong enough to go on any further. I remember what it was like to want to get more education and to have to be content with what little I was allowed to have."

Ralph saw his mother in an entirely new light. It was no wonder she seemed so excited about his desire to learn. Without waiting to listen to more of his parents' conversation, Ralph hurried away in the opposite direction. The feel of someone's hand on his shoulder stopped him. He turned to see Bob Parker standing **at his side.**

"Where are you going, Ralph?"

"As far away from Pa as I can get."

"Do you have a plan?"

"I'll make one."

"Look, Ralph, its Saturday and you really don't know what you're going to do. I'd like you to come home with me. You can stay with us until you make a plan for yourself. I'm sure once you both sleep on it, things will be clearer. I'll talk to Ruben and see if I can't change his mind."

"You won't be able to change his mind. It's made up. I guess I've always known that I wouldn't get to go to high school."

"Then you'll be coming home with us."

* * * *

Sunday morning, Ralph waited until the Parker family went to church before he went over to the home farm. He hoped he wouldn't run into any of the family. If he were lucky, they'd have left for church by the time he got there.

He noticed the truck was gone and breathed a sigh of relief. Going into the house, he made his way upstairs to get his clothes. He stuffed the things in his dresser into the feed sack he'd picked up in the barn.

Before leaving, he took a piece of paper along with the stub of a pencil to write a note to his mother.

Dear Ma,

> I won't be back for a while, but don't worry about me. I guess I've always known I wouldn't be able to go on to school. I'll give Pa a chance to cool down.

Ralph

There was so much more he wanted to say in the note, but he was afraid Pa would read it and he didn't want his feelings to be known.

He thought about going to visit Freddie and Marion, but decided against it. They would be getting ready to come over for Sunday dinner and he knew Freddie would ask way too many questions about why he left home.

Instead, he turned toward the Parker farm. It was sad to think everything he owned fit into a feed sack. There wasn't much considering he'd spent his entire life with his parents.

* * * *

All through the weekend, Ralph insisted on helping with the morning and evening milking. He figured it was the least he could do in exchange for room and board since he had no money.

After the morning milking was finished on Monday, Ralph went up to the house for breakfast. "I'll be going into town after I get done with breakfast, I have to find a job and pay you folks back," Ralph announced once Mr. Parker finished saying grace.

"You know you can stay here as long as you want to," Mrs. Parker said.

"It wouldn't be right, ma'am. Pa was right. I have to make my own way in the world."

"That's all well and good," Mr. Parker declared. "I don't agree with you but as far as we're concerned you don't owe us a cent. You've more than paid us back by helping with the chores. You're welcome to stay here with us until you get a job. How are you planning to get into town?"

Ralph thought for a moment. "I'll walk. It's not that far."

"Nonsense. I'll take you into town, providing you agree to stay with us until you find something."

The thought of someone doing anything so generous for him was an alien feeling. If the Parkers wouldn't take any money from him, he swore in the far distant future, if he ever got to a point where he could offer it, he would help anyone he could.

After breakfast, Ralph dressed in his best clothes and allowed Mr. Parker to drive him to town.

"I've got a lot to do today," he said as he got out of the truck. "There's no use in wasting your time. I'll try to be back at your place before it's time for evening chores."

He watched as Mr. Parker drove away shaking his head. Ralph knew his benefactor didn't understand the position Pa put him in. The sooner he was able to get a job and be out on his own, the better off he would be.

The first stop he made was the police department. "Can I help you, son?" the officer at the desk asked.

"How old do you have to be to get a driver's license?" Ralph asked. He prayed he looked more mature than his actual age.

"You have to be sixteen. How old are you?"

Ralph thought for a moment. He didn't want to lie, but he needed to get a driver's license if he wanted to get a car and find a job. "I'm sixteen."

"Do you have a car we can use for the driver's test?"

"No sir, I don't, but I need a driver's license to get a car."

"What about your folks' car?"

Ralph shook his head. It was hard not to laugh at the man's question. In no way would Pa ever let him use the truck to take a driver's test. "I couldn't use that."

"Well, I have my car out back. We can use it for the road test."

Ralph thanked the officer and followed him out the back door of the office. He was glad Pa used to let him drive the truck around the farm. At least he knew what to do.

After the test they returned to the office to finish the paperwork. "Now, how old are you really?" the officer asked once he handed Ralph his first driver's license.

"I won't lie to you, sir. I'm twelve. I'll be thirteen in August. My pa kicked me out of his house on Saturday and told me to get a job. I can't do that without a driver's license."

"What about a car?"

Ralph thought for a moment. "My Pa banks in Footville. I thought I'd try to catch a ride down there to see if I can get a loan for a car. Then I can start looking for work."

"Well, I can't help you with the money for a car, but maybe I can help you out with a job. I heard old Peter Templeton over by Evansville is looking for a hired man."

Ralph thanked the officer and put his new driver's license in his pocket. Once outside, he started walking toward Footville. It didn't take long for him to catch a ride with a passing motorist.

The bank was an impressive building. In the past he'd gone there with his folks, but this time he was on his own. Walking in alone seemed strange. Taking a deep breath, he walked up to the man standing at the teller's window. "My name is Ralph Derr and I'd like to take out a loan so I can buy a car."

The man behind the teller's cage looked at him skeptically. "I'm afraid I can't take care of that for you, Mr. Derr. You'll have to talk to Mr. Canary." He motioned toward the older man sitting at a desk in one of the offices.

Ralph turned toward the office. To his relief, the older man looked up from his work and smiled. "Can I help you, young man?"

Ralph entered the office and sat in the chair the man indicated. "I need to borrow money for a car."

"Do you have a job?"

"No sir. That's why I need the car. I've got a lead on a job but it's over in Evansville and I need a car to get there."

"You have to know the bank can't loan someone your age any money. I know who you are. I've seen you in here with Ruben and Amy Derr. You can't be much older than sixteen."

Ralph could feel his stomach knot. "I'm twelve and I'll be thirteen in August. After I graduated from the eighth grade on Saturday, my pa told me to go out and get a job. The way I see it, if I want to have a job, I need to get a car."

"What about a driver's license?"

"I got that before I came here."

"If I were to loan you this money," Mr. Canary said as he reached for his wallet. "How do I know you'll pay me back?"

"All I can do is give you my word. If I get this job, I'll make sure you get part of my pay."

"Do you have a car in mind?"

"Anything that's cheap and runs."

"Well, I don't do this for many people, but I think you need a

117

break. I'll loan you the money and take you down to the used car lot. If I'm going to loan you the money to buy the car, I want to make certain you get something reliable."

Ralph thanked Mr. Canary over and over again as he got up from his desk. He could hardly believe he'd been able to get a loan on his word alone. Of course, it wasn't a loan from the bank, but it was better. It was a personal loan from Mr. Canary. Ralph knew the two of them would become good friends over the months it would take him to pay back the money he'd borrowed.

At the car lot, he let Mr. Canary do the talking. After looking at several cars, Mr. Canary finally decided on a black Ford with a rumble seat in the back.

"Mr. Derr and I are going back to the bank. When you have his car ready and filled with gas bring it over and we'll get the money ready for you."

Ralph obediently followed Mr. Canary back to the bank. Once in the office, Mr. Canary wrote out a paper with the information about the loan. He made two copies and gave one of them to Ralph.

"Now, when you come in to make your payments, be certain you bring this paper with you so you have written proof of each transaction. I don't want either of us to be cheated."

They'd just finished the paperwork when the salesman arrived with the car. Ralph could hardly believe it when he held the keys to his first car in his hand.

"Before you leave," Mr. Canary said, "I think its lunchtime. I want to hear more about your plans so perhaps you'd go over to the café with me."

Overwhelmed was the only word to describe the feelings flooding through Ralph's mind. What Mr. Canary called lunch reminded Ralph of Sunday dinner at home. While he had the roast chicken, Mr. Canary ordered roast beef.

As much as Ralph wanted to keep his business private, it seemed as though Mr. Canary was really interested. By the time they finished eating, he'd told the older man the entire story of his life.

It was after one when Ralph drove out of town and headed for

Evansville. The officer who gave him the driver's test had also given him directions to Peter Templeton's farm.

Ralph soon learned there were two Peter Templeton's, young Peter and old Peter. He liked both of them immediately. "I can see you have your own car young man. Can you handle a team for doing fieldwork? What about cows, can you milk? I need someone to help us with the fieldwork as well as the milking."

Ralph assured the old man he could handle a team and could milk faster than his father.

"Show me how you milk," the older man demanded, as he held his hands with his thumbs pointing toward the ground.

Ralph began to imitate the act of milking a cow.

"You are good, but I'll teach you to be better. Now I want to know how you are with the horses."

Ralph followed Mr. Templeton out to the pasture. Before him were the biggest horses he'd ever seen in his life. In addition to the size of the animals, they each had shaggy feet. "I've never seen horses like these," he confessed. "I've seen Percherons before, but they aren't anything like these."

"They're called Clydesdales. I love them like they were my children. If you can handle a team, you shouldn't have any problem with these babies. Can you start tomorrow?"

Ralph tried to contain his excitement and merely nodded his head, holding out his hand to seal the deal, remembering what Mr. Canary told him about a firm handshake. "Do you need me for morning milking?"

"Nine will be early enough. I'll tell mama to have pie and coffee ready for you. My boy will be out in the field, but I'll be here to show you around."

By the time Ralph returned to the Parker farm, he was well satisfied with all he'd accomplished in one day. He hurried up to the room he shared with Bob's son to change into his barn clothes. "Am I too late to help milk?" he asked when he entered the barn.

"Hardly, I'm just getting started. Tell me about your day."

Ralph knew if he were at home no one would ask about his day or take any interest in his accomplishments. He started by showing off his new driver's license and the note from the bank He finished with the information about his new job.

"I hate to lose you, Ralph, but I know you have to do what you think is right. I'm proud of the way you've handled this."

Chapter Seventeen

Ralph had been working on the Templeton farm for about two months when Freddie came to the farm one rainy afternoon.

"I heard you got a job here," Freddie said as he got out of his car and stepped up onto the porch. "I also heard you got a car. How did you get Pa to buy you a car? For that matter how did you get a driver's license? You ain't old enough, even if you are about to have a birthday."

The smell of sour whiskey on Freddie's breath made Ralph cringe. "It's good to see you, too, Freddie," Ralph snapped. He'd hoped his brother came to the farm to wish him a happy birthday, not rub in the fact their father wanted nothing to do with him. "Pa doesn't have to buy my cars for me and I went into town, took a test and got my driver's license."

Ralph did his best to hide the anger building in his mind. He knew Pa always bought Freddie's cars and licensed them for him. What Mr. Canary did for him was a loan. Pa gave the same thing to Freddie without expectations of getting anything back.

"If Pa didn't buy it for you, how did you get it?" Freddie taunted. "I know for a fact you've never had any money."

"I don't think it's any of your business. Pa made himself quite clear on the day I graduated from the eighth grade. He told me to get out and I did. I got my driver's license on my own, just like I got the loan for my car."

"A loan? Who would give you a loan?"

"It came from a good man who believes in Ralph," Mr. Templeton said from behind them. "Ralph is a good farmer and I'm lucky to have him working for me. He's allowed me to help him manage the money from his pay."

Ralph's heart swelled at the words of praise from his employer. He knew Freddie came to see if he'd fallen on his face. If the tables were turned and Pa kicked Freddie out after the eighth grade, Ralph knew his older brother wouldn't be able to stand on his own.

"Pa knows you're working here," Freddie said as though he thought Pa knowing where Ralph was would be of any interest to him.

"I haven't made a secret of where I'm working."

"I told Harriett I was coming here today. She wants to know when you're coming home."

Hearing Freddie talk about Harriett brought a lump to Ralph's throat. They were so close and he missed her more than he did his own parents. Unfortunately, Pa made it clear he wasn't wanted at home. Ralph knew Freddie was playing his trump card when he mentioned their sister. Harriett was special. He wanted to see her, but he just couldn't go home, not yet.

"Be sure to tell her I miss her."

"You could come over for Sunday dinner."

Ralph shook his head. "Not yet."

"I could bring her over to see you."

Ralph could hardly believe Freddie would suggest something to make both Harriett and him happy. "I'd like that. I'd like it a lot, but what will Pa say?"

"Pa doesn't need to know anything about it. Marion is pregnant and Harriett's been coming over to help out. The doctor says this pregnancy isn't going to be an easy one. We really appreciate all her help. It was Marion who insisted I come over to make sure you're doing all right. She's also the one who suggested I bring Harriett over to see you. I'll bring her back with me tomorrow."

Ralph wanted to hug his brother, but they'd never been close enough for such a display of affection. Instead, he held out his hand in the manner of mature men.

The next day Mr. Templeton declared it was too muddy to do any fieldwork. As soon as Ralph finished breakfast, he went up to his room to take extra time in dressing, as he wanted to look his best when Harriett arrived.

Mr. and Mrs. Templeton went into town to go shopping and young Pete went off to be with his friends as Saturday was his time to himself. On any other Saturday when they couldn't do fieldwork, Ralph would have gone into town as well. If it had been a week when he got paid, he would make the trip to Footville to make his payment to Mr. Canary. Today would be different. He hadn't gotten paid, but something better was about to happen. Today he would have a very special visitor.

The house seemed very lonely with everyone in the family gone. To escape the quiet of the empty house, Ralph went out onto the porch. He lit one of the cigarettes young Pete introduced him to when he first started working at the farm. He knew Pa would never approve of him smoking, but it suited him much better than the Copenhagen chewing tobacco Freddie and Pa so enjoyed. He took a long drag and allowed the smoke to saturate his lungs. He made no bones about the fact he enjoyed smoking.

A light shower washed the air, freshening everything at about ten in the morning. It bothered him to realize Freddie and Harriett hadn't arrived by noon. Since the family would be staying in town for dinner, Ralph went into the kitchen to find something to eat. Rather than cooking something, he cut two slices of the fresh bread Mrs. Templeton served at breakfast and buttered it. It wasn't much, but it would have to do. If he knew Harriett, it was possible she'd bring him a plate of cookies when she came to visit.

After eating, he went back on the porch. It didn't take long for him to fall asleep and begin to dream of his reunion with Harriett.

When Ralph heard a car come into the driveway, he jerked himself awake. Certain Freddie and Harriett finally arrived, he got to his feet to greet them. To his disappointment, the car belonged to the Templeton family rather than his brother.

"Did you have a good visit with your sister?" Mrs. Templeton asked when they joined him on the porch.

123

"They didn't come. I was foolish to wait for him to keep his word when he never has in the past. Why should things be any different now? I guess I'd best go in and get changed for chores." He didn't wait for a reaction from his employer. In no way did he want his childish emotions to show.

"Why don't you go into town tonight?" Mr. Templeton asked once they finished chores, supper and the milking.

Ralph shook his head. "I think I'll just go up to bed." He turned toward the stairs suddenly so tired he wondered if he'd be able to make it all the way up to his room. The anticipation of seeing Harriett and having his hopes dashed exhausted him.

* * * *

After breakfast on Monday morning, Ralph went out to cut hay. The rain of last week was but a memory as the sun shone brightly making it a perfect day to do the haying.

At noon when they all came in for dinner, Ralph was surprised to see Freddie's car parked by the house.

"I didn't think you'd ever come in for dinner," Freddie greeted Ralph. "Harriett and I've been waiting for you for the last two hours."

"I waited for you all day on Saturday. You should know with good weather we'd be out in the field. For that matter how come you're not haying?"

"Pa had something else to do today. We're planning to get started tomorrow. I thought it was a good time to bring Harriett over for a visit."

Ralph's emotions filled his mind. Freddie was twenty-three years old and still couldn't do the work on his own farm without Pa. Even as young as Ralph was, he knew with or without Pa's help, he would have taken today to cut the hay. Even if they didn't get around to bailing it until tomorrow, at least that part of the work would be done.

"It's good to see you and Harriett, but your timing is bad. I've got just enough time to eat dinner before I have to go back to work." The fact Freddie hadn't answered him when he asked why they hadn't come over on Saturday grated on his nerves.

"Ma needed Harriett to help her make jam," Freddie said, as though reading Ralph's mind. "I figured today would be as good as Saturday to come over."

Ralph held his tongue. It didn't matter how little time he'd have with Harriett, he knew he'd enjoy every minute of it in spite of Freddie's inconsiderate attitude.

"Ralph!" Harriett exclaimed as she came out of the house. "I'm so glad to see you. Freddie said you were working here. I couldn't believe you weren't waiting for us to get here. Freddie said he told you we were coming."

"I'm sorry I wasn't waiting for you, but Freddie said you were coming on Saturday. I had the day off so I waited all day for you to get here. Today is a workday. You know how it is on a farm."

Tears ran down Harriett's cheeks. "I didn't think about that. I brought you cookies for your birthday. If I'd known, I wouldn't have promised Ma to help her with the jam."

Ralph reached up and wiped away the tears running down her cheeks. "Don't worry about it. I bet that jam will be really good."

"It is and I brought you a jar of it along with the cookies."

"Are you sure you won't get in trouble with Ma?" Ralph remembered snitching a jar of jam and getting caught. Ma certainly hadn't been happy with him about it and Pa made sure he never touched the canned goods again without permission.

"Of course I won't, silly. Ma sent this to you for your birthday."

Ralph expressed his thanks, knowing full well this was nothing his mother sent in honor of his birthday. In all of his thirteen years of life he'd never been given a gift. The only birthday he remembered at all was when he turned five and his father took him out to the barn to start doing the morning milking. He readily remembered coming back into the house and finding the picture of Flossie no longer on his dresser.

"You'll have to thank her for me."

Before Harriett could say more, Mrs. Templeton called them all in for dinner, including Freddie and Harriett. "If I would have known this was going to turn into a birthday celebration, I would have made a cake instead of pie this morning," she said as they all sat down to eat.

"It's not my birthday," Ralph protested.

"It's close enough for me," Harriett said, brushing a kiss across his cheek. "This is the first time I've gotten to see him since he left home over two months ago, so I figured it was an opportunity to wish him a happy birthday."

After dinner, Mr. Templeton insisted Ralph spend the afternoon with his brother and sister. When Ralph argued about the amount of work he thought he should be doing, Mr. Templeton shook his head.

"It isn't every day you get to celebrate your birthday with your family. You do far more than your share around here. Take the afternoon off. I saw how much hay you cut this morning. It will give us plenty to do just to get it baled. This way you can get the evening chores started so if we work longer than we thought we would, we won't have to worry about quitting before we've finished."

Ralph's annoyance at Freddie for interrupting his workday was overshadowed by being with Harriett. He knew most kids his age would miss their parents if they left home. Ralph, on the other hand, missed Harriett. In a strange way, he also missed Freddie's wife, Marion.

They spent the afternoon sitting on the porch and talking while Mrs. Templeton brought them out lemonade.

"Pa was sure you'd come home once you cooled off," Harriett said, as she sipped the lemonade. "When you weren't back by Wednesday night, he went over to Bob Parker's place. I was actually scared of him when he came back. I've never seen him so angry."

Ralph could feel his father's anger. "The only reason he wanted me to come home was so I could be his unpaid hired man in the barn. At least here I get paid for the work I do."

"I understand, but I still miss you."

Harriett's confession tore at Ralph's heart. His relationship with Harriett was so special. Throughout the afternoon, they shared childish memories, some good, some bad and some extremely funny.

"Remember when we went out to get the mail and there was a sample of candy." Harriett said, laughing so hard she could hardly continue. "I went up to the house crying to Ma and told her how mean

126

you were to me. When she found out it was Ex-lax she said it was okay because I didn't want that kind of candy."

Ralph joined Harriett in laughing at the memory, clutching his stomach in agony. "I remember spending hours in the outhouse. Pa said it served me right. When I finally stopped shitting, Pa gave me a whoopin' for being so greedy. At least I learned what Ex-lax was used for."

By three, it was evident Freddie was anxious to be going. Since none of the conversation revolved around him, soon became bored and insisted it was time they left for home.

Ralph walked them out to the car. Once there, he shook Freddie's hand and hugged Harriett tightly. He waved until the car drove out of sight.

"Did you have a good reunion with your brother and sister?" Mrs. Templeton asked when Ralph came back to the house.

"Yes it was good of Mr. Templeton to give me the afternoon off. I'd better go out and start the evening chores." He knew Mrs. Templeton wanted to comment, but he left the house rather than allow anyone to see how the reunion affected him. From what Harriett said, his father had written him off completely.

Ralph thought about his life as he brought the cows into the barn and prepared to start the evening milking. In his entire life, he'd never felt wanted. His parents usually fussed over Freddie and Harriett on their birthdays, but August 12th was never more than just another day when the farm work came before anything else.

With the end of August came the time for threshing the grain. Mr. Templeton joined with many other farmers to go from farm to farm to get the work done. Over a two-week period, Ralph worked for many different farmers while he collected his pay from Mr. Templeton.

It was a good way for Ralph to get more experience and meet the men who worked the farms in the midst of the depression. It was during this time, he received the nickname of 'Red'. It became a private joke between him and young Pete Templeton. With Ralph's dark black hair and piercing brown eyes no one could understand why Pete called him Red. To Ralph it was a great joke, since his initials denoting Ralph

127

Eugene Derr spelled out the word Red. Pete told him that if his initials spelled out a word it meant he would be a very rich man. With the depression he doubted anyone would ever be rich, but it made for a good joke on the men they worked with.

As the threshing crew made the rounds of the farms, Ralph enjoyed the good cooking of the wives. They made great meals and Ralph ate his fill. They'd been on the rounds for about a week when they came to a place where the men kept saying they didn't want to go.

"There's never enough to eat at this place," Pete cautioned. "Whatever you get, that's what you eat. If you pass it on, you won't get anything else passed to you. Everyone who has ever worked on this place knows they just don't put on the big meals like we've been getting."

Ralph decided Pete was joking until they sat down to eat dinner. In front of him was a small bowl of mashed potatoes. Looking around the table, he realized the remainder of bowls filled with food were equally small and the meat platter contained only one small chicken that had been fried to a golden crispness. Heeding Pete's warning, as soon as the farmer finished saying grace, he jealously guarded his trophy bowl of potatoes, eating them plain without so much as a pat of butter of any of the gravy he saw on the other side of the table.

With the threshing completed and the corn picked, Mr. Templeton told Ralph he couldn't afford to keep him on over the winter, but he would like to have him come back in the spring.

Ralph knew the winter would be a lean one, but soon heard about a young couple, Ben and Margie Sloan, who were running a farm over by Evansville. Ben had been brought up in Madison and knew nothing about farming. It had been the depression, coupled with an illness leaving Margie's grandfather unable to run his farm, which brought them out of the city to a life on a farm.

Ralph heard they'd struggled to make a go of things for the past year. Then everything changed when their bull gored Ben and he was unable to do the heavy work farming demanded. Since Margie had a new baby to tend to, she couldn't be much help in the barn either.

The farm was well kept, but from what he'd heard, the couple was trying to keep things going with help from their neighbors. It was one thing to accept charity on a short-term basis, but with the injury Ben incurred, Ralph knew it would be a long time before he could do for himself. Thank goodness it was winter and nothing more than caring for the stock would be necessary.

"We can't afford to pay you much," Ben said as they sat at the kitchen table sharing a cup of coffee.

Ralph assessed his needs. Over the summer, Peter Templeton had been a very generous employer and by the end of the threshing season Ralph had been able to pay back the loan on his car entirely.

"I don't need much. I need money for gas and to go out at night. Other than that I would appreciate a place to stay and my meals."

"Are you sure?" Margie asked.

"Positive. I just want you to know I do like to go into town at night."

"Oh dear, that might be a problem. I wouldn't want you waking the baby when you came home."

"I don't think that will be a problem. If you promise me you won't rearrange the furniture, I can come in at night and never turn on a light. I doubt you'll even know when I come in to say nothing of waking the baby."

Ralph enjoyed working for Ben and Margie. Even though Ben was fifteen years older than Ralph chronologically, Ralph was an old man if for no other reason than his experience.

Each night while Ralph did the milking, Ben came out and asked dozens of questions about farming. Even though Ralph was little more than a child, he'd been handling farm chores and milking for the past eight years and enjoyed sharing his expertise with Ben.

"I can't believe you're so much younger than me," Ben said one night, as Ralph was finishing with the last cow. "How do you know exactly what to do?"

Ralph smiled. "Been doing it all my life. It takes more physical strength than brains. Guess Pa thought I had exactly what he needed."

Ben shook his head, as though defeated. "Do you think you can ever teach me to be as comfortable as you are?"

Ralph tried not to laugh at Ben's question. "I guess the first thing I'd tell you is not to turn your back on your bull. Of course, you already know that."

Ben was the one to laugh. "I sure do. The way I feel I won't be ready to take over much before spring. I hope you can teach me everything I need to know by then."

Ralph smiled. With a long winter stretching ahead of them, he could teach Ben a lot of what he needed to know. The problem was that most of the things the man needed to know would have to come with experience. As much as Ben wanted to make a go of running this farm, Ralph was afraid things might not turn out the way Ben planned.

"Christmas is next week," Margie said one night at supper. "Ben's folks want us to come to Madison to spend a few days with them."

"That's great," Ralph replied, knowing his own family didn't want anything to do with him even at this special time of the year. "When are you leaving?"

"That's the problem," Ben said. "I'm thinking of just sending Margie and the baby to the city tomorrow."

"What about you?"

"I don't feel right about leaving you here alone. I realize you can handle the work, but Christmas is such a special time. I don't like the idea of making you work when you could be with family."

"Trust me, my family won't miss me. I haven't been home since the end of May, so to me Christmas is just another day of the week. The cows don't know it's supposed to be a holiday. They still need to be milked. I promise, I'll be just fine and will take good care of your place for you. Stay as long as you want."

Margie got up from her chair and came over to where Ralph was sitting to give him a hug.

The following morning, the family left right after breakfast. It would have been easy to stay in the warmth of the house, but the barn chores still needed doing, so Ralph went out to get busy with them.

When he returned to the house at noon, he saw an envelope on the kitchen table with his name on it. How he'd missed it before he went outside, he didn't know. Picking it up, he took a table knife and slit open the flap.

Dear Ralph,

Thank you so much for all you do for our family. I've left soup on the stove. All you have to do is heat it up for your supper. I know you usually go into town on Saturday nights, but in the root cellar, you'll find enough food to make satisfying meals.

Your Christmas present is under the tree. Please keep the tree watered and don't open your gift until Christmas.

Thank you again for everything you've done for us.

Margie

He read the note several times. Each reading brought thanks for bringing him to this farm.

Before he came here, he knew all about Christmas. His friends told him about the pine trees they put up in their homes for Christmas as well as the presents they received from their families and the ones they gave in return.

Christmas at home brought memories of Ma's Christmas cactus and how it would be in full bloom by now. The only presents he ever remembered receiving was maybe an orange or an apple in the stocking he left for Santa Claus. The one Christmas he did remember vividly had been when he was six years old. He and Harriett got the usual fruit and Harriett received ribbons for her hair.

The present that stood out the most was the one Freddie got. Just after his sixteenth birthday in February, Pa bought Freddie a car. In late fall there had been an accident and so Freddie's Christmas present had been a car to replace the one he wrecked. Back then Ralph didn't think much about the monetary value of the gifts they received. Now he realized things were never equal where he and Freddie were concerned.

After eating a bowl of the soup Margie left for him, he went into the parlor to relax until it was time to go out and do the evening chores. The Christmas tree in the corner enticed him. To him it was the most beautiful thing he'd ever seen. It was covered in silver tinsel as well as brightly colored glass ornaments and strings of popcorn and cranberries. Since the house had electricity, at night Margie would plug in the strings of lights bringing the tree alive. Beneath the tree was a present with a tag bearing his name. In a way it bothered him. He didn't think to buy presents for the family.

Rather than sitting down, he went upstairs and changed his clothes. He needed to make a trip into town to do the first Christmas shopping he'd ever done.

Even knowing he wouldn't be spending Christmas with his family, he bought presents for them just the same. For Pa and Freddie, he bought Copenhagen, for Ma, Harriett and Marion small bottles of toilet water and for the baby Freddie and Marion would soon be having, he found a small rattle. After buying presents for his family, he purchased a nice handkerchief for Margie, a pocketknife for Ben and a rattle like the one he bought for Freddie's baby for the little girl he'd come to love while working here. He was pleased when the woman at the general store offered to wrap his purchases for him. As she did, he wrote the name of each person on the packages when she finished.

Christmas was a quiet day. Although the present with his name on it pulled him like a magnet he refrained from opening it. He wanted to share his excitement with his employers, as he was able to give them the presents he bought for them.

The day after Christmas Ben and Margie returned with baby Sandra. "Did you have any problems?" Ben asked.

"None whatsoever. I did try to keep the house clean so Margie wouldn't have so much to do when she got home."

"You did a great job," Margie said. "I'm not at all interested in why the house is so clean. What bothers me is that you haven't opened your present."

Ralph laughed. "I decided it would be best if I waited for you two to get home. Then I could give you your presents."

Although Margie seemed upset about Ralph not opening his presents from them, her eyes lit up at the thought of receiving another present.

After Ralph helped Ben carry in several boxes from the car, Margie made a pot of coffee and cut into the mincemeat pie from Ben's mother. Ralph could feel his mouth start to water in anticipation of having a piece of pie. At home Ma made cakes and cookies. It hadn't been until he started working for Mr. Templeton that he first tasted pie. In his eyes no one could make a pie to match the ones that came from Mrs. Templeton's kitchen.

Margie brought their pie and coffee into the parlor, while Ralph proudly distributed the gifts he'd purchased at the general store. Once everyone had a present, Margie insisted Ralph open his present first.

Getting a present was such a special thing, Ralph fumbled with the colorful wrapping paper. Once he opened it, he saw a work shirt he knew Margie made especially for him. For the first time in his life, someone gave him a piece of clothing that wasn't a hand me down.

"I-I don't know what to say. Thank you seems to be far too little."

"It's us who should be thanking you," Ben said. "I'm learning more from you than I ever imagined possible. If it weren't for you I wouldn't have been able to spend the holiday with my family and still be able to send my milk to market."

Ralph smiled at the compliment. He knew these people couldn't pay him as much as he made working for Peter Templeton, but the words of praise meant more than all the money in the world. "Enough about me. I'm anxious for you to open your presents."

Margie carefully unwrapped her gift, meticulously folding the paper so it could be reused. "Oh, this is way to pretty to use," she declared holding up the handkerchief. "Thank you so very much, but you shouldn't spend your hard earned money on us."

Her response was the same for the gift for the baby. Ben was the last to open his present. He certainly didn't have to say a word to express his thanks. The expression on his face said it all. The pocketknife Ralph chose was the best one the store had to offer.

Being close to chore time, Ralph again thanked Ben and Margie before going out to the barn to start the milking.

He was almost half done when Ben joined him. "You'll never know how much we appreciate you staying here so we could go to my parents' place for Christmas. Something came up while were in the city. My folks don't think we can make a go of it out here, especially because of my accident. We also talked to Margie's grandfather. He's thinking about selling the farm. I know we'll be here for a little while, but my dad has found a position for me in town. I'm afraid we're going to have to let you go when we move."

Ralph could feel a lump forming in his throat, but he didn't want to make things any harder for Ben than they already were. Had this happened to him last summer, he would have been devastated, but since he'd been on his own he'd met several farmers who all said if he ever needed a job they would hire him. His work ethic was becoming well known and finding another job might take time, but according to Ben he did have the time to look for something different.

"It sounds like a good opportunity for you. I know working the farm has been hard for you. It has to be something you're born to, not thrown into without warning."

"I still feel bad about having to tell you like this, especially after you spent your money on us for Christmas presents. As far as we're concerned the best present you could have given us was staying here to do the chores."

"It wasn't anything special. My folks never made a big deal out of the holidays. I will have to ask for some time off during the day soon. My brother and his wife are expecting a baby and it's due to be born soon. When it is, I'd like to go over to see them, but of course I'd be back for the night chores."

"You amaze me, Ralph. I know how old you are. I can't imagine working seven days a week when I was your age."

Ralph shrugged his shoulders. "Ain't no different from being at home. Pa says it's the curse of being a farmer."

"What about school? Shouldn't you be going to high school?"

Ralph nodded. "I'd like to go to school, but Pa would have to sign papers for me to go and he said no. I know better than to go against him." Even though Ralph spoke the words, he knew he didn't mean them. More than anything else, he wanted to go to school, but what he wanted never mattered much to Pa.

* * * *

Ralph was in town the Saturday night after Christmas when he heard about Freddie and Marion having a little girl. He'd gone to the movies before stopping for ice cream. In the drug store, Ralph ran into one of Freddie's friends.

"I certainly didn't expect to see you here," Ralph greeted the man. "Why aren't you over at the tavern with Freddie?"

"Haven't you heard? I don't think Freddie will be coming into town on Saturday night for a while. Three days after Christmas Marion had a little girl. From what I heard, Marion didn't have an easy time with the birth. I ran into Freddie yesterday in town buying some things for Marion. He said his ma and Harriett have been coming over to help out."

Ralph finished his malt and headed for home. Tomorrow he would be seeing his parents for the first time in over six months. He had mixed emotions about what the next day would bring. On one hand, he was excited to hold his new niece. Being around Ben and Margie's baby had made him anxious to be part of Freddie's daughter's life. On the other hand, facing Pa would be difficult. Freddie and Harriett both said Ma worried about him, but never mentioned Pa's feelings.

By the time Ralph pulled into the driveway the house was completely dark. It was nothing new. He often stayed out late on Saturday night and arrived home long after the family went to bed.

After parking his car down by the corncrib, he crossed the snow-covered lawn to get to the house. Before going in, he scraped the snow from his boots and undid the laces. Once in the kitchen, he took off his boots and put them on the rug by the back door. In this way, he could cross the parlor to the stairs leading to his room without making any noise to disturb the family.

In the dark room, he tripped over something he would learn was a table, before falling onto the sofa. Without warning a woman screamed.

From upstairs the baby cried and Ralph could hear Ben's feet hit the floor. Within seconds, Ralph was on his feet as the lights came on illuminating the entire room.

On the sofa, a young woman clutched a sheet close to her neck. "What-what are you trying to do to me?" she shrieked.

"I-I'm sorry," Ralph stuttered.

It was Ben and Margie's laughter that defused the situation. "I'm afraid this is my fault, Ralph," Margie finally said. "This is my cousin, Katie. She stopped in after you went to town. I forgot to tell her you'd be coming home and not to move the furniture."

Ralph's embarrassment soon became a story he'd never forget, especially when he learned the red mark on Katie's face was a birthmark and nothing he was responsible for.

* * * *

The next morning after breakfast, Ralph hurried through his chores so he could get cleaned up to go to Freddie's and meet his new niece.

Driving from the farm where he was working around Evansville, to Freddie's farm outside of Brooklyn, Ralph experienced mixed emotions. He'd purposely stayed away from the area around his parents' farm.

He recognized Pa's truck parked up by the house and took a deep breath. After parking his car next to Pa's vehicle, he took the box of gifts from the back seat and stepped onto the porch.

Before Ralph could raise his hand to knock, the door opened and Harriett stepped out onto the porch to greet him. If it hadn't been for the box of gifts he carried, he knew his sister would have thrown herself into his arms.

"I'm so happy to see you, Ralph," she said, as she looped her arm around his elbow. "Marion had a baby girl. They named her Beverly Leila. I'm so pleased her middle name is the same as my middle name."

Ralph smiled. "I heard about it in town last night. I knew I couldn't stay away any longer."

Once inside the warm kitchen, Harriett focused on the box in Ralph's hand. "What's in the box?" she asked, sounding more like a small child than a fifteen-year-old woman.

"Christmas presents," Ralph proudly answered.

"Well, if that's not the biggest waste of money I've ever seen, I don't know what is," his father complained when Ralph set the box on the kitchen table. "You certainly didn't learn this extravagant nonsense in our home."

Ralph wanted to take the wrapped presents back to the car, but he knew it would break Harriett's heart. Instead, he handed his father and Harriett their gifts.

From the corner of his eye, Ralph saw his mother and Freddie enter the room. "Oh, Ralph," his mother exclaimed. "I wondered if you'd ever be coming over to see us again."

"I told Freddie I wouldn't miss getting to know my niece. I brought you all presents as well." He handed her the package with her name on it and picked up the one for Freddie.

"You shouldn't have spent your money so foolishly," his mother protested.

"I know Pa says it's foolish," Ralph replied, "but I've learned a lot these past six months. So many people have been generous to me, I feel as though I have to give something back. I gave gifts to the people I'm working for and couldn't believe how much enjoyment it gave me. Maybe it is foolish and a waste of money, but what else do I have to spend it on?"

"Freddie says you have a car," Pa said. "How in the hell did you get a car to say nothing of a driver's license?"

"I don't see why it matters to you, but I went into town and got a driver's license and then went down to Footville to the bank and took out a loan to buy the car."

"A loan! Who in their right mind would give you a loan?"

"I talked to Mr. Canary and he gave me a personal loan, not from the bank but out of his own pocket. I made enough money over the summer that I was able to pay him off before fall. I own the car free and clear. It didn't cost you anything, so don't worry about it."

"Please don't argue," Harriett pleaded. "This is a happy time. Come with me, Ralph. I want you to meet little Beverly."

Ralph obediently followed Harriett through the parlor to the downstairs bedroom where Marion and the baby occupied the large double bed.

"Ralph, it's so good to see you," Marion said, extending her hand to him. "This is our little Beverly."

Gently, Ralph picked up the baby and watched as she immediately wrapped her small fingers around his larger one. He knew from now on there would never be anything Beverly could ask him for that he wouldn't move heaven and earth to provide.

Marion, on the other hand, looked very pale and her voice was weak. He thought about what the man in town said the night before about the birth being hard on her. As he recalled, she'd always been a delicate woman. He'd even worried about how she would be able to keep up with Freddie and still run a home. Now the baby would complicate her life even further.

Beverly soon fell asleep in Ralph's arms and he handed her to Harriett so she could be returned to her cradle. Marion, too, seemed to tire. "I'd better let you get some sleep. I'll be back to see you before I leave."

"Can you stay for dinner?" his mother asked.

Ralph noticed the table was already set for five rather than four and the smell of roast chicken made his mouth water. They visited for a while but Pa made a point of not joining the conversation. It hurt Ralph, but he had too much on his mind to allow his father's actions to bother him too much.

By three in the afternoon, Ralph had been in to see Marion and Beverly again. He promised he come back soon, but wondered if it would be possible. With Margie's grandfather considering selling the farm and Ben and Margie moving back to Madison, he had no idea where he would be working or even where he would be spending the night. One thing was certain; it was far too cold to be sleeping in his car at night.

While he'd been in the house a snowstorm blew in. Ralph knew the roads would be treacherous making the trip back to the farm where he worked difficult. Harriett and his mother said their good-byes in the house, but Freddie and his father followed him out onto the porch.

"We weren't expecting to have to feed you today," his father said. "Times are hard for all of us. Freddie has a big burden now with Marion's health and the baby to consider."

Ralph knew what his father meant. He wasn't welcome, but since he'd been the one to come unannounced, he would be expected to pay his own way. Reaching for his wallet, he pulled out a dollar bill and handed it to his father. "I don't want you to ever be able to say I don't pay my own way."

Chapter Eighteen

Ralph sensed the indecision in Ben's voice when he first mentioned returning to Madison to do the work he loved. Farming seemed like a temporary solution for the young couple. The problem came in the knowledge Ben wasn't cut out to be a farmer. Even though the injury from the bull healed weeks ago, Ben made no move toward doing any of the chores, even the ones he could easily handle. Ralph knew Ben would be much happier in the city doing what he knew best.

Rather than wait for the inevitable to happen, Ralph started looking for another position. He'd just returned from a trip to a farm outside of Brooklyn, Wisconsin when Ben met him on the porch.

"I have good news and bad news," Ben said as Ralph neared the house. "Margie's grandpa was out today and said he sold the farm."

Ralph took the steps two at a time. "That's the good news, how soon before you and Margie will be moving to Madison?"

"That's the bad news. A man by the name of Ted Bumgartner bought the farm and he wants to be able to move in by February first. I asked if he'd be keeping you on, but he told Margie's grandpa he wouldn't need any hired help. I'm afraid we haven't given you much time to find another job."

"I didn't want to tell you, but I've been looking. I found a job over by Brooklyn. I was going to tell you he wants me to be able to start on February first. At least the timing worked out well."

Without further comment, Ralph went into the house to change his clothes so he could start his barn chores. When he'd gone over to see

Freddie and Marion's new baby, Harriett told him Ted Bumgartner had been coming over to see her and she expected to have him ask her to marry her after the first of the year. From what she told him, Pa approved of Ted, so it was entirely possible this farm would become Harriett's home as soon as she passed her sixteenth birthday.

By the last weekend of January, Ben and Margie moved from the farm to Madison. Since the cattle were being sold with the farm, Ralph stayed on to take care of them until the morning of the first of February. After he finished the milking, he packed his belongings into his car and left for Brooklyn. He certainly didn't want to let his family know he'd been working on the farm Ted bought in anticipation of his marriage to Harriett.

* * * *

Ralph had been at his new job for two weeks when he heard his parents and Freddie were moving from their farms near Albany to ones closer to Evansville and the farm where Harriett would be living after her August wedding to Ted.

After talking to his employer about it, he was able to head out early on the morning of March first to help with the double move. Since Freddie's farm was close to Pa's place, all he had to do would be to ask Marion which farm the men would be packing up first.

As soon as he pulled into the dooryard, Ralph noticed the trucks parked by the machine shed to start loading, eliminating the need for him to go to the house.

Like most of the tenant farmers, Freddie owned half the cattle, making it necessary for them to load them into the stock trucks.

Getting out of his car, Ralph walked down to the barn. "Can you use some more help?" he asked.

Freddie turned and broke into a wide grin. "You're the last person I thought we'd see here today. How did you know we were moving? The last time we saw you was just after Beverly was born. At that time, we didn't know anything about the move."

Ralph bit his tongue to keep from saying he'd heard about the move from one of Freddie's drinking buddies in town. "I went to the show the other night and someone mentioned it. I figured you could use an extra pair of hands. It looks like you have things under control here. Is Pa's place packed up yet?"

"Pa's been working over here, so we could get this stuff moved first. We're heading over to his place next. I doubt you'd be willing to help Pa so why don't you go with the trucks over to the new place to oversee settling my stuff."

Ralph nodded. By going over to Freddie's new place, he wouldn't have to contend with Pa. Rather than get into one of the trucks, he followed them to the new farm near Evansville and close to where he'd worked only a month earlier.

Once there, he found Ted waiting for them. "It's good to see you, Ralph," Ted greeted him. "Harriett was wondering if you'd come today."

"It's a family thing," Ralph commented. "I hear you and Harriett are getting married. I also heard you bought a farm, congratulations on both counts."

"I got lucky with the farm. The old man who sold it to me said his granddaughter and her husband were running it, but the guy had a run in with a bull and couldn't work. Guess they had a hired man working for them, but I said I didn't need any transient to help me."

Again, Ralph worked hard to keep his temper in check. It would do no good for him to admit to being the transient who lost his job when Ted bought the farm from Margie's grandfather. "I can understand why you would make such a decision. From what I've heard, you're a damn good farmer. Harriett's a lucky girl."

Ted beamed at the compliment. Leaving Ralph to work with the settling of the cows in the barn, Ted went over to the machine shed to oversee the men working there.

By noon, Freddie's cows were co-mingled with those belonging to his landlord. Ralph also stored Freddie's pails and other milking utensils in the milk house.

The noon meal was ready by the time Ralph went up to the house. The first person he saw was his mother. "It's good to see you, Ma," he said, genuinely pleased to see her.

"How did you find us?" Harriett inquired.

"I heard about the move in town, so I thought I'd come over to see if I could be of help."

"You look good, Ralph," his mother observed.

"So do you, Ma."

"Where are you working?"

Ralph thought about his reply. It would do no good to say he'd lost his job when Ted bought the farm where he'd been working since last fall. It was best if he made up a believable lie. "At the same place, but come spring, my boss is selling out. I'm looking for something else, but so far I haven't found anything. You don't have to worry about me. I'll be okay."

"I'm sure you will," Harriett said as she showed Ralph the way into the dining room to find a seat at the table.

After dinner, he went over to the place his parents rented. Like he'd done for Freddie, he worked mainly in the barn and milk house. By doing so, he stayed out of his father's way. The looks he received from the old man over lunch were anything but friendly. As soon as he finished with what he felt was his responsibility, Ralph sought out Freddie.

"I've got to be going. It's almost time to do the night milking," he said.

"I'm glad you came." Freddie extended his hand. "I know Ma would like it if you'd come over for Sunday dinner."

Ralph thought for a moment. Going home for Sunday dinner would be something to make his mother happy. He knew Pa would not be pleased to see him and would expect payment for what he ate. To again see the smile on his mother's face would be worth the price his father would extract in payment.

* * * *

On Sunday, Ralph waited until his employers left for church before he cleaned up to go to his parents' home. When he helped them move he'd worn work clothes. Today he wanted to dress up. Since he received room and board as part of his pay, the money he made was for him to spend as he pleased. With his car paid off, he reserved a portion of his salary to buy clothes that weren't handed down from Freddie.

On Saturday night, his employer's wife cut his usually unruly black hair. After putting in the Brill Cream, he worked hard at styling it perfectly.

When at last his appearance passed his meticulous expectations, he left the house to drive over to Evansville for Sunday dinner.

"What do you think of Ma's new house?" Harriett asked once she finished showing him through every room.

"I think it's one of the best places they've lived in. Ma deserves it."

"It is nice," Harriett agreed, "but wait until you see the place Ted and I are going to have."

Ralph remembered living and working at the farm Ted bought for Harriett. He enjoyed the memories of working for Ben and Margie. They'd been good people and the house was one of the nicest places in the area. "Ted told me about it. I'm happy for you. It's a shame Pa is making you wait until your sixteenth birthday before you and Ted can get married."

"I know, but Ma says it's best if we wait. I've been busy making a lot of linens. I'm even working on this apron." She stooped to pick up the blue and white checked apron she was adding decorating with cross-stitch embroidery.

Before Ralph could say anything, his mother announced she had dinner on the table. As usual his father sat at one end of the table with his mother at the other. To Ma's right sat Freddie and Marion, while Harriett and Ted had been moved close together to accommodate a place for Ralph to sit.

"Harriett showed me around the house," Ralph said, as he took the platter of chicken from his sister. "This is a really nice place, Ma."

"I don't know where you've been working," his father commented. "Wherever it is, they certainly haven't done anything for your table manners."

Memories of the silent meals he'd endured during his childhood assaulted Ralph's mind. He'd been gone from his father's home for less than a year and yet he felt as though he'd never belonged here. At the places where he worked, the families talked about their day at the dinner table and even smiled.

The remainder of the meal was eaten in silence. With dinner finished, the men went into the living room while the women cleaned up. Freddie and Pa each took a pinch of tobacco and Ted lit his pipe. Relaxed for the first time since his arrival, Ralph took a cigarette from his pack.

"When did you start smoking those filthy things?" Pa asked.

"Last summer," Ralph replied.

"Those things stink. If you want to smoke it, take it outside."

Without making further comment, Ralph stuck the cigarette back into the pack and put it back into his shirt pocket. He wanted to say that spitting the juice from the tobacco was nasty and that his cigarettes didn't smell any worse than Ted's pipe, but thought better of the idea.

"With the folks in a place like this, I'll bet you're sorry you left home," Freddie said.

"I'm doing okay. Like Pa said, I'm old enough to be on my own."

"What about that car you're driving?" Ted asked. "Does it belong to your employer?"

The question made Ralph bristle, but he refused to show it. "No, it belongs to me. I was able to pay it off last summer. I made good wages and did some outside work. I own it free and clear." He could see Freddie cringe at the thought of his being able to afford his own car, when Pa bought Freddie's cars and paid for his license.

When the women came in from the kitchen the tension drained from the room. Harriett prattled on and on about her wedding plans. Ralph listened intently, glad to have the attention turned away from him.

Checking his pocket watch, Ralph was relieved to see it was already three in the afternoon. "I have to get back to work," he said as he got to his feet.

"Will you be back for supper?" Harriett questioned.

"I'm afraid not. I'm doing the milking alone tonight. By the time I drive back and do the chores, it will be too late to come back for supper.

After putting on his coat, his father, Freddie and Ted followed him out to the car, saying they also had chores to do.

"When you're out of a job, don't think you can come back here," Pa said.

"I wouldn't think of it." Ralph reached for his wallet and pulled out a dollar bill. What hurt the most was that his father took it without saying it wasn't necessary.

Chapter Nineteen

In May Josh, the son of Ralph's employer, returned from the military, leaving Ralph again without a job. Even with the advance notice, finding a job had proven to be difficult. When he did find one, it was on one of the farms formerly run by Freddie and his pa. The owner of both farms decided to move to Freddie's farm and wanted to hire someone to help in running both of the places. Considering he had a competent tenant on the other place, they could exchange work and Ralph could be of help on both places.

The agreement was Ralph would have each Saturday as a day off. Although he didn't like someone else milking what he considered to be his cows, he did enjoy the freedom of having a day to himself each week.

When he took the job he already knew about the planned date for Harriett's wedding. With that knowledge, he made arrangements to have the entire weekend off. It meant working both days of the weekend following the wedding, but he didn't care, since he wanted to do something special for Harriett and Ted's wedding present.

A month before the wedding, Ralph paid Ted a visit. If his arrival at the farm just prior to the evening milking came as a shock to Ted, Ralph couldn't detect it.

"I've come with a proposition for you, Ted," Ralph began. "I'd like to take over your milking for the night of the wedding and the next day. You know, as a wedding present for you and Harriett."

Ted smiled at the offer. "I've been wanting to take Harriett away overnight for a wedding trip, but I didn't know how I'd be able to swing it with the milking. Of course, I know I'll probably lose a lot of money with someone different doing the chores. Cows are funny about things like that."

"I hear you there. Since I have Saturdays off, I thought I could come over every Saturday before the wedding and help you with your chores and the milking. That way I'd be familiar with your cows and learn how to do things the way you like them done. Then on the day of the wedding, I'd be ready to do your night chores as well as morning and evening chores on Sunday. The only thing I ask is for you to keep it a secret from Harriett, for that matter something just between you and me. I'd like it to be a surprise."

Ted agreed and Ralph pitched in helping his soon to be brother-in-law do the evening chores. Since Ted purchased the entire herd with the farm, Ralph knew there would be no drop in production. He was familiar with these cows and they knew him well.

When they finished the milking, Ted offered to round up something for their supper, but Ralph declined. Instead he went back to the farm where he worked and got cleaned up for a Saturday night in town, going to the movies and getting a bite to eat at the restaurant.

On Sunday, Ralph was just finishing his chores when he saw his employers returning from church. After changing from his barn clothes, he joined them for Sunday dinner.

"My husband tells me your sister is getting married," Ellie Baxter, his employer's wife said. "What are you giving her as a wedding present?"

Ralph tingled with excitement to be able to share his secret present. "I've already asked for the entire weekend of the wedding off. I'm planning to do the milking for her husband on Saturday night as well as Sunday so they can go away together."

Ellie sat quietly as her husband, John, congratulated Ralph for thinking of such a generous offer.

"I know this will be something your sister and her husband both appreciate," Ellie began. "I also think she deserves something a little more personal. I think I have an idea for the perfect gift."

By the time they finished eating Ellie decided she would be embroidering a set of seven dishtowels, one for each day of the week, to be added to Ralph's planned gift for Harriett's wedding.

* * * *

On the morning of the wedding, Ralph took extra care in dressing. He also put a set of barn clothes in the back seat of his car, so he could change before doing the evening milking. During the night he'd heard it raining, but as he drove toward Evansville, the sun shone brightly. Even the oppressive heat and humidity of the past week had disappeared.

Ralph could never remember his mother's garden looking more beautiful. Rows of gladiolas and zinnias were interspersed among the vegetables. Around the house petunias, pansies, geraniums and moss roses bloomed in a rainbow of colors.

Guests were already gathering in the front and side yards when Ralph made his way up to the house. He saw Harriett as soon as he entered. To him she looked more radiant than ever before. Behind her he saw Marion. She too looked lovely. Maybe what Ellie told him was true; weddings did bring out the best in women.

Causally, he placed his gift on the table with the others before going to greet his sister.

"I'm so glad to see you, Ralph," Harriett gushed. "I wondered if you'd be able to come today."

Ralph took her in his arms and gave her a kiss on the cheek. "I wouldn't miss your wedding for anything in the world." From the corner of his eye, he saw his father enter the kitchen. Rather than engage in an ugly confrontation, and ruin Harriett's special day, he went out to the garden to wait for the wedding to begin.

"The folks were wondering if you'd be here today," Freddie greeted him. "Considering you haven't been around much since you helped with the move, we thought you were avoiding us."

"You know I've been busy. Besides, I can't always afford the cost of eating Sunday dinner with the folks considering I can eat where I'm working for nothing."

Freddie got a strange expression on his face. "About that money I owe you…" he let the rest of what he started to say die on his lips.

Ralph remembered when he ran into Freddie three months ago in town. He'd come into town early on a Saturday afternoon to meet up with friends before going to the show.

From across the street, he saw Freddie leave the tavern. Hoping his brother hadn't seen him he kept walking.

"Ralph, Ralph, wait up," he heard Freddie call.

Turning around he waited for Freddie to cross the street.

"Boy am I glad to see you," Freddie began, his words slurred. "Marion asked me to get her a few things from the store, but I'm a little short. I don't like charging things. Do you think you could lend me a few dollars?"

Without hesitation, Ralph reached for his wallet. In the front he had just enough money to go to the show and get something to eat. It would be easy to tell his brother no, but his conscience wouldn't allow it to happen. Ever since he'd paid off his car, he'd saved part of his paycheck. Not always being able to get to the bank, he usually carried his extra cash in a hidden compartment of his wallet. "How much do you need?" he finally asked.

"I know it's a lot to ask, but I could use ten dollars. I'll pay you back, you know I will."

Ralph shook the memory from the corner of his mind. The ten dollars as well as all the other money he'd loaned Freddie ever since he'd been out on his own would never be repaid and Freddie knew it.

"Don't worry about it," he finally said. "You've got your hands full with Marion and the baby. I did see Marion in the house and she looked good. I didn't see Beverly, though. Where is she?"

"Marion's mother has her. This is naptime. Of course, she'll bring Beverly over so Marion can nurse her after the wedding."

Ralph knew it made sense, but he'd been looking forward to seeing his niece. It had been almost six months since the disastrous Sunday dinner right after the move. He was certain she'd grown and taken on a real personality in that amount of time.

Before Ralph could comment, he saw Marion start walking toward where Ted and his brother stood signaling the beginning of the wedding. By the time she stood across from Ted's brother, Ralph saw his pa and Harriett walk across the lawn so Harriett could join Ted and the ceremony could begin.

Once Ted and Harriett were pronounced man and wife the people gathered cheered. Men slapped Ted on the back and demanded kisses from Harriett. The women stood on tiptoe to lightly kiss Ted's clean-shaven cheek and hugged Harriett tightly as they wished her well in her marriage.

While the women went inside to watch Harriett open her gifts, Ralph joined the men to talk about farming as well as repeat stories about the various places he'd worked in the past year and a half.

After about an hour, Marion came out to say cake and coffee were being served in the house.

As soon as he stepped in the door, Ralph's mother pulled him aside. "The dishtowels were beautiful, where did you get them?"

Ralph smiled, pleased with her approval of his gift. "When I told my boss I wanted to have this weekend off, his wife insisted I needed a perfect wedding gift. She went right to work on making the towels for Harriett."

"Did you tell Ted about what you wrote in Harriett's card?"

Annoyance tugged at the fringes of Ralph's mind, but he refused to give into it. "You didn't think I'd write something like that without talking to Ted, did you? Like I said, I asked for the weekend off when I first heard about the wedding. Since I usually get Saturday off, I made a deal with my boss to work next Saturday to get this entire weekend to take care of Ted's chores."

"I don't see you taking off work to help me," Freddie complained.

Ralph knew his brother was trying to tease him, but the tone of Freddie's voice was aggravating. "As I recall, Pa and I milked your cows when you moved to your first farm. Of course, at the time of your wedding, you and Marion were living with the folks and didn't need to worry about chores when you went away to get to know each other better. It seems to me you rarely did any of the milking when you lived at home."

Ralph could tell their discussion was drawing undo attention, since Ted, Harriett and Pa had joined them.

"Well, I think it's a very generous offer," his mother said. "Where will you and Harriett be going, Ted?"

Ralph didn't miss the mischievous twinkle in Ted's eyes. "I made reservations for us in a hotel in Madison for tonight. I thought we could explore the city tomorrow."

After Ted and Harriett left for Madison, Ralph went over to Ted's place to do the evening chores. Without Ted being with him in the barn, Ralph felt as though he'd come home. Even though Ted told him he could stay in the house, Ralph drove back to where he was staying. Going into the house that would become Harriett's home would be more than Ralph could stand. No matter what, he would always consider this to be Ben and Margie's home.

Chapter Twenty

Over the next two years, Ralph worked on various farms around the area. During that time, he kept in contact with his family by showing up at least once a month for Sunday dinner. Although no one ever said anything about it, his father made a practice of following Ralph out to the car so he could receive payment for the meal his mother just served. Ralph always made sure he had a dollar bill to give his father, even though at times it constituted the only money he would have until his next payday.

Over the years, Ralph often saw Freddie in town. On several such occasions, he would end up loaning his brother even more money he knew would never be returned. If he were truthful with himself, deep down in his heart he admitted he'd stopped keeping track of the amount of the loans.

As Beverly grew from infant to toddler and then to adorable child, Ralph fell more and more in love with his niece. With Beverly at the table, the silent Sunday dinners were a thing of the past. It was evident the strict upbringing of the Derr home hadn't extended to Freddie and Marion's table. Beverly's childish laughter and endless chatter prompted the adults to join in the fun of family table talk.

In July of 1937, Harriett gave Ralph yet another niece to love. Donna Jean was born on July twenty-first. Although he knew Marion envied her sister-in-law, Ralph could tell having another child would be a burden for Marion. At three years old, Beverly was still nursing, even though it seemed to drain her mother completely.

In the fall of 1937, Ralph had made several new friends and went into town with them on a regular basis. His employment opportunities were also growing as many of the farmers in the area approached him to work for them.

Halloween gave Ralph and his friends the perfect opportunity to go out and do some mischief. They'd discussed what to do for weeks, considering everything from tipping over outhouses to smashing pumpkins. At last they decided to go to Argyle and see what was happening in the small rural community.

The first thing they saw was a democrat wagon. In reality it was a two-wheeled milk cart with long handles so the farmer could pull the cans of milk from the barn to the milk house with very little effort.

Ralph drove through town as one of his friends sat in the rumble seat pulling the cart behind them. At the top of the hill his friend let go of the handles and sent the stolen cart careening down the hill. Without giving thought to what happened, Ralph and his friends drove out of town, pleased with the mischief they'd participated in.

The next Sunday, all his family could talk about was the horrible hoodlums who did so much damage in Argyle on Halloween.

Ralph listened as Harriett told how someone had driven through town pulling a democrat wagon behind their car. At the top of the hill they'd let it loose. "It wouldn't have been so bad if it hadn't gone through the window of the Argyle Atlas and smashed into the china shop. They've posted a twenty-five-dollar reward for the capture of these hoodlums." She went on to describe Ralph's car perfectly.

The more she said the more Ralph's stomach churned. "I-I'm not feeling well," he finally said. As he hurried out of his parent's house, he almost forgot to leave the money to pay for his meal on the library table.

Once back at the farm where he was working he pulled his car into the machine shed. Tomorrow would be soon enough for him to drive down to Footville and trade it in on a different model.

* * * *

By February, all talk of Halloween pranksters and rewards came to an end. Ralph found work closer to Evansville and the rest of his family, to say nothing of farther away from Argyle.

He'd just come in from doing morning chores when he heard his boss' phone ring. "It's for you. Ralph," the man said.

Receiving a call was something Ralph never experienced. "Hello," he said tentatively.

"Ralph, Ralph, this is Freddie. I called the doctor for Marion and he says he won't come out this time. Marion is so sick she has to go to the hospital. Can you come over and stay with Beverly?"

Ralph swallowed hard. Once he agreed, he left his breakfast uneaten. He hurried out to his car to drive the three miles to Freddie's place. He got there to find Beverly nowhere in sight and the kitchen littered with the remnants of breakfast.

After cleaning up the mess, he went to the bedroom where he knew he'd find Marion. When she wasn't there, he knew they'd already gone to the hospital. It was possible Beverly had been taken to the folks' place.

Instead of cleaning up the mess, Ralph hurried over to his parent's farm, relieved to find Beverly in his mother's care.

"Freddie called me to come over and watch Beverly," he said. "I panicked when I couldn't find her. Thank goodness she's over here with you."

"I'm sorry Freddie took you away from your job," his mother said. "He wasn't thinking right. At least he had enough sense to bring Beverly over here when he was on the way to the hospital to join Marion. Her parents took her before Freddie brought Beverly here."

"How bad has it been for Marion?" he asked.

"I doubt if you know it or not, but Marion has been sickly ever since Beverly was born. I told her she shouldn't be nursing Beverly past the age of four, but she wouldn't listen to me. I swear that's why her health is so poorly. I saw her a few days ago and I haven't seen her looking so terrible before. I'm afraid this is something far worse than just being run down."

"Since you're taking care of Beverly, I'll go back to Freddie's place. I'm certain he hasn't finished his morning chores. Once I get them done, I'll clean up his house. He needs to be with Marion at the hospital now."

From the corner of his eye, he saw his father join them in the parlor.

"I hope you're man enough to know what your responsibility in this is. You don't have any roots put down, but Freddie does. He has Beverly to think of to say nothing of the owner of his farm. I think it would be best if you quit your job and moved in with him. With Marion so sick, Freddie will be in no shape to do his daily work."

Without giving his father an answer, he left the house and went out to his car. On the drive back to the farm he now called home he came to the conclusion he needed to quit his job and stay with Freddie. He had enough money saved to see to his needs and being February, he knew his boss would be relieved not to have to pay his salary during the slow time of the year. He also remembered talking to Marion at Christmas time. She wasn't feeling well that day and asked him to promise to take care of Beverly. Knowing Freddie, he wouldn't be responsible enough when he didn't have Marion at his side.

As he suspected, his boss sympathized with the situation and even paid him the last of his wages before Ralph left to go back to Freddie's farm.

The house was strangely silent, even though the dooryard was filled with cars. He recognized his father's car as well as the ones belonging to Freddie and Ted.

Trying to be as quiet as possible, he put his belongings in the spare room off the kitchen and prepared to go out to the barn to see if he could be of help.

"Pa said you left," Freddie said from behind him.

"I went over to where I've been working to quit my job. I thought you might need me here."

Freddie smiled weakly. "I do. I can't expect Pa and Ted to keep doing my chores."

"How's Marion?"

"Her folks are at the hospital with her. I think they blame me for this. If she hadn't given birth to Beverly, her heart wouldn't…" Freddie sunk down on a kitchen chair and put his head in his hands, sobs wracking his body.

"That's nonsense and you know it," Ralph said, trying to comfort his brother. "Marion's always been weak. Having Beverly was her heart's desire. I know she loves that little girl more than she loves anything else in the world."

Ralph left his brother to think about what he'd said.

After cleaning the manure from the gutters and spreading the lime, he filled a feed cart with silage and threw down hay and straw to feed the cows and get the fresh bedding.

By the time Ralph checked his pocket watch he realized it was time to do the evening milking. It amazed him how quickly the day slipped away from him.

With the milking finished and the milking utensils rinsed, he finally went up to the house. Suddenly hungry, he hoped he could find something to eat. Going without breakfast and lunch left his stomach growling in protest.

After he finished with the night chores, he came back into the house. A pot of stew bubbled on the stove and the smell of it make his mouth water. It had been over twenty-four hours since he had his supper last night. Freddie's morning phone call had interrupted his breakfast and lunch had been non-existent.

Mr. and Mrs. Walmer came out to the kitchen. "I thought you and Freddie would need something to eat," Mrs. Walmer said, her voice laced with tears.

"I do appreciate it, Ma'am. How was Marion when you left her?"

"The doctor said she's stabilized and after she rests tonight she should be ready to come home tomorrow. We told Freddie we'd be over in the morning to go to the hospital with him to bring her home," Mr. Walmer said.

"It's good Freddie has you to lean on," Ralph replied. "I doubt if he'll be in any shape to drive there on his own. As for Beverly, my folks will take good care of her and I'll be doing the chores. I've quit my job so I can be here to help any way I can until Marion is back on her feet."

Mrs. Walmer left the house and for the first time Ralph noticed Freddie sitting at the dining room table. Filling his bowl with stew, he went into the adjoining room to sit with his brother. As he did, he saw tears forming in Freddie's eyes. "Why are you doing this?" Freddie questioned.

"Because you're my brother and that's what families do." What he left unsaid was his father demanded he do what was right for Freddie.

After supper, Freddie excused himself from the table. Ralph knew his brother was more than likely going out to have some of the whiskey he'd stashed in the wood box on the back porch.

The house was quiet when Ralph got up the next morning. Rather than check on Freddie, he went out to the barn. Milking took the better part of an hour. When he finished, he fed the cows and cleaned the barn before going up to the house for breakfast.

A pot of oatmeal sat on the stove and a note on the table said Mr. and Mrs. Walmer had left with Freddie to go to the hospital to pick up Marion. It was evident the note had been written by Mrs. Walmer since he knew Freddie wouldn't think to do anything so considerate.

Ralph finished eating his breakfast and cleaning up the kitchen. He knew he needed to get back out to the barn to finish the chores, but for some reason, he lingered in the warmth of the kitchen. He wondered what it would be like working here and doing the chores he knew were Freddie's responsibility. He doubted Marion would ever be strong enough to be of any help to her husband, leaving the lion's share of the work for him. Ralph didn't care. As long as Marion and Beverly were cared for, he could handle the outside work.

From the dooryard, he heard tires crunching against the crusty snow of the driveway. He hurried to the front door in time to see Mr. and Mrs. Walmer in the front seat of the car and Freddie slumped in the back. Marion was nowhere to be seen.

Mr. Walmer got out of the car and went around to open the passenger's door for his wife. Ralph held open the door, knowing the worst had happened and yet not wanting to believe it.

Mrs. Walmer nodded at him and went to sit at the kitchen table where she began sobbing bitterly while her husband tried to comfort her.

"Marion's gone," Mr. Walmer said his voice flat and emotionless.

It was hard for Ralph to believe, but at the age of twenty-one Marion had finished her lifespan and left Freddie alone with Beverly. "I thought she was coming home today," Ralph said, his voice hardly louder than a whisper.

"She was," Freddie said as he came through the door, tears running down his cheeks. "When we got there, she said she was feeling much better. Her mother was going to help her get dressed, but when she stood up she collapsed. Within minutes she was gone. The doctors told us there was nothing they could do. Her heart was just too weak. What are we going to do, Ralph? How are we going to take care of Beverly without Marion?"

Ralph hurried to his brother's side and supported him as his knees buckled. Before he could sink to the floor, Ralph guided Freddie to a chair Marion's father held out for him.

As much as Ralph wanted to retreat to the barn to do his own mourning in private, he forced himself to stay at Freddie's side. He was at a loss for any words of sympathy for his older brother, especially in light of the fact it was only eleven o'clock in the morning and Freddie already reeked of whiskey mixed with the chew Freddie always kept between his lip and his gum was enough to sicken Ralph.

"Beverly," Freddie's voice sounded frantic. "Where's Beverly?"

"You took her over to stay with Ma yesterday."

"But Marion needs to nurse her. Ma can't nurse Beverly. She should be here."

"Beverly is a big girl. Ma's taking very good care of her, but we do have to tell both the folks and Beverly about Marion."

Reluctantly, Freddie got to his feet, leaning heavily on Ralph for support. Seeing Freddie close up, Ralph noticed the stubble of a two-day growth of beard. "You need to get cleaned up and rinse out your mouth. You don't want Beverly to see you like this."

Freddie allowed Ralph to lead him out of the room. As though Ralph was the parent and Freddie the child, he helped his brother to get cleaned up, shaved and put on clean clothes.

Whether or not Freddie completely understood Marion wouldn't be coming back to the farm Ralph didn't know and to be truthful, didn't want to know. At Mr. Walmer's suggestion, Ralph followed them into town to go to the funeral home to make the necessary arrangements. With that done, they went back out to their parents' farm. Their mother met them on the front porch, with Beverly at her side.

"Daddy, Daddy, you came to get me. Where's Mama?"

Ralph watched as Freddie knelt in front of his daughter and pulled her into a tight embrace. His tears fell so quickly it was Ralph who delivered the news about Marion's death.

"What does dead mean, Uncle Ralph?" Beverly asked in her childish way.

"I know your Mama takes you to Sunday school and there they tell you about God and Jesus. Well, God sent his angels to bring your Mama to be with him. He needs her with him."

"I want my Mama," Beverly wailed.

"We all do," Ralph said, "but God needs her more. Now, your daddy and I have to go into town. We have lots of things to do, so you need to stay with Grandma and Grandpa for a few days. Can you be a good girl for them?"

Beverly sniffed loudly and wrapped her arms around Ralph's neck. "I still want my mama," she cried.

Ralph lifted her high in his arms and kissed her cheek before handing her back to his mother. The hardest thing he ever had to do was to leave this dear little girl with his parents when he knew she needed to be with her father. Unfortunately, Freddie was in no shape to take care of his daughter and probably wouldn't be until long after the funeral.

As they were getting into Ralph's car, Pa came up to the passenger's side to talk to Freddie. "I know you don't have enough money for a cemetery plot. I'll go out to the cemetery and purchase it for you."

Freddie merely nodded, indicating to Ralph his brother hadn't given any thought to where his wife would be laid to rest.

On the morning of the funeral, the amount of family, neighbors and friends who came was almost overwhelming. One of the neighbors, he'd been told, had stayed at Ma and Pa's place to take care of not only Beverly, but also Harriett's daughter, Donna Jean.

While Ralph sat next to Freddie, Marion's parents sat across the aisle from them, their faces washed with tears and their expressions ones of overwhelming grief.

At the cemetery, Pa said he'd not only purchased one lot, but a block of six. Ralph took a mental count of the family. There would be spaces for his parents, Freddie and Marion as well as Harriett and Ted, leaving him, as always the odd man out. In reality it didn't matter where he spent eternity. What hurt was being on the outside of the family he'd grown up with and been kicked out of so easily.

With the graveside services complete, Ralph helped Freddie back in the car and drove back to the folks' farm. The neighbors had come in and brought enough food to feed the entire county.

Someone filled plates for the family, allowing Ralph to keep a close watch on his brother.

"What are you going to do now, Ralph?" Harriett asked, as they sat at the table to eat their dinner.

"I've quit my job and moved over to Freddie's place so I can help him with Beverly," Ralph said when Freddie sat with his head in his hands sobbing silently. "I talked it over with the people I'm working for and they agreed with me. With winter, there's not much for me to do there and paying me has become a hardship. If Ma can keep Beverly for a few more days, it will give me time to get settled in and familiar with Freddie's needs." Again he thought of Pa's insistence he be the one to help Freddie, but made no mention of what was on his mind. It would do no good for him to complain. Even if Pa hadn't told him what to do, he knew it was for the best. Freddie was in no shape to run a farm and take care of his daughter at the same time.

161

Chapter Twenty-One

March brought the first warm winds of spring. Ralph could see Beverly beginning to heal and overcome the loss of her mother. On the other hand, Freddie spent his days in the bedroom he shared with Marion drinking himself into oblivion. By evening he shared supper with them and went into town to drink with his friends at the tavern and purchase another bottle to make it through the next day.

Since Beverly slept until Ralph finished the milking, he got her up when he came in to prepare breakfast. After that, she became his constant companion. She sat on a hay bale and watched as he cleaned the barn and fed the cows. She helped him slop the pigs and with spring, she helped him get the equipment ready for the planting he knew would have to begin within the next couple of weeks.

As spring turned to summer, Ralph knew he was unable to trust Freddie with Beverly's care. Becoming her sole caregiver, Ralph found she wormed her way into his heart. He took her to the barn while he did the evening milking and into the field while he planted oats and corn, and did the cultivating and haying. Even the big horses didn't frighten her, but on Sunday when they went to dinner with his parents, aunt, uncle and cousin, she was all girl.

Although Ralph missed his evenings in town, he loved his niece more than he ever thought possible. By the end of September, Ralph's car was acting up, so he took Beverly on a trip to Footville to look into getting a new vehicle. He delighted in introducing Beverly to Mr. Canary.

"My, what a lovely young lady you are, Miss Beverly," Mr. Canary greeted her. "Would you like a piece of candy?"

Beverly's eyes shone with excitement as she looked up at Ralph to see if it would be all right. Once he nodded, she smiled brightly. "Yes please," she replied, making Ralph proud of the manners Marion taught her and he reinforced.

With Beverly occupied by trying to decide which piece of chocolate to choose from the box, Mr. Canary turned his attention to Ralph. "What are you looking for in a car, Ralph?"

"I'm hoping to get a good trade in on a new car. I have enough in my account to put a dent in the cost after my trade in. I was hoping to be able to finance the remainder."

Mr. Canary nodded. "Your timing is very good. The new models for 1939 just came in and that means the dealer will want to get rid of the remainder of 1938 vehicles he has on his lot. Would you like me to call over there and talk to the owner or go with you like I have in the past?"

Ralph beamed. "I'd like to have you go with me. I think they give me a better deal with you looking out for my interests."

An hour later, Ralph and Beverly headed for home in a new car with a small lien payable to the Footville State Bank.

"Grandma and Grandpa will be excited to see your new car, Uncle Ralph," Beverly said as they pulled out of town.

Clouds of doubt crowded Ralph's mind. His parents had never been excited about anything he'd done in his life. In his heart, he knew this time would be no different. "I hope they are."

On Sunday, October second, everyone gathered at the home farm for dinner. Beverly was thrilled to be able to play with her younger cousin, Donna Jean.

Although Freddie drank heavily throughout the week and on Saturday night, Ralph insisted he at least stay sober on Sunday when the family got together.

"Uncle Ralph got a new car," Beverly said as soon as they sat down to eat.

"How could you afford that car?" Ruben asked.

"I've been saving for it for a long time," Ralph replied, annoyed with his father's tone. "I got a good deal on it and with my trade in they didn't need that much money. What I didn't have, Mr. Canary was able to finance for me."

"I think it's great," Harriett said. "Can I drive it?"

Ralph couldn't say no to his sister. He'd always been her protector and whenever possible he'd tried to give her anything she wanted, within reason.

"Sure you can."

Harriett was overjoyed. "You know, I wish I'd have an accident."

"Why would you say such a thing?" Freddie inquired.

"You and Ralph have both had accidents and you're good drivers. I think I'd be a better driver if I had an accident."

"Oh, honey," Ma lamented. "Don't wish for such a thing. Freddie and Ralph have more experience driving than you do. That's why they're better drivers. I don't see why you want to drive anyway."

"I tell her the same thing all the time," Ted commented. "She keeps saying it gives her more independence. It's all the fault of this modern society we live in."

Everyone laughed at the statement, but Ralph didn't miss the look of concern on his mother's face.

Since it was such a beautiful October day, the men all went out to sit in the yard so they could watch Beverly and Donna Jean play on the lawn.

"Are you ready to go for your ride?" Ralph asked, when Ma and Harriett came out to join them.

Harriett's eyes sparkled. "Are you kidding? Of course I'm ready to drive your new car. Can I go into Evansville and get us some ice cream?"

Ralph laughed at her enthusiasm. After giving her his keys, he reached into his back pocket and pulled out his billfold to give her the money for ice cream.

"Can we go with you, Aunt Harriett?" Beverly begged, holding tightly to Donna Jean's hand.

"Of course you can," Harriett replied. "It will be a great

adventure."

Ralph smiled at the enthusiasm of his sister and the children as Harriett slid behind the wheel and the little girls got into the passenger seat. Once they were seated, Harriett pulled out onto the gravel road and headed toward Evansville.

With Evansville just two miles up the road, it seemed as only a few minutes passed when Freddie pointed toward the road. "Here they come!" he shouted.

He no more than spoke the words when the shrill whistle of an oncoming train rent the air. Everything seemed to move in slow motion as the two little girls waved toward the family gathered in the yard. To everyone's horror, Harriet crossed the tracks at the same time as the train applied the brakes to avoid smashing into the car.

Ralph's heart sank, as the huge train seemed to block the entire scene. He knew the house stood next to the tracks but never realized just how close it was until this minute. If he'd taken a minimum of steps he could have touched the passing train. Seeing it smash into his car he knew the lives of his sister and nieces came to an end.

By the time the train finally came to a halt, the car had been pushed almost a mile down the tracks. Ralph felt sick and knew in that one brief moment their lives would be forever changed. It was apparent not one of the people in the car could have survived. In the blink of an eye the three most important women in this family's lives were gone.

Ralph was the first to reach the wreckage, the first to see the mangled bodies of Harriett and the children. "Don't look," he advised the rest of the family.

"It's all your goddamned fault," Freddie shouted. "If you hadn't bought that goddamned car none of this would have ever happened."

Ralph looked at his brother in disbelief. How could Freddie say such a thing? How could he be to blame for Harriett not seeing the train coming before she crossed the tracks?

As shock became painful reality, Ted along with Ralph's parents all placed the blame on his shoulders. They had lost their loved ones and Ralph was at fault.

Everyone remained in a daze as the Rock County Sheriff's

Department as well as the Evansville police, reporters from the area papers and lastly the officials for the railroad questioned them. With all of his family members pointing their fingers at Ralph, he left the family to deal with the incessant questions.

He left the front yard and walked the two miles to Freddie's place to do the evening chores. With them done, he walked over to Ted's farm to do the same for him. It was the least he could do and he knew he had to keep his hands busy. Being in the barn without Beverly's never ending questions was hard, but at least here he could shed his tears without the family seeing this crack in his demeanor.

The next few days were a blur. With the infrequency of car versus train accidents, the railroad agreed to pay for all three funerals, give Freddie and Ted cash settlements and replace Ralph's car. Newspaper reporters interviewed all of them over again. They came from Janesville as well as Madison. No matter how many articles they wrote, it would never bring back Harriett, Beverly and Donna Jean.

While Ruben, Freddie and Ted mourned their losses, they also continued to verbally blame Ralph for the accident. If he hadn't bought the car, if he hadn't allowed Harriett to take it to Evansville, the accident wouldn't have happened.

As a defense mechanism, Ralph avoided the family. As he had on the night of the accident, he took over not only Freddie's chores but also the ones that needed to be done for Ruben and Ted.

Freddie and Ted spent most of their time sitting around his mother's dining room table trying to decide what to do about the funerals and burials. When Ralph did stop in for meals, he learned that since his parents purchased the six cemetery plots at the time of Marion's death, they offered them to Freddie and Ted. Freddie immediately said he wanted Beverly buried beside her mother, but Ted insisted on buying a separate plot for Harriett and Donna Jean.

The night of the visitation, neighbors offered to do the chores so the family could all be at the funeral home. Ralph would have, instinctively turned down the offer, but he knew he had to be there to say good-bye not only to his sister, but also to his beloved nieces.

When his mother hesitated to walk into the flower filled room,

Ralph took her arm and supported her. Two caskets, one opened and one closed sat at the front of the room. Looking at the smaller one, Ralph knew it contained Beverly's remains, making him wonder where Donna Jean was. Upon looking into the open casket, Harriett looked like she was asleep and could easily sit up to talk to them. In reality she had been taken away forever. Tucked into the casket at Harriett's side, was a pink blanket that held Donna Jean's remains. Even though the funeral director had done a good job of restoring his sister's beautiful face, he couldn't help noticing the thick pancake make-up that covered her skin and hid the stitches holding her face together as well as the bruises he knew were there.

Ralph seemed to suffer in silence, unlike Freddie who sobbed loudly. Ted broke down often and Ruben spoke with family and friends while tears rolled down his cheeks. There seemed to be no end to the line of mourners who passed by the two caskets. It became hard to tell the actual family and friends from the curiosity seekers.

The next day the Methodist Church in Evansville was packed to overflowing. While Ralph sat with his family on one side of the church, Ted sat with his family on the other side of the aisle. The man his sister loved and became another brother to Ralph over the past several years acted as though he wanted nothing to do with any of them.

Ralph sat between his parents and Freddie on one side with Mr. and Mrs. Walmer on the other. Throughout the church, men and women alike sobbed, as the service seemed to drag on forever.

For the second time in the year of 1938, a line of cars drove from the church, out Highway 14 and up Cemetery Street to the final resting place for the last of the girls of the Derr family.

At the cemetery, Ralph stayed at Freddie's side as they laid Beverly to rest. He knew Freddie needed him more than Ted at this time.

The minister did the graveside service for Beverly first. Ralph was surprised to see a little boy come up to Freddie's side. He immediately recognized him as the son of one of Marion's cousins. To his surprise, he heard Freddie speaking in hushed tones to the little boy.

"Would you like to come and live with me?" Freddie asked. "I don't have a little girl to love anymore. I could love you like I did Beverly."

Ralph ached for his older brother. Over the past eight months, Freddie had hardly even known Beverly existed. Today he realized his daughter, like his wife, would rest in the cemetery for eternity and never physically be in his presence again.

Ralph finally guided his older brother away from the small casket containing his daughter's remains. When they rejoined the family for the second graveside service of the day, Ralph helped him stand and not buckle at the knees.

He watched as his mother gratefully sat down on one of the chairs provided by the funeral home next to Ted and his mother. Behind her, Ruben sank to his knees and cried bitterly. In comparison, Ralph remained dry eyed. He'd shed his tears in the barns and would continue to do so in the future. For today he needed to be strong for not only Freddie, but also his parents

Chapter Twenty-Two

The next two weeks were a nightmare. Mr. Canary, from the bank came over from Footville with a new car for Ralph and news of how the railroad had paid off his loan. In the back of his mind, Ralph remembered the people from the railroad questioning him about what kind of car he'd purchased and how much he owed on it. He certainly never expected getting the newest model of his car and having his loan paid off.

Although Ralph lived in the same house as Freddie, he saw little of his brother. The drinking increased until Ralph could hardly stand to be around Freddie. They also didn't eat meals together or even speak.

On Sunday, Freddie still went over to their parents' place for dinner, but Ralph opted to stay at the farm or even go into town.

"What are you planning to do now?" the owner of the grocery store said when they met on the street one Sunday.

"I don't know. I'm doing Freddie's chores, but I can't continue living with someone who doesn't even speak to me."

"I'd like to offer you a job. I ran into Freddie the other night at the tavern and I don't know how you can live with that man to say nothing of working for him. I need someone reliable to work for me on the City Delivery. The pay isn't a lot, but I do supply you with a vehicle to drive for the deliveries and there's an apartment above the store where you can stay. It would be a stable job for the winter and I know there are other places around town where you can pick up odd jobs."

"Who's doing the deliveries now?"

"My kid was doing them, but he's going to Madison to college since the first of September and he doesn't have the time to spend delivering groceries for me. Until I can find someone, I've been doing them myself. I can tell you my customers don't like to wait until the store closes to get their groceries."

"I'll have to give Freddie some notice, but I'll talk to him when he gets back from the folks' place today. This is the one time I know he'll be sober. I'll let you know what I'm going to do tomorrow morning."

Ralph drove back to the farm, wondering how he would approach Freddie about leaving. It wasn't fair to Freddie and yet working under the conditions he'd been forced to endure wasn't helping him much either.

It came as a surprise to see Freddie sitting on the porch waiting for him to arrive. With the drop in temperature, Ralph knew Freddie must have something important on his mind.

"I've been waiting for you," Freddie said, as Ralph mounted the steps to the porch.

"It's pretty cold out here. Why didn't you wait in the house?"

"There's whiskey in the house, and I didn't want to be tempted to have a drink before I talked to you. I had a long talk with the folks over dinner today. I talked to my landlord and under the circumstances he's agreed to buy me out. He said he's been thinking about it ever since Marion died and you took over the work here. He has a new tenant who can move in right away. I'm moving over to stay with Ma and Pa. I know it doesn't give you much notice, but I'm packing up and leaving tomorrow. The new people will be moving in as soon as I'm gone."

Under normal circumstances, Ralph would have been put out for the short notice, but considering the offer he'd received in town, he knew it was for the best. "I heard Ted is selling out as well. Was he at the house today?"

Freddie shook his head. "He ain't been there since the day of the accident. Pa did hear Ted was able to find a tenant to take over and he moved back with his parents. I know Pa is thinking about selling out as well. I think they want to retire from farming and move into town. So what will you do?"

"I've been offered a job?"

"What farmer in their right mind takes on hired help at this time of year?"

Ralph wanted to make a scene, but he refrained. It would do him no good. "I was in town this afternoon and ran into the man who runs the grocery store. He needs someone to work on the City Delivery. The pay isn't much, but it does come with a furnished apartment over the store." What Ralph left unsaid was that he'd been working for Freddie for the past almost nine months without any pay whatsoever so no matter what was being offered, it would be more than he'd been making.

"Good. I hope you can start right away. I'd like you gone after morning milking tomorrow."

Ralph bit his tongue. He could have been gone tonight, but he knew Freddie wanted him to do morning chores so he wouldn't have to be bothered.

As soon as Ralph agreed, Freddie went into the house to begin his packing. Ralph wondered what he'd be doing with not only the furniture he and Marion had accumulated or Beverly's possessions. It was entirely likely Freddie would leave everything where it had been all the time they lived in this house.

By the time Ralph finished milking, Freddie's car was gone. It was entirely possible he'd gone into town to either buy a bottle of whiskey or to drink with his friends at the tavern.

Instead of going to his room, Ralph went upstairs to the bedroom that once had belonged to Beverly. Seeing the boxes Freddie must have packed earlier, he looked around the room until he found a doll he'd missed in the packing. Picking it up, he took it down to his room so he could include it with his belongings.

It was almost ten when Ralph finished his packing and put his belongings into the car. The only things left in his room were the barn clothes he intended to wear in the morning as well as his boots. Everything else, including Beverly's forgotten doll, now rested in his car.

Just before going to sleep, he heard Freddie stumble through the

171

back door and curse the scatter rug Marion insisted keeping at the door, to keep her kitchen floor clean. When Freddie was finally in the room directly over the one where Ralph slept, the house once again became quiet.

With sleep came dreams of happier times before all the tragedies of 1938. Marion was alive and pleased to be preparing dinner for them. Beverly and Donna Jean played in the front yard and a truce of some sort had been called between Ralph and his family.

* * * *

By the time Ralph finished milking, Freddie's car was gone and the new people were already moving into the house.

"Have you been doing the milking here, son?" the man of the family asked as Ralph left the milk house.

"Yes sir, I have."

"Can you tell me about the cows?"

Ralph nodded. He had no place he needed to be. He didn't even know if he could start work as soon as he arrived at the grocery store.

Going into the barn with the man, Ralph went from cow to cow telling the new man how each of them liked to be handled.

"I appreciate you doing this. It's hard coming onto a farm to take over a herd you aren't familiar with."

"How did you hear about this place?" Ralph asked, unable to contain his curiosity.

"The owner of this farm was talking to my folks about how he wasn't happy with his tenant. Something about him losing his wife and drinking so much he couldn't keep things up. He did say the guy's brother was doing all the work, but he worried about him doing everything considering his age. I take it you're the brother."

"I am," Ralph replied.

"To make a long story short, I just got married. We were afraid we were going to have to wait until March to get a place of our own. This is a godsend."

"This place is just right for a young couple," Ralph agreed. "I wish you luck."

"What will you be doing?"

Ralph glanced at the house longingly. All that was left of the happy life Freddie and Marion once had in this house were the memories. Those same memories would have to be enough to last him, knowing he was no longer welcome in the home of the people he once called family.

"Ah, I have a job waiting for me in town. I was afraid I would have to make them wait until Freddie could replace me, but now I have no reason not to be on my way. I hope you enjoy living here. The corncrib is full and so are the silo and grain bin. There's also a couple of good cuttings of hay not to mention the straw in the loft."

Without saying more, he turned from the man and went to his car. The sooner he could be away from this farm, the better he would like it.

Chapter Twenty-Three

Working on the City Delivery opened a whole new life for Ralph. He no longer got up at the crack of dawn to milk cows. He started working at eight in the morning and had all his deliveries made by five in the afternoon. Along with his hourly pay, he also made tips from the customers who appreciated his ready smile and the way he brought in their groceries and helped them put everything away.

Along with his lighter work schedule, Ralph also heard all the gossip circulating around Evansville. He soon learned Ted had finally been able to sell his farm and Ralph's parents were planning to move into Evansville. The talk was they bought a large rooming house on Madison Street and his father had applied for work with the city. The farming they'd done all their lives now brought only bitter memories of the daughter and granddaughters they loved and lost on one sunny October Sunday afternoon.

Just after the first of the year, Ralph finished work on a Saturday afternoon and went to the diner for a late lunch. The sandwich he ordered arrived just as Hiney Hosely sat next to him at the counter.

"Hey Ralph, what do you have planned for tonight?" Hiney asked. "There's a dance over in Brooklyn. How would you like to go with me? I hear there will be a lot of eligible girls there."

"What time does it start?" Ralph inquired.

"I think I heard seven. I can pick you up and take you over with me."

Ralph thought about Hiney's offer. He didn't like the man to begin with and having to share a car with someone who would, undoubtedly, be drinking didn't appeal to him. "I'll come over, but I think I'll drive myself. I like to be able to leave when I want to. I might be ready to come back to Evansville before you're ready to leave. I'll meet you there."

He took special care in dressing for the dance. Over the weeks he'd been living in town, he'd been to several dances and enjoyed getting dressed up to meet with the girls who went there to dance and have a good time.

The hall where the dance was being held was brightly lit and the band played with great gusto. After dancing with several of the girls he'd seen at other Saturday night dances, Ralph saw Hiney enter with a woman on his arm. From the resemblance he knew she had to be Hiney's younger sister.

"Ralph, I see you made it. I want you to meet my sister, Leona. I think the two of you are perfect for each other."

Ralph assessed Leona. She certainly wasn't his idea of someone who would be perfect for him. Pulling Hiney aside, he glanced back at Leona. "Nothing against your sister, Hiney, but I'm just too young to be tied down to a wife. I'm only seventeen."

"So what? Leona's only eighteen. She's practically an old maid. You've got a good job working on the City Delivery. She could have a hot meal ready for you when you get home at night. Wouldn't that be better than having to cook for yourself? Besides, she'd keep your bed warm, if you get my drift." Hiney poked Ralph in the ribs with his elbow and winked wickedly.

"Sorry, Hiney, but you're barking up the wrong tree. I'm not interested in marriage and I'm certainly not interested in your sister. I think it's time I went back to Evansville."

The look on Hiney's face was one of shock and disbelief. "I figured after all that shit between you and Freddie, you'd be glad to have a wife to take care of you."

"I guess you figured wrong," Ralph replied. "Good luck finding Leona a husband. I'm not interested in getting married."

Ralph turned to leave the hall when Leona approached him. "Don't youse want to dance with me?" she asked.

"Not tonight, Leona. There's a lot of guys here, I'll bet you'll be able to get one of them to dance with you."

The look on Leona's face was one of dejection, but Ralph didn't care. He had no desire to take her as his wife. Like everyone else in the area, he'd heard all about how old man Hosely raped all his daughters and the state had them sterilized. When he first heard about it, Ralph wondered why, but seeing Leona tonight he didn't question it further.

It was evident Leona was retarded. He could understand completely not wanting her to produce more children like herself. He felt sorry for her, but the only way any man would marry her would be if they were drunk out of their mind and did not know what they were doing.

Throughout January, Ralph often saw Hiney at the dances held in various halls around the area. It was sad to see Hiney trying to find someone to marry his sister.

In March, Ralph heard some news that came as a complete shock. First, he heard his brother had contacted Plenty Tolls about renting his farm. Considering Freddie had enough money from selling his half of the stock and equipment when he left the farm in October in addition to the settlement from the railroad, he would have no problem getting back into farming. Along with that news came the announcement Freddie married Leona Hosely. Ralph had no doubt Freddie had been drunk and in no way would remember the ceremony binding him to Leona for the rest of his life.

With the coming of spring, Ralph found an additional job in town. He started working on Friday nights, Saturday afternoons and Sunday evenings at the movie theater. In addition to the extra money in his pocket, he got to see all the movies that came to town without spending the money to buy a ticket.

From what he heard, Freddie was trying hard to be a successful farmer as well as a good husband to Leona. What hurt Ralph the most was the fact Leona would never be able to give Freddie another child. He knew it was something his mother desired more than anything else in the world and it was now evident her favorite son wouldn't give her more grandchildren.

* * * *

Ralph celebrated his eighteenth birthday by going to Janesville with a friend on Sunday afternoon to go skating at the Ace High Roller Rink. As soon as they arrived, his friend pointed out two girls who were attempting to skate.

"What do you think of those girls?" his friend asked.

Ralph watched the girls, hardly hearing his friend's question. As he did, the brunette lost her footing and landed on the hardwood floor of the rink. Without giving an answer, he skated over to help her up.

"Hi," he said, staring into her incredible brown eyes when she was at last on her feet. "My name's Ralph Derr. What's yours?"

The girl giggled and looked to her friend, as though too shy to give a reply on her own.

"She's Norma Howard and I'm June Hall," her friend said. "Are you from Janesville, Ralph?"

Concentrating on Norma rather than June, he flashed what he hoped was a brilliant smile. "No, I'm from Evansville. How about you?"

"I live out east of town in Johnstown," June replied. "My dad owns I G Hall Implement."

Ralph nodded. He'd heard good things about I G Hall from the many farmers he'd worked for in the past. "What about you, Norma?" he inquired. He liked the way she blushed when he asked her a direct question. "Are you from town?"

Her blush turned to shock. "Good grief, no. I go to school here, but I live in LaPrairie Township. My dad has a farm and runs a dead stock truck."

"Where do you go to school, Ralph?" June asked.

For the first time, Ralph was embarrassed by his status in life. "I don't go to school. I've been working on farms as a hired man, but this year I'm working on the City Delivery in Evansville and at the theater."

Thoughts of why he was working in town crowded his mind. With them were memories of the accident that took the lives of his sister and

177

nieces. Rather than dwell on the past, he concentrated on the smile crossing Norma's lips.

"It's too bad you aren't farming anymore," Norma commented. Her voice sounded like the singing of a bird and bordered on being flirtatious.

Ralph stared deep into her eyes. "Why would you say that?"

"My dad is just starting his new business and has been looking for someone to do the work on the farm while he concentrates on building it up. He hasn't had any luck finding anyone."

Thoughts of working on a farm again, especially a farm where Norma lived ran rampant in his mind. "What would I have to do to get that job?"

Norma's eyes widened with surprise at his question. "Would you really be interested?"

Ralph nodded.

"I could talk to my dad. Will you be coming here next Sunday?"

"I can," Ralph replied. "For now, would you like to skate with me? I promise I won't let you fall."

She smiled and slipped her hand into his. Together they skated as a couple for the remainder of the afternoon allowing Ralph to feel young for the first time in too many months and forget all about time.

"Ralph, Ralph," his friend said as he skated up to them. "Do you have any idea what time it is? We have to get back to Evansville for the five o'clock show."

As much as Ralph wanted to stay with Norma, he also took his responsibility to his employer seriously. "I'll be here next Sunday at two. Promise me you'll be here."

"I will," Norma promised.

He wondered if it was his imagination or if she didn't want him to leave. Rather than just touching her hand, he wanted to take her in his arms and kiss her, but he knew this was neither the time nor the place.

After taking off his skates, Ralph and his friend went out to the car. "That's the girl I'm gonna marry," Ralph said as they pulled out of the parking lot onto Highway 11. Knowing how late it was, he pushed the accelerator all the way to the floor and prayed the Rock County

Sheriff's department wasn't patrolling the roads between Janesville and Evansville.

"How can you say such a thing? You just met her. You don't even know her. Besides why would a beautiful girl like her want anything to do with an ugly cuss like you?" His friend playfully punched him in his right arm.

Ralph knew his friend was teasing, but the words still hurt. They reminded him of all the barbs he'd heard from his family for as long as he could remember.

They pulled up in front of the theater with only minutes to spare. Although Ralph ran the projector, he paid little attention to the film. He'd seen it before, he didn't need to watch it again, especially since his thoughts centered on a beautiful girl by the name of Norma Howard.

* * * *

On Wednesday afternoon, Ralph returned from his morning deliveries and his boss said someone had been in looking for him. "The man said he'll return after eating dinner at the diner."

Ralph wondered who would be looking for him and what the man wanted. Still mulling it over in his mind, he took time to eat the sandwich he'd packed for himself earlier.

He was boxing up the afternoon deliveries when a large man entered the store. "I'm still looking for Ralph Derr," he said. "Is he back from his deliveries yet?"

Ralph set aside his work and came out from behind the counter. "I'm Ralph. How can I help you?" he asked, extending his hand to the man.

The man looked at him skeptically. "I'm George Howard. My daughter says you do farm work. How would you like to come down to LaPrairie Township and work for me?"

Ralph swallowed hard. This man was Norma's father. "What would you need me to do?" he asked, hoping he sounded more confident than he felt.

"I milk about twenty head of cattle and own an eighty-acre farm. I plant corn, oats and hay. To be truthful, I've started a new business with Woody Traxler and I don't have time to keep up with the chores on the farm. I have three boys, but they have no interest in farming and from the way Norma takes to schooling, she doesn't either."

"What do you pay?" Ralph inquired.

"That would depend on your references. I'd like to have the names of the farms where you've worked in the past. I can't be expected to take the word of my sixteen-year-old daughter. From the looks of you, I doubt there would be many people to contact."

"I wouldn't expect you to take her word, sir." Ralph took a piece of paper used to wrap groceries and wrote down the names of his past employers along with directions to each of the farms. He deliberately left Freddie's name from the list.

George took the paper from Ralph's hand and stared intently at the names and addresses of the places where he'd worked. "Just how old are you?" he asked.

"I just turned eighteen last week."

"Then I don't think I can use you."

Disappointment filled Ralph. "Why would you say that?"

"You're too young to have worked all these places. The one thing I can't tolerate is a liar."

Ralph could feel his anger building. "I may be a lot of things, Mr. Howard, but I'm not a liar. If I say I worked those farms you can bet that I did. My word is my bond. I learned a long time ago that if you tell the truth you don't have to remember which lie you told to which person." Thoughts of the one lie he'd ever told his mother crossed his mind. He'd never told her the truth, but the guilt he'd experienced dogged him so badly, he vowed to never tell another lie as long as he lived.

"If the boy says he worked those places, he did," his employer said, making Ralph proud to have this man take his side. "The way I heard it, old Rube kicked him out when he graduated the eighth grade at the age of twelve. He's been on his own ever since. I've never heard anything but good about him from every man he's ever worked for."

"If he's such a good farmer, why is he working for you?" George questioned.

"That's a long story, and if you want to hear it, I think it should come from the boy. Let's just say, if you want to hear the story, it's best Ralph told you himself, in his own time. Are you here to offer him a job on a farm?"

"Yes sir, I am. I need help, but it looks like he already has a job, with you."

"I know you're needing help, but so am I. I also know Ralph has been itchin' to get back to farming ever since last spring. That's the only fault I can find in him. Once he signs on at a place, he doesn't leave as long as he's needed. If he wants to work for you, give me a week to find someone to take his place and he's free to do as he pleases. If he doesn't want to work for you, he's always got a job here with me."

Ralph didn't know what to say. He certainly didn't expect his boss to give him such a glowing recommendation.

"Look son, you want the job, it's yours. I should check with your past employers, but either this man thinks a whole lot of you or he wants you out of his business. Whichever it is, I'm prepared to take his word. Just so you know, we're church-going folks and we expect the same of you. No one in my family smokes, but if you do, that's your business. I expect you to take the filthy habit out of the house. My wife's name is Gertie and they don't call her 'Old Dutch Cleanser' for nothing. The job pays twenty-five dollars a week and room and board. To be fair to your employer, I'll expect you a week from Monday. Norma told me she'd see you on Sunday at the roller rink. When she does she can tell you how to get out to our place."

"Thank you, Mr. Howard. You won't be sorry. I can do everything you need and more if you want. I'll see you a week from Monday."

Ralph thanked his employer and went back to the job of packing the afternoon deliveries.

"About what I said," his employer commented as he joined Ralph behind the counter. "I meant every word of it. I've also heard about that little girl you helped up at the skating rink on Sunday. If I'm not mistaken, that man was her pa. Look, I know you've stuck with me because you knew I needed the help. I also knew you wanted to be working on a farm more than you wanted to be here. I've got someone in mind for your job. Why don't you go over to the theater and talk to the manager? He may want to start looking for someone to take your place as well."

Ralph picked up the box he just finished packing. "I'll stop over there tonight when I'm done working for you. I do thank you for what you said. I hate to leave you in the lurch, but working for George Howard could be a great opportunity. At least I'd be able to get to know his daughter, Norma, better. I doubt I have a snowball's chance in hell with her, but I want to give it a try. She's the prettiest girl I've ever seen and she's well educated, too. She's going to high school in Janesville."

Ralph couldn't stop smiling as he took out the afternoon deliveries. He was just about done when he saw his father coming toward him. In all the time his folks lived in town, he'd managed to avoid running into the old man, so why did it have to happen today, of all days?

"It's good to see you, Ralph," his father greeted him.

"You look good too, Pa. I hear you got a job working for the city of Evansville. How's that going for you?"

"It's not as hard as farming. I'm getting too old to be up at five in the morning milking cows. Your Ma sent me out looking for you. She wants you to come to Sunday dinner. She was mighty upset when you didn't come over around your birthday."

"I didn't think I'd be welcome. If Ma wants me to come over, I'll be there. I just have to be in Janesville at two. I've just gotten a new job and I'm going to be getting the details on it then."

"Are you going back to farming?"

Ralph nodded.

"I wondered how long it would take you to want to get your hands dirty again. Freddie's out working for Plenty Tolls on his place."

"I heard that. I also heard he married Leona Hosely. That came as a surprise."

"It surprised us too, but I think they're happy. From what Freddie says, she's not much of a cook, but she's learning. Since you have to be in Janesville at two, I'll tell your ma to have dinner ready at eleven."

Ralph agreed and watched as his father went back to his parked car for the drive home. The thought of seeing his folks and Freddie again weighed heavily on his mind, but he knew he'd have to do it sometime and this seemed as good a time as any. He'd made his way without their help for the past five years and done nothing to shame them. Even though they blamed him for the accident that took Harriett's life to say nothing of those of the two little girls, his only blame was having bought a new car and allowing his sister to drive it into town.

* * * *

On Sunday morning Ralph took extra care with his appearance. He'd used his paycheck on Saturday to buy a new set of clothes as well as a new hat. He not only wanted to appear prosperous to his parents but he also wanted to impress Norma Howard when he met her this afternoon at the skating rink.

"I'm glad to see you, son," his mother greeted him when he came into the house.

Ralph entered and looked around the living room. "This sure is different from your last place. It looks like you got a nice house here."

When Freddie and Leona arrived, Freddie didn't seem at all shy about questioning Ralph's intentions. "So what brings you here?"

"I'm tired of living in town. I signed on at a farm in LaPrairie Township."

"LaPrairie?" Ruben echoed. "How in the hell did you get a job way down there?"

"Well, I met this girl and she said her dad needed someone to milk and run the farm while he takes care of his new business."

"Does this mysterious girl have a name?" Freddie teased.

"Of course she does, she's Norma Howard."

"Are you telling us you're going to be working for George Howard? I heard he was working with Woody Traxler picking up dead animals. I think this time you might have fallen into a pile of shit and came out smelling like a rose. From what I've heard, those old boys are both loaded. Of course, everyone knows the Howard's practically own

LaPrairie Township."

"So," Freddie began, nudging Ralph with his elbow and winking broadly. "Is this girl special. Are you going to marry her? With all that money, you'd be a fool not to get hooked up with her. I'll give you a word of advice, though. Be careful marrying above yourself. I did that with Marion and came to regret it."

Ralph knew his mother was listening intently to the conversation between himself and Freddie.

He didn't dare tell anyone in his family of his plans to marry Norma Howard. She may be too good for him, but he'd show everyone what a good man he was and how well he could support her.

Chapter Twenty-Four

The following Monday, Ralph started work on the Howard farm. He soon learned what his brother meant about the Howard's owning most of LaPrairie Township. George Howard had six brothers and three sisters all living in the area. His father also lived close by and his farm sat less than half a mile up the road.

While old Ralph Howard was a farmer, only a few of his sons seemed to follow in his footsteps. Like George, they had businesses other than farming to occupy their time. Ralph soon learned they were all excellent horse and cattle traders. He knew living and working here would be an experience as well as an education. These men were not the tenant farmers he'd worked with before. They each owned their farms. It didn't take long for Ralph to learn the farms had been wedding presents from their father for which they paid a dollar to keep things legal.

The crops Ralph saw growing in George's fields promised to be bountiful and the grain bin was filled to the brim with the oats George harvested before Ralph arrived at the farm. In the barn, he found neatly stacked hay and top producing Holsteins just waiting for him to milk them.

Gertie Howard lived up to the name her husband gave her. Ralph was certain he could eat off her kitchen floor without worrying about germs. Her cooking rivaled any he'd ever tasted and her cakes and pies made his mouth water at the very thought of them.

His only complaint was that George, a true Englishman, enjoyed tea with his meals, while Ralph preferred coffee. The first chance he got, Ralph went into town and purchased a small coffee pot and three pounds of coffee.

Gertie looked at him skeptically when he came home with his purchases and proceeded to make himself a pot of coffee. "I didn't think you'd mind if I made myself some coffee," he said, when he caught her eye.

Gertie smiled and then started laughing. "Of course I don't mind, but why don't you let me make it for you? It's been a long time since I made coffee, but I do drink it when I go to visit my parents. I miss the smell of it, but I've learned to drink tea."

It didn't take long for George to start drinking Ralph's coffee, sending him back to town to buy a larger pot.

Although Ralph and Norma lived in the same house, he saw little of her. After breakfast, George would take Norma to school while Ralph took care of the morning chores and went out to do the fieldwork. By the time he returned to the house, Gertie had supper ready. There was always pleasant table talk, but rarely time for a private moment between the two of them. After supper, Ralph would go out to do the night milking, while Norma studied for her next day at school. Ralph envied her opportunity for higher learning, yet if he'd gone to high school, as he wanted, he would have never met the beautiful Norma Howard.

Just prior to Thanksgiving, an early blizzard hit the area paralyzing everything but the ever-present duties of the farmers like Ralph. With the roads closed, Norma spent the day at the house. Ralph was thankful he'd finished picking the last of the corn and could relax once he finished his barn chores.

When he came into the kitchen, Ralph found Norma sitting at the dining table, pouring over some hen scratches he couldn't make out.

"Are you learning a different language?" he asked, when he sat down next to her to enjoy a piece of chocolate cake and a cup of coffee.

"You might say that. It's called shorthand."

Ralph had heard about French, German, Swedish, Norwegian and even Spanish, but this shorthand was unfamiliar to him. "Where do they speak that language?"

Norma laughed and Ralph feared she was making fun of him.

"It's not a language, not really. The girls at school all take secretarial classes so they can get jobs after high school. Shorthand is one of those classes. It makes it so we can take dictation in an office."

Norma's explanation bewildered Ralph. "Is that want you want? To be a secretary?"

Norma shook her head. "I don't *want* to be a secretary, but after graduation I have to do something. Pa says in this modern age girls have to either get married or get a job."

"I can't see that you have much of a problem. There have to be any number of young men beating a path to your door."

Norma blushed at his comment. "Do you see any boys coming to the farm? Even if there were, there's not a young man in the area I would take as a husband."

Her declaration took him by surprise. "Who would you take?" he finally asked.

"Now you are being silly. I'd take you, of course, that is if you were to ask me."

Ralph's heart beat so loudly, he feared Norma could hear it. "I fell in love with you the first day we met. I told my friend I planned to marry you. I just didn't know if you felt the same way about me."

On an impulse, Ralph leaned over and gave Norma a kiss. Her lips tasted sweet and he longed to take her in his arms, but seated at the table, this would have to suffice.

"What are the two of you doing out here?" George asked as he came into the dining room.

Ralph pulled away, embarrassed to be caught kissing his employer's daughter.

"Oh Pa, Ralph just asked me to marry him."

"Marry him!" George bellowed. "He's just a hired man. If you marry him, you'll never have anything. You'll ride around in a rusted out old car with a dozen kids hanging out the windows."

Ralph bristled at George's comment. With Norma as his wife, she would never have to want for anything. For her, no matter what the cost, he would provide only the best.

The early snow melted quickly as the temperatures reached into the forties and by Saturday, Ralph and Norma were able to go to the movies and get some ice cream. At the drug store, Ralph insisted they have their picture taken separately as well as together in one of the new mechanical picture machines that were becoming popular.

"Would you like to meet my family?" he asked as they drove home. "I'm going to Ma and Pa's tomorrow for Sunday dinner."

"I have to go to church. Pa says so."

"Ma usually doesn't plan dinner for any earlier than noon. She knows I go to church with your folks. She also knows I come up there once a month. I'd like to have them meet you. I've talked about you so much, I feel like they already know you."

"I'll ask Pa and see what he says."

Ralph was relieved to see lights on in the living room when they arrived back at the farm. With luck both George and Gertie would still be up so Norma could ask for permission to go to Evansville with him on Sunday after church.

Gertie immediately asked if they enjoyed the movies and if they would like some pie and coffee before going to bed. Even though they'd enjoyed chocolate sodas at Adamany's Restaurant in town, Ralph didn't turn down the offer. He knew George enjoyed having something to eat before going to bed and it was possible the food would put him in a more receptive mood when Norma asked about what they'd planned for tomorrow.

"We had our pictures taken while we were in town," Norma said, instigating the conversation with her parents.

"I don't put too much stock in those new machines they have," George commented. "I'm surprised the damn thing didn't blow up in your faces."

"Oh Pa, they're perfectly safe. Look how good they turned out." She took the strip of pictures from her purse and handed it to George.

Ralph was pleased he'd suggested they have two sets of poses taken so he could have a set as well. He doubted she would be receptive to him taking away any of the pictures of which she was so proud to use for his own purposes.

"Oh," Gertie gushed. "Those turned our really well."

"After we had them done, Ralph asked if I'd like to go to Evansville with him tomorrow for Sunday dinner. Is it all right if I go?"

George glared at Ralph. "You have to go to church tomorrow."

"I know she does," Ralph said, coming to Norma's rescue. "I go to church with you every Sunday. On the weeks when I go to Evansville to see my folks, I leave right after church. My ma plans dinner for noon so with church getting out at eleven, we have plenty of time to get there. We'll be back long before it's time for supper and to do the chores."

"Please, Pa. I want to go with Ralph and get to know his family. We told you we want to get married, but how can I get to know his family if you don't let me go?"

George shook his head in defeat, but it was Gertie who gave them the answer they wanted. "I don't see any problem with you going to Evansville with Ralph. He's a responsible young man and if, and I do mean if, the two of you get married you should get to know his family."

* * * *

On Sunday morning, Ralph and Norma sat with George and Gertie on the left side of the church at the outside of the pew. As the congregation was singing the last hymn, they discreetly slipped out the back door and got into Ralph's car for the trip to Evansville.

Ralph drove past the farm and up County Trunk J until he reached Highway 14 where he turned left and headed toward Evansville.

"I've never been out this way," Norma confessed. "Pa would say it all looks like good farm land."

"It is. I haven't farmed out this way much, but I did work Freddie's farm for a while as well as one just down the road from his. They were on this side of Evansville on County M."

Talking about Freddie's farm brought to mind the reason he'd worked for his brother from February to November of last year. Even driving past the intersection leading to the farm where his folks lived at the time of the accident, brought visions of the train smashing into his car and taking away Harriett and the girls.

"Before we get to the folks' place for dinner, there's something I want to ask you," Ralph said.

Norma snuggled closer to him making it easy for Ralph to snake his right arm around her shoulders while driving the car with his left. "The other night you said you would marry me. Did you mean it?"

She kissed his cheek. "Of course I meant it. I knew I was going to marry you the first time I saw you at the roller rink."

"I'd like to get married right away. Your pa gives me Saturdays off and I thought we could go to Iowa and get married."

"Do you mean it?"

He liked the sound of excitement in her voice. "More than I've ever meant anything in my life. There's just one thing. I think this is something we have to keep secret."

"Secret? But why?"

"Because you have the opportunity to go to high school. That's something I always wanted to do. I want to see you graduate in the spring."

"But, if I'm your wife, why do I need to finish high school?"

"Because it's important. If anything were ever to happen to me, you'd be able to take care of yourself. I don't have an education. The only thing I know is farming. If I were to have to give that up, I don't know what I'd do."

"Then we'll keep it a secret, but won't Pa and Ma have to know?"

"We can tell them, but no one outside of the family. If anyone found out, you might not be able to finish school and I don't want that for you."

Freddie's car was already in the driveway when Ralph pulled up in front of the house on Madison Street. He could sense Norma getting nervous. Before getting out of the car, he reached over and took her hand in his.

"They don't bite too hard. I just hope you like chicken. That's the only thing Ma makes for Sunday dinner. It's Freddie's favorite."

"What about your favorite?" she asked.

"It don't matter much. I eat anything anyone puts in front of me.

It's something I learned when I was working out. Sometimes all I got was the mashed potatoes, but I soon found out if I wanted to fill my stomach I'd eat what they gave me."

Ralph got out and went around to Norma's side to open the passenger's door for her. Taking her hand, he walked up the front sidewalk and then up the steps leading to the porch. Without knocking, he opened the door and entered the house. If Norma was nervous, it couldn't hold a candle to how he felt concerning the meeting about to take place.

"Is it too late for you to set another place at the table, Ma?" Ralph asked once they stepped into the overly warm living room of the house.

"Of course not. There's always room for one more."

Ralph took a deep breath. "Norma has agreed to be my wife. I wanted her to meet my family."

After the introductions were made, Norma insisted on going out to the kitchen to help Ralph's mother put dinner on the table, leaving Ralph alone with Freddie and his father.

"We weren't expecting extra company," Ruben complained.

"I'll pay for the extra food. I doubt there will be any shortage of things to eat, considering Ma always makes more than enough for everyone."

"Did you say she 's going to marry you?" Freddie inquired. "Isn't that working a bit too fast?"

"No faster than you, big brother. As I recall, none of us even knew you were seeing Leona when the two of you got married."

Freddie mumbled something about things happening rather quickly between the two of them. Ralph knew exactly what happened. Hiney got Freddie drunk and the rest as they say was history.

"I've been spending most of my days now breaking a new mustang George brought home from the sale barn last week," Ralph said, trying to put the conversation on neutral ground. "I have to admit she's a beauty. I'm sure George will get top dollar for her when he takes her back there for sale."

"What about you? What do you get out of it?"

"I get paid. Even if they weren't paying me in cash money, the food is good and there's always lots of it."

"There's something else there to hold your interest, isn't there?" his father asked. "Norma is a pretty girl. I can't believe she agreed to marry you. Good grief Ralph, she hardly knows you."

"We're getting to know each other. We want to get married as soon as possible."

Before anyone could say more, Leona came into the living room to tell the men dinner was ready.

Ralph was glad he'd warned Norma about the fact his family didn't say table grace before eating as was the custom at the Howard table. Food was passed and Norma took a small portion of everything, in direct contract to Leona who heaped her plate with everything from chicken to mounds of mashed potatoes.

"This is delicious," Norma declared after tasting her chicken. "It's especially good to have asparagus. Ma has an asparagus bed in the side yard, but she's never canned it. I miss having it after it's gone to seed in the spring."

Ralph cringed. This asparagus hadn't come from a family asparagus bed. He knew his mother bought it in cans at the store, just as she bought already molded gelatin, windmill cookies and the angel food cake she would serve for dessert. The meal in no way resembled the freshly made dishes Gertie served at her table.

The talk around the table was the same things Ralph heard every time he shared a meal with his family. Pa talked about his job, Leona looked down at her plate without saying a word and in Freddie's drunken state all he could say was the only thing he liked better than chicken was more chicken.

Ralph endured the meal, as he always did and wished he'd never brought Norma here. Of course, if he intended to make her his wife next Saturday she'd have to meet his family sometime soon.

With dinner finished, Norma was the first on her feet to start clearing the table. Ralph studied his mother's reaction. In the past he couldn't ever remember anyone other than Marion so readily anxious to help in the kitchen.

Even though he knew his mother's long narrow kitchen was about the same size as the one at the Howard farm, he also knew it was nowhere near as neat and clean. What would Norma think of the way his parents lived?

Once the men were settled in the living room, Freddie talked about the snow and Pa explained how he would be running the warming house up at Lake Leota for the winters' skaters.

"You're quiet Ralph," Freddie said. "Did Norma tell you to keep your mouth shut?"

"Of course she didn't. I was just enjoying listening to what you and Pa had to say."

"Did you get much snow down there?" Pa asked.

For some reason the question annoyed Ralph. He lived twenty miles from Evansville not hundreds of miles away. Of course, the weather would be the same in LaPrarie Township as it was here. "We were snowed in for a day. Thank goodness I got all the fieldwork done before the storm hit. Did you get all your corn picked, Freddie?" He knew the answer to his question, but wanted to hear Freddie's answer for himself.

"Well," Freddie slurred, "I didn't quite get finished. I've still got one field to pick. Of course, I don't have all the help you do."

Ralph chafed at Freddie's words. "Where did you get the idea I have help?"

Freddie laughed. "Don't tell me old man Howard makes you do everything alone."

"Why not? He does. That's what I'm paid to do. George is a dead stock dealer as well as a cattle dealer. He doesn't have the time for fieldwork or barn chores for that matter. It's nothing I can't handle. Seems to me I did quite well when I was working for you last year."

Freddie opened his mouth to say something but the women came back into the living room. As soon as they did, his mother went into the parlor to bring out another chair to put in the doorway separating the two rooms. He certainly didn't want to be so far away from Norma, but he had no other choice.

"Ralph asked me to marry him," Norma declared. "It's supposed to be a secret, but he said we could tell our families. We're going to Iowa next Saturday so we can get married there."

"Aren't you a little young?" his mother asked.

"She's the same age as Harriett was, when she married Ted," Ralph said, coming to Norma's rescue."

"Well, I think it's pretty quick for you to be getting married," Freddie said. "She doesn't even know you."

"How well did you know Leona when the two of you got married? I've known Norma for almost four months, not four hours like you and Leona."

Rather than answering Ralph's question, Freddie got up and made an excuse to go out to his car. In his heart, Ralph knew his brother needed a drink and would be able to get it from the bottle he kept in his car.

"Telling you was the reason we came up here today. We were wondering if you'd come with us as a witness, Ma?"

His mother beamed at his invitation. "I don't see why not?"

"Can I come too?" Leona asked, sounding like an excited child.

"Of course you can," Norma agreed.

"Maybe Norma has a sister she'd rather take or perhaps her mother," Ma commented.

Ralph knew his mother was trying to keep Leona from going. She made no bones about her dislike for Freddie's choice in a wife considering Marion had been dead less than a year when he married Leona. He also studied Norma and saw her cringe, but being who she was, she said nothing to upset any of his relatives. The idea of keeping their wedding a secret from her friends left her with few options for people who would be willing to witness their wedding.

"I don't have any sisters and I doubt my ma would want to come. Her and pa think I'm too young, especially since I'm still in school. I told her I'm almost the same age as she was when she married Pa. As for school, Ralph and I both agree I should get my diploma."

The glimmer of admiration Ralph saw in his mother's eyes made him proud. He always knew she'd craved higher education but it had been denied to her, just as Pa denied him the chance he wanted so badly. By the same token, George and Gertie's main concern was

Norma's education. There was no way he would ever consider keeping her from graduating and getting her diploma.

As they got ready to leave, Ralph reached for his wallet, but his mother stopped him. "You're going to be married soon. It's not like when you were single."

Ralph watched the expression on his father's face and knew the old man wasn't happy with Ma's declaration. In the past he wondered if Ma knew about the money he paid for his meals in her home. Now all doubts ceased.

By the time they were on their way home, the plans for the following Saturday were made. Ralph's biggest regret was the thought of Leona coming along with them.

"Your family is nice," Norma commented as they neared Janesville.

"If you say so. I don't see them that way."

"Why were you going to give them money before we left?"

"You might as well know before we get married. My pa kicked me out right after I graduated from the eighth grade, I was twelve at the time. Since then Pa has insisted I pay for every meal I've ever eaten in their home. The only time I didn't pay was when I was working for Freddie. Since he wasn't paying me, they thought I couldn't afford it. Guess that's why they were so upset when I got a new car with my savings."

"Oh Ralph, I didn't know."

Her concern opened the floodgates, allowing Ralph to tell Norma everything about his life, including the accident that took the lives of Harriett, Beverly and Donna Jean. The accident his family blamed him for, even though he wasn't driving at the time the car was struck by the train.

Chapter Twenty-Five

The following Saturday, December 9, Ralph and Norma took off for Iowa. To her parents they only said they were going for a long ride and wouldn't be home until late. Although her parents protested, Norma told them she had all her homework finished and would be free for the weekend to have some fun.

Ralph fingered the locket he'd had made in town last week. He knew he wouldn't be able to give her a wedding ring, but considering they'd had their pictures taken in one of the booths at the dime store, he knew exactly what he wanted to do with his copy. Norma thought it was a terrible waste of money, but he assured her it was nothing he couldn't afford.

Last Monday, after dropping Norma off at school, he went downtown to the Dewey and Bandt jewelry store and ordered the locket with their pictures in it. They'd promised him it would be ready by Wednesday. By taking Norma to school, it was easy for him to stop and pick it up without her knowing anything about it. Until they could tell the world of their marriage, it would have to be the wedding ring he couldn't put on her finger.

After a stop in Evansville to pick up his mother and Leona, Ralph headed for Dubuque. They'd no more than crossed the bridge when Ralph saw a sign for a Justice of the Peace.

Pulling up in front of the unassuming white house, Ralph watched as Norma fussed with her hair and pinched her cheeks to add color while looking in her compact mirror.

"Can I help you folks?" the man who met them at the door asked.

"We want to get married," Ralph explained once they were crowded into the small front room of the house.

"Well Son, that's what I do. How old are you?"

"I'm eighteen and my girlfriend is sixteen."

"Then I can't be of help to you. In Iowa you have to be twenty-one and eighteen."

Ralph thought Norma was going to cry, but instead she held out her hand and thanked the man for his time.

"What are we going to do now?" she asked, after they got back into the car.

Ralph thought for a minute. "We're going to the next town. The way I read the map, that's Maquoketa. Once we get there, we'll tell the Justice of the Peace I'm twenty-one and Norma is eighteen."

"But that's lying," Norma protested.

"It's the only way we can get married. Do you want to wait two years until you're of age or worse yet three years until I'm twenty-one?"

"No, but what if they ask for proof?"

Ralph turned and looked at his mother. "Ma will vouch for us, won't you, Ma?"

"Well, I don't know Ralph. I really shouldn't, I…"

"Look Ma, you've done everything for Freddie for as long as I can remember. When Harriett wanted to get married right after her sixteenth birthday, you moved heaven and hell to make it happen. What have any of you ever done for me? The way I see it, you owe me. Even though there's ten years difference in age between Freddie and me, in experiences I'm much older than he is. You know I can make my own way. I'm ready to get married and so is Norma."

The look on his mother's face was sobering. From the expression on her face, he could tell she knew he was right and finally agreed to attest to the fact he and Norma were both older than their actual ages.

"I never asked," she finally said. "Do you have a ring to give to Norma?"

Ralph looked at her in disbelief. "We have to keep our marriage a secret until Norma graduates from high school. There's no way I can give her a ring as a symbol of our marriage. I have something else."

"You do?" Norma asked, excitement sounding in her voice.

"I do, but it's a surprise, so don't ask me any more questions."

Norma giggled, but Amy persisted. "You have to have a ring for the ceremony. I know it will be way too large but you can use the ring your father gave me when we got married."

Ralph watched as his mother dug in her purse and brought out a beautifully etched wedding band. It was surprising, since he'd never seen her wear the ring or any jewelry for that matter. The only piece he'd ever seen on her was the pendant watch she wore to church, but he never knew where it came from.

"It's only for the ceremony and merely something symbolic, but it should be enough to satisfy the Justice of the Peace."

"Oh, Mrs. Derr," Norma gasped, as she took the ring from Ralph's mother. "It's beautiful. I'll be honored to use it for the ceremony. This is something that must mean so very much to you."

Ralph wondered what his mother thought about the sentiment Norma just put voice to. He doubted the ring held much meaning for his mother. From what Freddie said, once all of the children were out on their own, his parents had started sleeping in separate bedrooms. With the house in Evansville being filled to capacity with the men who were the roomers, the old man more than likely either slept in the back storage room or on the daybed in the parlor adjacent to his mother's bedroom.

Without further discussion, Ralph pulled away from the curb and headed for Maquoketa. After arriving in town, it took only a matter of minutes to locate the Justice of the Peace. As the man in Dubuque had done, the man asked them their ages.

"I'm twenty-one and my girlfriend is eighteen," Ralph said.

"Who are your witnesses?" the man asked.

"I'm Ralph's mother and this is his sister-in-law, Leona."

"Can you vouch for the ages of these two young people?"

Ralph held his breath. It was entirely possible his mother would refuse to lie for them about the one thing that could keep them from getting married.

"It's as my son says. They're both of age."

Ralph exhaled slowly and listened as the Justice of the Peace said the words that would make the two of them one for the remainder of their lives.

"Do you have a ring for your lovely bride?" he asked.

Proudly, Ralph produced the ring his mother gave him only minutes earlier. As she predicted, it was much too large for Norma's slender finger, but it didn't matter. Once they left, he was going to present her with the special locket he'd picked up at the jewelry store earlier in the week.

"Where are we going from here?" Leona asked.

Ralph was certain she hadn't grasped the importance of what just happened in his life. From what he'd learned, when she married Freddie it had been a late night affair with only Hiney as witness to the event. He hadn't asked Freddie about the ceremony, since he knew his brother was, more than likely, too drunk to remember what happened to join him to Leona.

"We're going to the bluffs overlooking the river," Norma said. "I've never been over here, but when my dad heard we were coming to Iowa for the day, he said we had to see them. I'm sure they're much more beautiful in the summer, but they should be spectacular today as well."

Ralph drove in the direction of the bluffs, hardly able to believe his good luck at having Norma as his wife, even though he couldn't tell anyone other than his folks and Norma's parents.

At the park by the bluffs, they all got out of the car and Norma gave Amy her camera. "It's such a beautiful day, would you take a picture of Ralph and me up on the bluffs? It will be our wedding picture."

His mother agreed and Ralph helped Norma to climb up the slightly inclined rock walkway.

At the top, he reached into his pocket and produced the locket. "I know it isn't a wedding ring, but I promise, as soon as I can afford one, I'll buy you any one you want. For now, this will have to do."

He held out the box from the jewelry store and watched as she opened it. The gold of the locket on the delicate chain caught a stray sunbeam and glistened, inviting Norma to loop the chain around her fingers and pull it from the box.

"Open it," Ralph suggested.

She slid her fingernail into the grove that held the case shut. When it opened, she squealed with delight when she saw the pictures of the two of them, one on each side of the case. "When it's open it's so beautiful, but when it's closed, I can pretend the pictures are kissing each other," she declared.

Allowing her to admire the necklace for a few more minutes, he finally took it from her hands and clasped it around her neck. It would be a symbol not only of their secret marriage, but also their undying love.

* * * *

It was almost milking time when they returned to the farm. Ralph noticed George heading toward the barn and waylaid him so they could tell Norma's parents about their wedding.

"Can't see why you wanted me to come back to the house," George grumbled. "Those cows won't milk themselves."

"Even though it's my day off, I'll take care of the milking, but there's something Norma and I want to tell you and Gertie first."

In the house, Norma and her mother sat at the table. Ralph knew Norma was having a hard time not to blurt out the truth about their excursion to the bluffs along the river in Iowa.

"Ma, Pa, Ralph and I have something we want to tell you," Norma said once her father and Ralph were seated at the table. "This morning when we went to Iowa we got married. I know this isn't what you wanted for me, but I love Ralph so much, I didn't want to wait. We aren't going to tell anyone, not even the boys, until I graduate in May. We just didn't want to wait."

"You—you aren't going to have a baby are you?" George accused.

"Pa! How could you ask such a question? Of course I'm not going to have a baby. Ralph and I haven't done anything we shouldn't be doing."

"Well, see that you keep it that way until you graduate from high school. I don't know why the two of you couldn't wait until spring, but what's done is done. By God Ralph, if you hurt her, you'll have me to answer to."

"You don't have to worry, George. The last thing I would ever do is hurt Norma. I fell in love with her the first time I saw her. You'll see I'll make her happy or die trying."

Chapter Twenty-Six

Ralph debated what to do about Christmas. Both Gertie and Norma insisted he should join the family for dinner, but he didn't agree. Since they'd decided to keep their marriage a secret it would look strange for the hired man to eat with the family.

If things had been different, he could have gone to be with his family for Christmas, but they had never really celebrated the day. It was only at Norma's insistence they had gone to Evansville on the Sunday before Christmas with the car loaded with presents for everyone. Norma had spent every free minute since their wedding embroidering linens to give to both his mother and Leona. He'd taken it upon himself to buy cans of Copenhagen chewing tobacco for his father and Freddie. As he did he remembered the first time he'd purchased Christmas presents for his family. Then he bought presents for Harriett and Marion. Thinking back on that joyous Christmas brought a lump to Ralph's throat.

Together, they also bought presents for George and Gertie. Norma told him her mother loved frogs and when Ralph saw a glass frog at the dime store, he immediately purchased it. For George, he found a leather wallet. Pleased with his purchases, he concentrated on what to give his new wife. He finally decided on a box of chocolates along with a pair of earrings he thought she would like.

On Christmas Eve, Gertie made oyster stew and Ralph exchanged his gifts with the family. He'd been thrilled to be able to put his small gifts under the beautifully decorated tree in the parlor. Norma was thrilled and he decided George and Gertie were shocked when he gave them each a present. Money was always tight and yet he'd spent part of his meager wages on things for them.

From Norma, he received a flannel shirt. He was certain she'd made it especially for him, since she seemed to be very talented with a needle and thread. From George and Gertie, he got a whole carton of cigarettes. In all the years he'd been smoking, he'd never had an entire carton of cigarettes at one time. Even though he knew Gertie hated what she called his nasty habit, she had wrapped his present in colorful paper. It meant a lot to him to be accepted by Norma's family.

While the family ate breakfast, Gertie was already working in the kitchen. Pans of rolls were shaped, had risen and were now in the oven while she labored over getting the turkey ready to replace the rolls as soon as they were done. On the buffet were several pies along with Christmas cookies for dessert. Although all the smells were tantalizing, Ralph knew he needed to go back out to the barn and not intrude. Next year he would be able to rightfully claim a place within this family, but for now, he was nothing more than the hired man.

"I wish you'd change your mind about eating with us," Norma said as she stopped him in the back room. "The boys won't bite."

"I know they won't, but there'd be too much explaining to do. It's best this way." He took her in his arms and kissed her hoping to put her at ease with his decision.

"But what will you do all day?"

"It seems to be fairly mild, so I plan to work with that new mustang your pa bought last week. I also have enough work to do in the machine shed to keep me busy for at least a week."

"What about your dinner?"

"With the amount of food you and your ma fixed for breakfast, I'll be good until supper or when your brothers leave, whichever comes first." Before going out the door, Ralph kissed Norma one last time. He knew she wanted him to join them, but he also knew it wouldn't be right. Above all else, he didn't want to put her in a compromising position.

The mustang George brought home last week from the sale barn nickered a challenge to Ralph. They'd already had one go around where Ralph hoped he'd showed the horse he was the boss. "I've got chores to finish," he said aloud, acknowledging the challenge. "After that we'll see what you can do."

By the time Ralph finished feeding the cows and liming down the barn, his pocket watch read well past noon. Although his stomach growled, he refused to give in and go up to the house. Instead, he prepared to take down the bridle for the mustang.

Before stepping into the stall, he glanced out one of the few windows at the front of the barn. To his surprise, snow fell heavily. "This wasn't what I expected. Guess we won't be going out today after all."

The horse nodded, as though pleased not to have to go out in the storm that raged outside.

Checking the storm again, he noticed the three cars parked up by the house. He'd only ever met Norma's older brother, Ralph, but he knew the others belonged to Herman and Edmund. He closed his eyes and imagined Gertie in all her glory with her adoring family around her. The thought brought a lump to Ralph's throat. He certainly didn't have an adoring family and his mother didn't get excited about anyone other than Freddie coming home.

He wondered if things would have been different if the accident hadn't happened. Harriett would have accepted Norma and perhaps his mother wouldn't have told him that she prayed he wouldn't have children. Her true and beloved granddaughters were dead and buried. There would never be room in her heart to accept another grandchild and if her worst fears were to come to life, a boy would be tolerated but never another girl.

Thinking of the children he and Norma would one day have made him sad. He knew George and Gertie would love these children, but how would his parents react? Norma would insist they continue going to Evansville at least once a month. Maybe those visits would endear his mother to his children.

Shaking his head to rid himself of the thoughts of his family, he contemplated what to do now considering the weather changed his plans for the day. He could always go up to the haymow to throw down hay and straw for the cows.

Even with the storm raging outside, weak light shone through the cracks in the drop door of the loft, making the dust motes sparkle.

Although he'd been to the loft many times before to throw down hay, there had never been time to contemplate the rich harvest these eighty acres provided. By being married to Norma, he was sure his moving days were over and next year he could claim this crop as his own.

Sitting down on one of the bales, he allowed his mind to wander and he closed his eyes for just a moment of rest. Even with the cold of winter, this loft remained warm from the body heat of the cows beneath him.

"Ralph – Ralph!" Someone calling his name startled him from a deep sleep.

"I'm up here," he hollered back, getting to his feet and rubbing the sleep from his eyes.

"The boys are stuck in the snow," George said as soon as Ralph came down the ladder. "Can you harness a team to snake them out?"

Ralph nodded and grabbed his winter coat before hurrying to get the team from their stalls on the far side of the barn. The mustang whinnied his protests at being left behind, but Ralph ignored him.

Outside, he saw Norma's brothers all together for the first time. They were each different from the other. Ralph was tall and had darker skin than the others. He'd met Ralph's wife, Frieda as well as his daughters Judy and Barbara in the past. It was the other two boys who represented the unknown. Herman was a little taller than Ralph and from Norma he'd learned that Bernadine was his second wife and they were expecting a baby to be born in the coming year. The youngest of the three, Edmund, was shorter in stature and shared Norma's striking good looks. His wife, according to Norma, was Lillian.

Ralph smiled to see all of the young men dressed in topcoats over what he decided must be suits and highly polished shoes. They certainly weren't dressed to pull cars out of the snowdrifts and get them ready to pull out onto the road.

One by one he pulled the cars out of the snowbank and for the first time met the last two of Norma's brothers.

"You look like you're half frozen," Herman said. "I know Ma is putting out stuff for supper, why don't you come in and join us and warm up? Besides, we have to let the cars warm up before we take the girls out in this storm."

Ralph was uneasy about going into the house with the family. He could easily use the excuse of having to do chores, but the three young men who, although they didn't know it, were his brothers-in-law caught him up in their enthusiasm.

"Norma hasn't stopped talking about you all day," Edmund commented, once they were seated at the dining room table. "I was beginning to think you were nothing more than a figment of her imagination. Maybe it's a good thing this storm hit. It gave us a chance to get to know you."

Ralph was uneasy. Everyone was dressed in their Sunday best and he wore his barn clothes. It was evident they were the businessmen and he nothing more than the hired man. What would they think if they knew Norma had become his wife three weeks earlier?

"Norma says you've worked at a lot of farms," Herman said as he slathered one of Gertie's rolls with butter and peanut butter. "You don't look old enough to have worked at many places."

Ralph took a deep breath. "I've been out on my own since I graduated from the eighth grade. I was twelve at the time."

"Did you skip a grade like Norma did?" her oldest brother asked.

"No. I started going to school when I was five. I followed my sister to school and the teacher said I could stay. By the time I was old enough to actually go to school, I'd completed all the work for the first grade."

Herman shook his head. "I can't even imagine living that kind of a life. We were so lucky that Ma and Pa insisted we all had to go through high school."

"Maybe I was wrong about that," George said. "I don't see any of you boys clamoring to take over this farm."

Ralph watched the expression on the faces of Norma's brothers.

None of them had the look of a farmer. It was just as well. Without them having an interest in farming, he could run this place the way he always wanted to run a farm of his own.

"Just what are your intentions toward my sister?" Norma's oldest brother, Ralph, asked.

Ralph contemplated his response. "Do you believe in love at first sight?" From the corner of his eye, he saw Norma fingering her locket.

All three of Norma's brothers looked surprised and then smiled. "I know what you mean. I loved Lillian when I first saw her," Edmund confessed.

"Then you know how I feel about Norma. I fell in love with her on the day we met and have loved her more every day since. I have to admit when I learned your dad needed help, I would have moved heaven and hell to get this job so I could be close to her."

The brothers all seemed to accept his explanation defusing what could have become an explosive situation. One by one they started packing up their families with no idea their baby sister, the prettiest girl in LaPrairie Township, was a married woman and he was her husband.

"I was afraid we were going to have to tell the boys about our marriage," Norma said, once everyone left.

"That was the reason I didn't want to come in and share the day with your family. It was hard, but I didn't tell them a lie. I do love you more every day we're together."

* * * *

As January wore on, Ralph found being married without anyone knowing about it was getting harder by the day. As much as he wanted to see Norma graduate and get her diploma, he also enjoyed the weekends when she was in the house when he came in for meals.

It was late February when Ralph woke up one morning with the same sore throat he'd experienced for the past week. The difference this morning was he felt overly warm. Not willing to give into the weakness his body felt he went out to the barn to begin the milking. Even though the thought of going back to bed crossed his mind, he could hear his father telling him that a farmer didn't have time to be sick with a cold or even a sore throat.

By the time he came in for breakfast, he was beginning to feel lousy. Never having been sick a day in his life, he shrugged off the feelings.

A few minutes after Ralph finished cleaning the barn George returned from taking Norma to school. "You look tired, Ralph," George commented. "It looks like we might get some more snow. Why don't you call it a day and come in where it's warm?"

Ralph nodded. He didn't need to be asked twice. All he could think about was sitting down in one of the chairs in the living room close to the big floor register that would be putting out enough heat to warm the entire house.

"I have pie and coffee for you, Ralph," Gertie said, once he entered the kitchen.

"I don't think I want any. I just want to sit down for a while."

Gertie hurried over to his side and put her hand on his forehead. "Why didn't you say you were sick this morning at breakfast? You're burning up. I'm going to make you a nest on the couch in the parlor and call for the doctor. The way your neck is swollen, it's possible you have the mumps."

"Mumps?" Ralph questioned. "Isn't that a kids' disease?"

"Have you ever had them?"

"I've never been sick a day in my life."

"Then if you've got the mumps, it's something we need to have checked out. I'll call into town and have Dr. Overton come out and check on you. Mumps in an adult man can go down on him and cause sterility."

Gertie's comment about sterility, brought to mind his mother's admission of not wanting any more grandchildren. It was possible she would be getting her wish. As much as he wanted children with Norma, those dreams could have been dissolved because of this sudden sickness.

"I have your nest ready," Gertie called.

Laboriously, Ralph got up from the dining room chair and made his way through the living room to the parlor. As though she was caring for one of her own, Gertie spread blankets over the couch so once he lay down, she could cover him up. He felt like a small child but it was soothing to have someone fuss over him.

Once he lay down, he rested his head on a fluffy pillow covered with one of Gertie's beautifully embroidered pillowcases. Just as he closed his eyes, he heard George come into the house.

"I'm afraid Ralph is terribly sick," he heard Gertie say. "I'm going to call for Dr. Overton to come out. I'm certain he has the mumps and you know how bad those can be when you're a grown man."

Ralph quit listening to the conversation between his in-laws. It was so much easier to close his eyes and when he did, he fell into a deep sleep.

"Ralph, Ralph, you have to wake up," someone in his dreams said.

"Please let me sleep, Pa," he muttered.

"Dr. Overton is here, Ralph."

He shook the cobwebs from his mind as he recognized George's voice. With great effort he opened his eyes to see the doctor standing next to the couch.

"How long have you been feeling like this, Ralph?" Dr. Overton asked.

"I've had a sore throat for about a week. I figured it was just a cold."

"Have you been resting?"

Ralph laughed, even though it hurt. "I'm a farmer, Doc. Farmers don't get sick. They just don't have time."

"Well, like it or not you're going to have to take the time. You do have the mumps and you've let it go so long it's gone into pneumonia. I'm going to tell George you have to rest and that's all there is to it."

"But if I rest, I won't get the work done and that's not what he's paying me for. I have to work if I want to earn any money."

"And you have to rest if you want to live long enough to see your nineteenth birthday. This is serious. I know Gertie will take good care of you. Your main job is to rest and get your strength back before it's time for spring work to start."

Ralph could see there was no use in arguing. For one thing, Gertie wouldn't allow it and for another, he was too tired to even try to argue.

When he awoke the next time, Norma sat by him in one of the overstuffed chairs. "Oh, Ralph, why didn't you tell us you were so sick?"

"I'm not paid to be sick. I have to go out and do the chores."

"You have to stay in bed and Ma and I are here to make sure you do it."

"But I have to do the milking."

"No you don't. Pa talked to Grandpa Howard and he said Pete would be down to help with our milking when he gets done with the chores up there."

Ralph thought about the offer. Pete Petersen was one of the first friends he'd made when he first arrived at the Howard farm. He was the stepson of Norma's Grandpa, Ralph Howard, and only a little older than Ralph. He thoroughly enjoyed being with Pete. He had an easy manner and was always whistling. To be truthful he was one of the first really good friends he'd had in a long time.

"I don't know how I'll ever be able to repay him for helping me out."

"This is a family thing," Norma assured him. "Pete is more than a friend, he's family. He's doing for you exactly what you did for Freddie when Marion died. Did Freddie ever pay you for the eight months you ran his farm for him?"

Ralph closed his eyes as he remembered the horrible day when Marion died leaving Freddie alone with Beverly. Without even giving it a thought he'd quit his job and moved in with his brother in order to keep the farm running and to help raise Beverly. At the time, he thought he was doing what his family expected of him. Now he knew it was because he wanted to help his brother, no matter what financial sacrifice he had to make.

"No, he didn't. Maybe this is pay back for what I did for Freddie, and what I'll be ready to do for anyone else who needs my help in the future."

Chapter Twenty-Seven

By the middle of March Ralph was back doing his own chores. The only lasting reminder of what he'd been through was the threat he might never be able to father children. He had so much love to give to a child. He'd proved it when he'd taken care of Beverly from the time of her mother's death until death snatched her as well as Harriett and Donna Jean from the loving arms of their family. It wasn't fair that the line of his family would die out because there was no one left to carry on. Leona would never have children and now he'd sentenced Norma to the same fate.

Norma had wanted to nurse him back to health, but he'd insisted her studies were the most important thing for her to be concentrating on. It was Gertie who made certain he rested and regained his strength, while Norma worked on her homework. He was pleased when she received the high grades he'd wanted to achieve for himself.

As the day of her graduation drew closer, Ralph knew they would be revealing the secret of their marriage. In preparation for this announcement, he went into town and stopped at the jewelry store where Norma had been looking at a beautiful diamond set wedding band. On one Saturday, they'd even gone into the store and Norma asked to try on the ring she wanted so badly, but knew they couldn't afford.

"There's a ring in the window," Ralph said, tongue-tied over engaging in such a large purchase without the assistance of his mentor, Mr. Canary. "How much do you want for it?"

Mr. Bandt looked at him and then smiled knowingly. "I've seen you in here with Norma Howard. I know she's in love with that ring. Are you planning to do something honorable with it?"

"She's my wife."

"Wife?"

"It's supposed to be a secret, but next Saturday she'll be graduating from high school and we can tell everyone we've been married since December. I can't see the harm in you knowing about it a week early."

The older man nodded his head. "It all makes sense now. I remember the day you bought her the locket and insisted you needed the pictures of the two of you put inside it. Is that what she's been wearing in place of a wedding ring?"

"Yes, it is, but I want her to have the same thing every other married woman has. She needs a symbol of our love and I want it to be one of the most beautiful rings in your store."

Mr. Bandt went to the front window of the store and pulled out the ring Norma wanted so badly. "Norma is a very special young lady. I know because one of her teachers was in here the other day to buy her a pink sapphire for her graduation gift. That's how I know her size. She has such small fingers, I'm certain she's one of the few people who could even wear this ring. I'll gladly give you a good price on it, since I doubt I'd ever be able to sell it and have to send it back to the goldsmith who made it when his new designs come out this summer."

Ralph held his breath as Mr. Bandt named his price and was relieved when he was able to pay cash from his billfold for the ring he would present to her as soon as they made their announcement.

"Thank you, Mr. Bandt. I won't ever forget this."

"Consider it a wedding present. Every so often there's someone in my life who is so special I know they deserve the very best piece in my shop. Norma is one of those people. I can see the love you have for her in your eyes when the two of you come in together. All I ask is for you to love her as much on the day you die as you do today. It's what she deserves."

* * * *

The following Saturday, Ralph sat in the audience as the graduating class of 1940 walked across the stage to receive their diplomas. When Norma's name was called, he was immediately on his feet, cheering louder than even her parents and brothers.

With the ceremony completed, her friends surrounded Norma when Ralph joined them. "I have a wonderful announcement to make," Norma said. "Ralph and I have been married for five months. It's been so hard to keep it a secret from you."

"Married?" June echoed. "I can't believe it. Even so, I should have known it considering he came to work for your dad shortly after the two of you met. I'm so happy for you. I'm also getting married. Ole Hanthorn proposed to me last night. We're getting married in June. You and Ralph just have to be there."

"You bet we will," Ralph said. He knew Norma hadn't seen him join the group. "Before we go back to the farm and the party your mother is planning I want to give you your present. I can't think of a better time to do it than now."

He watched as Norma's hands trembled as she opened the small jewelry box. "Oh Ralph, it's the ring I wanted. I was so upset when I saw it wasn't in the window of the store any longer. I just knew Mr. Bandt sold it to someone else."

"This ring belongs nowhere but on your finger. I was afraid I wouldn't be able to afford it. The next time we come to town, you'll have to be certain to stop in and see Mr. Bandt so you can thank him for his wedding present. He gave me a good price so this ring could belong to you."

The diamonds of the ring, although smaller than most stones set in such rings, sparkled in the sun. He enjoyed the way her friends gathered around her to ooh and aah over the beauty of not only the ring but also their love for one another.

At the farm, Norma's brothers, sisters-in-law, and parents waited for them to arrive. Also there were her Grandpa Howard, his wife Christine, Norma's Howard aunts and uncles, Pete and Gen Petersen, as well as her Grandpa and Grandma Kellogg and her Kellogg aunts and uncles.

Gen was the first to notice the new ring now gracing the third finger of Norma's left hand. "What's the meaning of this?" she asked, bringing the attention of the entire family to Ralph and Norma.

Ralph pulled Norma into an embrace at his side. "In December Norma and I were married. Today I was finally able to give her a symbol of my love for everyone to see. She is now and will be forever Norma Jean Howard Derr."

"Did you know about this, Pa?" Herman demanded.

"We knew. That doesn't mean we approved of it. Of course, you boys all know your sister. When can you ever remember her not getting her way? I happen to know this is the ring she's been wanting for the past several months. When I picked her up from school the other day I had to stop downtown and she went right to the store to look at it. I was certain she planned to ask Ralph to buy it for her. She came back to the truck crying, since it was no longer in the window. At the time she was devastated and I realized for one of the first times in her life she wouldn't get what she wanted above all else. Ralph has worked for me since last fall and I couldn't ask for anyone better to do the work on this farm while I run my other business."

Ralph appreciated his father-in-law's words. Even so, he knew there were a lot of the women who were counting the months as they contemplated Norma's slender figure. In no way would she be giving birth to his child in August or even September. Unfortunately, because of the cruel turn of fate that infected him with the mumps had probably made her ever having his child impossible.

With their secret out, Ralph now pondered having to introduce Norma's family to his. It was Norma who suggested a picnic and extended the invitation to his parents as well as Freddie and Leona.

Ralph's worse fears were realized when his family arrived and it was evident Freddie had been drinking. Ralph knew his father-in-law was dead set against drinking and George became more and more uncomfortable throughout the afternoon as Freddie made several more trips out to the car so he could have yet another drink.

"We're so pleased to have Norma in the family," Amy gushed to Gertie.

Ralph wanted to puke to listen to his mother saying only what she thought her hostess wanted to hear. On more than one occasion, she'd told him he'd married above his station in life and she believed Norma considered the entire family as beneath them.

With the news of Ralph and Norma's marriage now public knowledge, Ralph met more and more of the neighbors. In addition to old Ralph Howard, his son Everett and Pete from one road over were the Rehbiers, the Ackermans, and the Hodge brothers. Just down the road were Bob and Beulah Baker, Everett Howard, Bob and Marge Ransom and the Atkinsons. Some were related to Norma, but most were friends who had known the family for years and many of the young men had, at one time or another fancied themselves as being in love with her.

"You're one of the luckiest son of a bitches in the county," Alan Hodge said when they first met. "You have the prize of LaPrairie Township. I doubt there isn't one young buck around who wouldn't give anything to have married Norma Howard. She has to be the prettiest girl I've ever seen. Besides George's farm is some of the richest land in this part of the country."

Ralph smiled. He knew exactly how lucky he was. He'd gone from being a kid with a wild streak, to a young man with a price on his head, to being married to the girl of his dreams. He must have done something right in his life, but he'd be damned if he knew what it was.

By mid-summer Ralph and his neighbors worked together doing the haying as well as the combining of the oats. It was good to have someone to work with, someone to depend on. With everyone helping each other, the work seemed to be done with much more ease than he'd ever expected in the past.

The only thing to mar what Ralph saw, as his perfect life was the fact Freddie literally demanded help with his crops. On most Sundays when Ralph and Norma visited his parents, the two younger couples left right after dinner to go out to Freddie's farm so Ralph could help with planting and cultivating corn, baling hay and combining oats. With all the work Freddie needed help doing, the trips to Evansville were made every other Sunday.

On the opposite Sundays, Norma's brothers came for dinner at the farm, leaving Ralph with no day of rest. Even though milking was a twice a day seven day a week job, during the winter Ralph had been able to have at least one Sunday a month for himself. Even when the boys came for dinner, he'd been able to slip away to the barn and pretend these people meant nothing to him. Now that was impossible. Norma's brothers and their families were his family as well. No matter what they thought of him, he was pleased to have someone he could be proud of to call family.

Chapter Twenty-Eight

Days blended into weeks and weeks into months. With each passing month when Norma didn't get pregnant Ralph knew she was disappointed. He ached at the fact his sickness was the cause of her inability to get pregnant.

"Maybe we were wrong to get married," he whispered one night after they made love.

Norma raised up on one elbow and looked at him in the soft light coming through the window from the full moon. "Are you sorry you married me? Do you want a divorce?"

"Oh, Norma, never, but it seems like I can't give you what you want the most. I can't give you children. More than anything else in the world I want a child to love and raise. But I know the fact we haven't made a baby is hard on you."

Norma's earlier tears turned to a broad smile. "We can always adopt a baby. If we can't make one of our own, we can still have a family. I was just afraid you didn't want to be with me. I love you so much I think I'd just die if you were to leave me."

They had just begun the paperwork to adopt a baby or even an older child when the news the Japanese bombed Pearl Harbor in Hawaii came across the radio. Ralph knew he was of an age where he would be eligible for military service, but leaving Norma was almost more than he could stand.

The next Sunday, the family gathered at the farm and the main discussion was about the impending war and the need for the nation's young men to fight for freedom.

"I checked into the draft," Norma's brother Herman said, "but they said I'm too old. As a matter of fact, we're all too old. At least this family won't be torn apart by the war. Now that we all have children it's for the best."

Ralph thought of the nieces who had been born over the past few months. In addition to Judy and Barb, Herman and Bernadine had given birth to a girl named Gaye, while Edmund and Lillian had a daughter by the name of Jacquie. Only he and Norma were childless and that was enough to break his heart. "I'm not too old," he said. "Norma and I've talked about it. As much as I hate to leave her, I know she'll be well taken care of."

Norma and Gertie cried, even though they'd talked of nothing else all week. Seeing his wife's tears nearly broke Ralph's heart, but it couldn't be helped. His country was at war and as a citizen of that country it was his duty to do his part.

On Monday morning, after the chores were finished, Ralph and Norma drove into Janesville and went to the draft office. The man at the desk looked at him skeptically. "Name?"

"Ralph Eugene Derr."

"Age?"

"Twenty."

"Hair color?"

"Black."

The man jerked his head up from the paper where he was recording Ralph's answers. "Only niggers have black hair. I'm marking it down as brown."

"But it's black," Ralph argued.

"Brown," the young man insisted. "Eye color?"

"Brown."

"Occupation?"

"I'm a farmer."

Again the man looked up at Ralph, only this time his expression was one of exasperation. "Well, this has been a waste of my time to say nothing of yours. As a farmer you're exempt from service. I thought everyone knew that."

"But I want to serve."

"It looks to me like you've got a nice wife here and I'm sure she'll be happy to have you at home rather than off getting yourself killed in some godforsaken place a million miles away from home."

Ralph thanked the man and walked out of the office to the waiting room where he'd left Norma minutes earlier.

"Are you going to war?" she asked. Even though she was now almost nineteen, he marveled at how childlike she sounded. It was as though she'd been praying he wouldn't be able to go and fight for his country.

"They won't take me. They say because I'm a farmer, I'm needed to milk cows and plant crops, not fight either the Japanese or the Germans."

"I know you wanted to go, but we have so much here. I'm glad you won't be going to war. I don't know what I'd do without you."

Although disheartened, Ralph tried not to show it. Instead, he took Norma out to lunch at one of her favorite restaurants, Adamany's. The thought of sharing one of her favorites, an olive nut sandwich helped to dampen his disappointment over not being able to fight for his country.

* * * *

Throughout the winter, men from all over the county were shipped overseas to fight in the biggest war the world had ever seen. The most notorious of these men were the Janesville 99, who while defending Bataan in the South Pacific, were captured by the Japanese and forced into imprisonment in what was called the Bataan Death March. Of the ninety-nine men who went to war only thirty-six would return in 1945. At the time there were many families in the area that knew at least one of the men who went to the South Pacific in 1942 and were prisoners of war.

Ralph felt the loss more than most, because if he had been able to enlist, it could have been him who was being held prisoner or perhaps even dead for all anyone knew.

In the spring of 1942, construction began just down the road from the Howard farm. In a field owned by Rock Atkinson, a Quonset hut was being constructed. The hump shaped building was intriguing to Ralph prompting him to go down to the neighbors to find out why the new building was being built.

"They're going to start running a glider school here," Rock said. "I know they're looking for people to help with the schooling. It would mean learning how to teach these recruits how to handle the gliders. Would you be interested in training to do the job?"

Ralph could feel his spirits soar. He could remain on the farm and yet do his part in the training of young men to go to the front and fight the war. After checking things out, he learned he would be working as a mechanic rather than a glider pilot trainer. It didn't matter. At least he would be doing his part for the war effort.

The family was horrified when they realized what he planned to do. He would finish the morning chores and then go down to the school to work throughout the day. After evening chores were finished, he did the necessary fieldwork, not coming in until almost midnight to fall into an exhausted sleep. All thoughts of trying to get Norma pregnant were put aside as work for not only the farm but also the war became a top priority.

One group of students that stood out the most in Ralph's mind, were the young men who came from Texas. It was fall and they had never seen snow. On the first frosty morning, they were certain it had snowed. When they found out it was only frost, they were very disappointed.

Within a month of them finishing their training, the school got word that they'd all been killed on their first mission over Germany. Again Ralph realized how lucky he was to have been a farmer and exempt from serving.

With all the work he now had to do, trips to Evansville were cut to once a month. When they did go, Freddie complained bitterly about not having any help with the fieldwork. Even Ralph's parents didn't understand his obsession with the things he was doing for the war effort.

Eventually, the school shut down and Ralph's workload became lighter. With the war ending, Ralph and Norma again started looking into the possibility of adopting a child. At the middle of October 1945, they learned they were being considered to become the parents of a two-year-old boy. It wouldn't be the baby Norma dreamed of, but it would be a child and for them it was all that mattered.

They no more than got the news when Norma woke up one morning sick. They both chalked it up to the flu, but when it continued for a week straight, they suspected it to be more. At Gertie's insistence, Ralph took Norma into Janesville to see Dr. Overton.

Ralph sat in the waiting room while Norma went in for the examination. He feared the worst and prayed for the best. Norma just couldn't be sick, but the persistent illness in the morning could mean she was terminally ill. After what seemed like an eternity, the door to the inner office opened and Norma motioned for Ralph to join her.

"I have some good news and some bad news to tell you," Dr. Overton said.

Ralph held his breath.

"The good news is that you and Norma are going to be parents. I figure the baby will be born in April next year. The bad news is that little boy you were going to be adopting will have to go to another family. Since you've proved you can have children of your own, your petition for adoption will no longer be considered."

"A-A baby," Ralph stammered. "Are we really going to have a baby?"

Norma nodded, affirming what the doctor had just told them. "This is what we've been hoping and praying for ever since we got married. Everyone was wrong. Even with you having the mumps right after we got married, we are able to have a baby of our own."

Ralph's heart leaped for joy, but it was short lived once he realized now he would have to tell his family about the child they were expecting. He knew his mother wouldn't take it well and neither would his father. Their granddaughters had died in 1938 and they had no intention of accepting another grandchild. His parents had even tried to dissuade them from beginning the adoption proceedings before the war. This wouldn't set well with them.

Chapter Twenty-Nine

While every one of Norma's friends and family were excited about the upcoming birth of their child, Ralph's family was less than enthusiastic.

"I can't understand your parents' reaction to our news," Norma said as they left the house in Evansville after making their announcement at Sunday dinner.

"There's something I think you should know. My mother told me a long time ago she would never accept another grandchild. In her eyes, the sun rose and set in Beverly and Donna Jean. I hope when our baby is born she'll soften, but I can't guarantee it. As for Freddie, he knows what a mistake he made in marrying Leona. He will never have another child to love. As much as he loved Beverly, I know the last months of her life were extremely difficult for him. That was when he started drinking. It was hard for me to lose Marion in February and the remainder of the younger female members of our family in October. It had to be ten times harder for him. I know he loved both Marion and Beverly with all his heart."

"Why in the world did he ever marry Leona?" Norma asked, as they turned onto Highway 14 to head toward home.

"I'm sure he was drunk out of his mind and merely woke up married to her. I have no doubt he doesn't even remember the ceremony. Her family was desperate to get her married off. They even tried to get me to marry her, but I wanted no part of it."

"If that's the case why does he stay with her?"

"He feels he has no choice. A long time ago our pa told us marriage is forever. He said we should be very careful who we chose to marry. Once the vows are said it is something no one can ever change. I was certain about you and I know Freddie was certain about Marion. As for Leona, he said the words binding him to her and now he has to abide by them."

"What about our child?"

"If my family isn't as attentive as yours toward our child, so be it. There will be enough love to go around and he or she will never know how their grandparents on my side of the family feel."

Ralph knew the actions of his family were hard for Norma to comprehend but this was nothing new as far as he was concerned. They acted like this when they kicked him out once he graduated from the eighth grade, when the accident occurred and now that he was getting what he desired more than life itself, a child to complement the love he felt for Norma.

* * * *

By April, Norma had gained more weight than Ralph thought possible. She was over eighty pounds heavier than she had been when they were married but the joy radiating from her eyes overshadowed her physical appearance.

"I wish this baby would be born soon," Norma lamented as they ate breakfast on the morning of April 23.

Ralph smiled. He, too, was looking forward to having the baby born and to be able to begin the new job of being a father.

Gertie reached across the table and put her hand over Norma's hands and looked deeply into her eyes. "Just remember, honey, you're carrying this child in the easiest place you'll ever carry it."

Ralph smiled at the gesture between mother and daughter. He could only imagine such a tender scene happening between his own mother and Harriett, since he'd never seen anything close to this tenderness.

"What are you planning to do today?" he asked. "The weather is perfect, so are you going to relax on the porch swing?"

Norma looked at him as thought he had made an obscene suggestion. "I'm sick to death of resting. Ma had Pa plow up the garden yesterday while you were working out in the field. I'm planning to start planting the seeds."

"Do you think that's wise?" Gertie inquired.

"Of course it is. I always make a garden at the end of April. It seems to me you like it when the peas and lettuce are ready to be eaten fresh out of the garden."

Ralph shrugged his shoulders in defeat. Her father hit the nail on the head when he told her brothers Norma always got exactly what she wanted. He'd learned about it first hand when they'd been on their way to Watertown to visit Herman and his family. As they passed through Fort Atkinson, Norma saw a beautiful fur coat in the window of the Fort Fur Company. He knew the minute she saw it he would be buying it for her. He certainly had no idea how he would be able to afford a mink coat, but if Norma wanted it, then she would have it.

Weeks later, on a rainy day when there could be no work in the field, they'd again driven to Fort Atkinson and gone inside the store to look at the coat that so captivated Norma's imagination.

"We're interested in the coat you have in the window," Norma said as they entered the store.

"Oh, I'm sorry, that's a discontinued model. I'm afraid we have nothing like it in stock," the man who ran the store advised them.

"What about the one in the window?" Ralph questioned.

The man looked at them as though they had lost their minds. "There's no way we can sell that one. It's been in the window so long the sun has faded it. Besides, the size is so small I doubt anyone can wear it."

Tears formed in Norma's big brown eyes as the coat of her dreams was slipping away from her.

"Can Norma try it on?" Ralph asked.

The man looked at him as though he'd completely lost his mind. "You can try it on, but I'm certain it won't be up to your expectations."

Ralph squeezed Norma's hand as the man opened the door leading to the show window. When he returned, Ralph helped Norma out of her

224

old coat and held the fur for her to try on. As though it had been made especially for her she looked like a princess.

"I see nothing wrong with the coat or the way it fits my wife. How much are you asking for it?"

"It's three hundred dollars."

"Oh Ralph, it's way too expensive. We can't afford anything this elegant."

Refusing to leave the store without the coat that Norma wanted so badly, Ralph turned to the shopkeeper. "What would you do with this coat if we don't take it off your hands?"

"I'd have to either leave it in the window forever or send it back. I'd at least get half of my investment back."

"How much would you be willing to sell it to us for, considering the size as well as the discoloration from being in the sun for so long?"

"Well, let me see. What is your budget?"

"Right now I have seventy-five dollars in my billfold. For Norma I'd be willing to use that as a down payment. What amount do you have in mind?"

"Because of the condition of the coat, the designer wouldn't be able to give me anywhere near what I paid for it. I'm sure I couldn't return it for more than seventy-five dollars, so I think we have a deal."

Ralph smiled at the memory. Norma had been the envy of all her friends and he had the satisfaction of knowing he'd made her dream come true for a lot less money that he ever expected to spend for the coat of her dreams.

After breakfast, Ralph went out to finish dragging the field he'd disked yesterday in preparation for the planting of the corn next week. Rather than coming to the house at noon, he'd asked Norma to pack him a sandwich for lunch. It was about two when he saw George driving his truck over the freshly prepared field.

"I'll take over here," George declared. "Take my truck and go back to the house. Norma's in labor and she's ready to leave for the hospital."

Ralph abandoned the team to his father-in-law and jumped into the still running truck to drive back to the farm. He would have wanted to take a bath and change his clothes, but Norma was in tears for fear they wouldn't make it on time.

As he helped her get into the car, he remembered how much she hated the 1937 Terrplane Coupe he'd purchased last summer before they ever thought they would be parents within less than a year. He knew he would have to replace it with something more modern and more to Norma's liking in the near future.

Once at the hospital, Norma was settled into a comfortable room. "I know you have chores to do, Ralph," the doctor who was there to help with the birth said. "It will be a while before your baby is born. I suggest you go back home and do your chores, have some supper and then come back. I'm sure there will be plenty of time, besides there is nothing you can do here."

Ralph was reluctant to leave Norma's side, but through her tears, she agreed with the doctor. He would have felt much better about it if Dr. Overton was overseeing the birth, but he'd taken ill and was unable to be there. The doctor who was taking over for him, assured them his specialty was delivering babies and Norma would be in good hands.

By the time Ralph returned to the hospital dedicated nurses as well as the nuns who ran Mercy Hospital were caring for Norma.

"What are you planning to name your baby?" one young nurse asked as Ralph sat beside the bed.

"If it's a boy, we're going to name him Darrell," Norma replied. "Of course if it's a girl it will be Cheryl and we'll call her Sherry."

Ralph chafed at the mention of the girl's name. "I don't like the fact you want to name her one thing and call her something else," he said. "If you want her to be Sherry, then I think we should name her Sherry."

Norma agreed and endured the labor that seemed to be never ending. Ralph slept fitfully in the chair next to the bed, all the while holding onto her hand. By five in the morning, the contractions dwindled to one every ten minutes, giving Ralph an excuse to go back to the farm in order to do the morning milking.

Once there, Gertie insisted he take time to change his clothes, eat some breakfast and place a call to Evansville to inform his family of the impending birth.

At eight, he walked back into Norma's room, to find her in full-blown labor. "The doctor says the baby will be born soon," she said between contractions.

Finally, at nine-thirty, the nurse came and wheeled Norma into the delivery room, directing Ralph to the father's lounge to wait for the doctor to come and tell him the baby had finally been born.

To his surprise, when he entered the father's lounge, George and Gertie, as well as his parents were waiting for him.

"After you left," Gertie began, "I called Amy and we decided this was something we've waited so long to see, we should both be here. My only daughter is going to make me a grandmother, just as her youngest son is going to do the same thing for her. I hope you don't mind us being here."

Ralph shook his head no. The very fact his parents came to be with him today meant more than he could ever say. The only thing he could remember his parents doing for him was when his mother accompanied them to Iowa for their wedding. Of course, his father hadn't been there, but at least his mother went along with them for their special day.

It was almost ten thirty when a nurse came in to inform them the baby had been born. "Mr. Derr," she said, prompting both Ralph and his father to get to his feet. From the corner of his eye, Ralph saw his mother reach for her husband's hand and force him to sit back down. "You have a beautiful daughter. She weighs nine pounds seven ounces and is twenty-one inches long. Your wife will be ready to see you in a few minutes. Do you know what you're going to be naming her?"

Ralph smiled. "We've decided on Sherry Lee."

"Sherry Lee," Gertie echoed. "What about Cheryl?"

"We talked about it last night and decided to call her Sherry."

Leaving his parents and in-laws in the waiting room, he hurried down to the room where Norma and Sherry were ready to meet him.

"She's beautiful," Ralph said when Norma pulled the blanket away from the baby's face.

"She has blue eyes," Norma said. "The nurses tell me all babies have blue eyes, but wouldn't it be fabulous if they stayed blue, just like my father."

For a short minute he thought about the picture of Flossie that had been on his dresser for so long. Even though it was black and white, he was certain her eyes were also blue. Perhaps blue eyes ran in his mother's family.

After ten days in the hospital, Ralph was finally able to bring Norma and Sherry home on Thursday. Gertie fussed over them and at supper suggested Norma should rest.

"I've been resting for days. You know Thursday is our night to go to the movies and I made Ralph promise to take me to Clinton so we can see the new show. I think it's supposed to be a John Wayne movie, but not getting to go last week, I don't know for sure."

Against the protests of Norma's parents Ralph hurried through the chores and bundled Norma and the baby into the car in order to go to the movies.

"I'm so glad to be alone with you," Norma said as they pulled out of the driveway.

"Alone?" Ralph questioned glancing down at the baby sleeping in Norma's arms.

"You know, just the three of us. I couldn't believe the number of neighbors who were waiting for us when we got home. I was completely overwhelmed. It's bad enough having Ma and Pa watch our every move, but to come home to a houseful of people was a bit too much. I'm afraid it's not going to let up any time soon. Ma says the boys and their families will be coming after church for Sunday dinner. I know you probably wanted to go to Evansville, but…"

"Don't worry about going to Evansville. We can go up there next Sunday. I'm in no rush to share our daughter with my family."

As he usually did, Ralph bought a large bucket of popcorn and ushered Norma to one of the plush seats so they could enjoy the movie. Even all the noise in the theatre didn't seem to bother Sherry, as she slept through the entire show.

Afterwards, they went across the street to the drug store where they both had chocolate malts. Considering they went there every Thursday night, they were met with great enthusiasm and everyone wanted to enjoy their first glimpse of Ralph and Norma's baby.

On the first Sunday after they returned home Norma's family arrived to get their first looks at their newest niece. Ralph and Frieda had expanded their family with yet another daughter, Cathy. Herman and Bernadine finally gave George and Gertie two grandsons, Tony and Mike, bringing the number of grandchildren, including Sherry to eight.

Gertie was in her glory and Ralph beamed at the congratulations from his brothers-in-law. He watched, as each sister-in-law and niece took a turn at holding the baby. This was the kind of family he wanted all his life and had been denied. In his mind's eye, he could see Beverly, at the age of twelve and Donna Jean nine welcoming their cousin into the world.

From the corner of his eye, he caught a flash of black as another car pulled into the driveway. His heart sank when he realized it was not only his parents but also Freddie and Leona coming to welcome Sherry home. It wasn't as though Norma's family hadn't met his family in the past, but he dreaded Freddie's drunken antics that would be so embarrassing with Norma's more sophisticated family.

Gertie greeted Amy warmly and invited them all in for dinner. It didn't take her long to add another four places at the table, making everyone squeeze in just a bit more.

Although his mother held the baby, he saw none of the admiration in her eyes he'd witnessed when she held either Beverly or Donna Jean. It was Freddie who was the most surprising of the group. To Ralph's relief, his brother hadn't been drinking and when he took Sherry in his arms it was as though he was once again staring into the face of his fair haired little Beverly. Other than Sherry's blue eyes, Ralph could see no resemblance whatsoever. Where Sherry had lots of long downy black hair, Beverly had beautiful blonde curls. Beverly had also been much smaller at birth, weighing in at just a little over seven pounds.

"She's beautiful," Freddie declared. "You don't know how lucky you are to have a daughter. Sons are nice, but daughters are always much better. Just remember how quickly things can change. I'd give anything to have Beverly and Donna Jean here today to meet their new cousin."

Freddie's words brought tears to Ralph's eyes. As much as Freddie missed his daughter, Ralph suffered the loss of his sister and nieces just as deeply.

By the time everyone went home for the evening, Norma was exhausted and Sherry was ready to be put down for the night.

"It was a beautiful day," Norma whispered as they snuggled into bed.

"It really was. I'm so glad Freddie was sober and didn't make a spectacle of himself in front of your family."

"I don't know why you're so worried. I happen to know Ralph and Frieda aren't above having a drink in the evening and so do Herman and Bernadine. I'm sure it will be the same with Edmund and Lillian."

"Well, it won't be the same with us. After living with Freddie and watching him drink himself drunk every day, I have very little tolerance for drinking. I guess I'm a lot like your dad in that department."

Chapter Thirty

Ralph found life fell into a predictable pattern. Norma kept busy with the house and Sherry, while Ralph kept up the chores, worked the land, broke mustangs to be taken back to the sale barn for auction, and took on extra work for many of the farmers in the area who needed his help.

The only thing to mar his perfect life was the fact his parents remained cold where Sherry was concerned. They tried, even having a gift of a Little Golden Book for her each time they came for Sunday dinner. The comparison to George and Gertie was like night into day. Gertie doted on Sherry and even George played with her whenever she pestered him.

In Evansville, Sundays were as tense and formal as he always remembered them being. While the women sat at the far end of the room in a row of stiff chairs, he sat at the other end in one of the three comfortable chairs along with Freddie and his father. Whatever the talk on the other end of the room centered on Ralph had no idea. What he did know was Freddie spent most of the afternoon complaining about the amount of work he had to do all alone and how unfair it was Ralph wouldn't come up and help him, when he was helping others down in LaPrairie Township.

"What I do for my neighbors is no concern of yours," Ralph finally said, one Sunday when he could no longer take Freddie's baiting. "I help my neighbors and they help me back. In addition, I work on several farms to make extra money. You know if you drank a little less and socialized with your neighbors a little more, you might have the same kind of help I do. Haying takes more than one man and so does threshing. Down in our neighborhood, we all help each other and don't have to be doing everything alone."

"You know, it wouldn't hurt you to help your brother," Pa commented. "Freddie has always had things come to him a lot harder than you have. Ever since I can remember, you've always been a little bastard who never wanted to help the family. Everything has always been for you and you've never missed an opportunity to show off what you have and we don't. You've always driven flashy cars and worn clothes that are better than ours."

"Pa's right. Hiney told me you turned him down when he offered to have you marry Leona. Seeing Norma, I know you think you're too good for Leona. Well, she's a good wife and I guess I don't mind taking your leavings. I can tell you one thing, I don't spend my money as foolishly as you do. There's no I way I would ever go out and waste good money on diamond rings and mink coats."

Ralph could contain his anger no longer. "No Freddie, you don't buy nice things for your wife. You spend all your money on whiskey. If you didn't drink so much, you wouldn't be so far behind with your fieldwork. I bust my ass to support my family. I've never asked for a handout before and if you want me to start paying for our Sunday dinner again, I'll be glad to oblige. Everyone asks about my family and it breaks my heart to say I really don't have one. I get more love and respect from Norma's family than I've ever felt in this house or any of the other places you've ever lived. Maybe Harriett, Marion and the girls are the lucky ones. They don't have to live in the shadow of this family and know how little you think of anyone but yourselves."

The front door opened signaling the women had returned from their walk uptown to look in the store windows. "It's time to go home, Norma," Ralph said, getting to his feet. "I've got a lot to do to get ready to do the cultivating tomorrow."

Norma looked at him skeptically but said nothing. Instead, she started to pack up Sherry's things in preparation to leave for home.

"What happened while we were gone?" she asked as soon as they pulled out of town.

"I couldn't take any more of Freddie's whining about how unfair it is I had a great job and a beautiful wife, while he lives in his bottle, can't get his farm work done and is saddled with a woman like Leona who will never give him any children."

"Did they bring up about you working at the glider school again?"

Ralph shook his head no. "The subject's been hashed over enough during the war. Freddie could never understand why I took on something like working for the war effort when I could have been helping him. I just couldn't make him or Pa understand it was the least I could do for my country. If I couldn't fight, I needed to help out in some way."

"I'm glad you did it. I'm also happy you weren't able to enlist. If you had, you might have gone with the Janesville 99. Losing so many of the young men I went to high school with and knew most of my life was hard enough without thinking about losing you too."

"I guess things do turn out for the best. I can't imagine being away from you and Sherry."

"What about your family?"

"They aren't family, Norma. I call them Ma and Pa and acknowledge Freddie as my brother, but they've never been as much of a family to me as your folks have."

"What about Harriett and Marion?"

"I loved Harriett more than anything else in the world. She was sweet and even though she was older than me, I fancied myself her protector. As for Marion, I never knew why she married Freddie. She was a frail little thing and almost as pretty as you. I think I loved her from afar. Of course, she was much older than me and couldn't see me for anything other than Freddie's younger brother. I do think Freddie loved her and Beverly too, but when Marion died, part of Freddie died as well. I don't know what would have become of Beverly if I hadn't quit my job and moved over to his place to do the work and take care of her while he drank himself silly."

Just thinking about the girls who now rested in the Evansville cemetery brought a lump to Ralph's throat. He knew he couldn't ever forget them. It was Norma who insisted that in order to keep their memories fresh in his mind, he would have to make amends with his family. If that wasn't reason enough, she told him, Sherry deserved to know of her family. If he had a day when it was too rainy to get out into the field, he'd go up to Evansville and once again apologize because he'd let his temper get the better of him.

* * * *

The differences between Ralph and his family were glossed over. Even though his parents remained cool, Leona fussed over Sherry and Ralph's mother bought her beautiful little dresses at the Junior Shop. Being one of the most expensive children's shops in the county, Ralph decided his mother was pretending she was still purchasing clothes there for Beverly and Donna Jean. Although their names were never mentioned, pictures of them were taped to the inside of the china closet in the parlor. It was one reason Ralph rarely went into that room.

"Why doesn't Grandma Derr have a Christmas tree?" Sherry asked one snowy Sunday as they drove back home after celebrating Christmas with their Evansville family.

Ralph contemplated the answer to his daughter's question. "I don't think your grandpa's family every celebrated Christmas and neither did your grandma's. Other than the Christmas tree we had at school, I never even saw a real one until I was out on my own."

"Where did Santa put the presents?"

Ralph thought about the Santa Claus he played at church during the Christmas program. It was so different from his upbringing. There hadn't been a Santa in his household. There hadn't even been presents. "You've seen Grandma's Christmas cactus. That was our Christmas tree and where Santa left the gifts."

Norma looked skeptically at him over the top of their daughter's head. She knew the entire story and he decided she didn't mind him bending the truth a bit so as not to taint Sherry's opinion of her grandparents.

Chapter Thirty-One

Once Sherry started school, Ralph became even more involved in the community. Along with his chores, he took on more outside work including the repairs at the school. It was good to be involved and above all else, he wanted Sherry to have the best education possible.

It came as no surprise when, in the early 1950's, Freddie announced he'd taken a job at Highway Trailers in Edgerton and was quitting farming. Since he no longer wanted to be a farmer, he and Leona moved into the basement apartment of Ralph's parents' home.

Although Ralph wasn't astonished that his brother had once again moved home, it was still annoying. The worst part of it was that Bert, the old man who lived in the basement apartment was being forced to move. Where he went, Ralph would never know.

Pa made no secret of the fact he paid for Freddie's cars, registration, and driver's license. Now it was evident, Freddie would be living with their parents rent-free. It was more than likely they took all of their meals together as well, since Leona was not what he would consider a good cook.

It was Norma who told him to just accept Freddie's relationship with his parents. They were well settled on her family farm and would always have a roof over their heads and were able to support themselves.

In 1954, Ralph's well-ordered world started to come to an abrupt halt. Everything started when Norma was diagnosed with diabetes. While they were still reeling from that revelation, her father's mind snapped.

George was a big man and after being admitted to a facility in Oconomowoc, WI, the conclusion of the doctors came as a shock. George was suffering from hardening of the arteries to the brain, later known as Alzheimer's disease.

The Sunday before George was to be released from the hospital, the entire family gathered at the farm to discuss what would happen in the future.

"You know I love George as if he were my own father," Ralph began. "That's why this is so hard. I can see now he's been slipping for years, but the night we came home and found Gertie and Sherry barricaded in Sherry's bedroom, George was downstairs stark naked. I just can't have that around my daughter."

"I understand," Herman said, "but where do you think he should go?"

The question hung in the air like an elephant in the room no one wanted to acknowledge.

"I think I have a solution," Edmund suggested. "We bought that house in Tiffany recently and I've been checking things out. If Ralph and Norma can put up with Pa's care for a little longer, we have an area we can make into a separate apartment for Ma and Pa."

Gertie wrung her hands, as though the decisions being made were more than she could handle. "That would be such an imposition on you and Lillian."

Ralph held his peace. He'd just said it would be an imposition on his family, but for some reason it didn't matter. In the end Edmund remodeled his house to accommodate the new apartment, but the solution didn't last.

In less than a year, George became harder and harder to handle. Finally, the decision was made to put him in the County Farm where he could have around the clock care without exhausting Gertie.

"What are we going to do about the farm?" Norma's oldest brother asked when they met at the farm to discuss the future.

"George has always said the farm should belong to Norma and Ralph," Gertie said, smiling sweetly at her daughter. "They've been the ones to run it for the past sixteen years."

"But that's not fair," Herman protested. "It should stay in the Howard family."

"I agree," Edmund said. "I've been talking to Gary Howard and he'd like to buy it. That way it will still be owned by a Howard."

Ralph's temper threatened to boil over. In no way did he want to move. He'd considered this his home for longer than he'd been anywhere else in his entire life. "I know it will break Norma's heart to leave this farm, but if you don't want us to stay on, at least I have enough time to find a place to rent so we can move the first of March. As far as I'm concerned, you can do, as you want with this place. Since you'd rather have the money in your pocket than keep it running and taking away the only home your sister has ever known, so be it. As for Norma and me, I can guarantee we'll leave this farm and we won't look back."

Beside him, Norma and Gertie cried, but the deed was done. In no way would he jeopardize Norma's relationship with her family, but he certainly wouldn't stay where he wasn't wanted.

The following spring, with the help of their neighbors and friends, Ralph, Norma and Sherry moved from LaPrairie Township to a larger farm in Johnstown Township owned by Ross Mansur. The home farm was sold to Norma's cousin, Gary.

Although it was hard, both Ralph and Norma adjusted well to the move and Sherry went from going to a one-room school to a consolidated school just down the road from the farm. They also changed churches since driving all the way to Shopiere to attend the Congregational Church made no sense since a half-mile from the farm was a lovely Presbyterian Church in a country setting.

Just prior to Thanksgiving, Ralph had all his top teeth pulled and was waiting for the swelling to go down so he could be fitted for an upper plate.

The next Sunday when they went to Evansville, his mother put a dish of something finely ground in front of him.

"What the hell is this?" he demanded.

"I ground up a piece of chicken so you could eat it," she replied.

"You can take this shit back to the kitchen. I want to eat chicken, not this dry carp. Norma thought she was doing me a big favor by serving me soup. That lasted for one meal. If I'm going to be working like a man I have to eat like one."

After dinner, when the women left to go uptown window-shopping, Ruben took the opportunity to admonish Ralph for his outburst at the table. "Your mother was trying to do something nice for you."

"I know she was, Pa, but so was Norma and I like I said, I told her the same thing."

"How is it renting that big farm of yours?" Freddie asked, apparently trying to change the subject. "I can't see you taking orders from anyone. George pretty much let you have free rein in running his place."

"It's not much different. Ross and I get along just fine and now that he's left for Florida, things will go on as they always have. Even being gone he'll continue to get his share of the milk check and half of whatever animals I send to market. As a matter of fact, after the first of the year, Ross and Ruth want us to drive down and stay with them for a week."

"You'd take Sherry out of school for that long?" Ruben inquired, his voice sounding with an agitated tone. "The way you go on about an education I can't believe you'd ever consider doing such a thing."

Ralph sighed deeply. "I had the same concerns, but when we talked with her teacher, she told us Sherry could take her schoolwork with her. She's such a good student that shouldn't be a problem."

"Well, it all sounds like a waste of time and money to me," Freddie observed. "Of course, you always were able to spend more money than Pa and me. Guess it helped when you married old George Howard's daughter. There has to be plenty of money there. Didn't you say Norma's brothers sold that farm? How much did Norma get out of it?"

Ralph fumed. "If you want the truth, we were supposed to inherit the farm. Once we did, I told Norma I wanted to remodel the house and give Gertie a place to live for the rest of her life. The boys had other ideas. When they sold the farm, we gave Norma's portion of the money to Gertie. Lord knows she can use it."

Before Ralph could continue, the women returned and all discussion ceased. Within several minutes Ralph announced they were ready to leave to go back home so he could do evening chores.

"What did they say this time?" Norma asked, once Sherry was engrossed in The Shadow Knows, a radio drama they usually listened to on the way home from Evansville.

"They wanted to know how much money we got when the boys sold the farm. I'm so tired of Freddie thinking he has to know everything we spend our money on. I told them the truth, we gave the money to your mother. If he wouldn't drink so much, he'd have money to take vacations and buy nice things for Leona."

Norma wrinkled her nose. "I doubt Leona would know what to do if Freddie treated her any differently than he does now. She's had a rough life. She doesn't know what it's like to have nice things or be treated like a special lady. I'm so lucky you didn't fall into Hiney's trap. If you had, I wouldn't have been able to meet you and marry one of the most generous and loving men I've ever known."

Ralph winked, like he usually did when Norma said something to make him feel special. "No, honey, I'm the lucky one. I married the perfect girl and have the perfect life."

"But you should have had the farm."

"As far as I'm concerned, this was all for the best. I know the farm had good land, but this land is just as good. I have more acreage, therefore, I don't have to take on extra farm work to make ends meet. Along with that are the new friends we've made. Pete and I were close and still are, but here we have Lloyd Schroeder, Robert Mansur, and even Milo Moore. I'm a firm believer that whatever happens is what God has in mind. Guess he wanted us to move here so we could run a larger farm and Sherry could go to a good consolidated school, rather than the one room school back in LaPrairie."

Chapter Thirty-Two

The trip to Florida had been a good break, but Ralph contended it cost him much more than he spent along the way. Not only did his cows produce less milk but also the young man who came to stay at the farm had no idea how to regulate the wood furnace. In the time they were gone, he'd burned through not only all the stored wood but also two loads of coal, while having all the doors and windows open with the temperatures below zero.

Once back Ralph got everything under control again and prepared to plant his crops in the spring.

By fall, Ruben took to his bed. The doctor diagnosed him as having cancer. After several weeks, the only nourishment he could take was beer.

On September 30, 1957, Ralph just finished milking when they received a long distance phone call. "It's for you," Norma whispered holding out the receiver to Ralph.

Tentatively, Ralph took the receiver. On the other end of the line, he could hear his mother crying in the background. "I think you ought to get up here, Ralph," Freddie greeted him. "The doctor just left and told us Pa won't make it through the night."

It took all the restraint Ralph could muster not to tell them all to go to hell. "I'll be right there," he said.

"Is it bad?" Norma asked as soon as Ralph hung up.

Ralph nodded. "They don't think Pa will make it through the night. Freddie wants me up there. I guess they need someone who is sober. I don't know when I'll be back. Hopefully it will be in time for morning milking. If I'm not, give Lloyd a call. He'll come over and get the chores done."

Without another word, Ralph hurried up the stairs to change his clothes and then got in the car to make the drive to Evansville.

The scene at the house reminded him of the hushed pall hanging over the farm after the accident. Leona sat in one of the dining room chairs, as though to sit in one of the comfortable chairs on the other side of the room would be a sin. In the parlor, his mother sat next to the daybed and Freddie stood behind her, drinking from a glass filled with what Ralph decided was whiskey.

Nothing ever changes. Ma clings to Freddie for support, even though he's too drunk to be of any help. When they really need someone, they call on me. I don't know if I'm strong enough to handle much more of this.

It was close to midnight when Dr. Gray was once again called to the house. Ralph finally made the decision to call the man back at this ungodly hour, since his father's breathing became more and more shallow.

"It won't be long now," Dr. Gray said after listening to Ruben's heart.

To everyone's surprise, just after midnight, on October 1, Ruben sat bolt straight up in bed. "I see them," he said, his voice hardly more than a whisper. "Can you see them? It's Harriett and the little girls, they're waiting for me. I'm coming girls, I'm coming home to be with you."

He laid back down, closed his eyes and his breathing stopped. It was Dr. Gray who pronounced him dead.

Ralph thanked the doctor and showed him out while his mother clung to Freddie. Leona sat twisting her handkerchief and crying, leaving Ralph to call the funeral director to come and get his father.

I should be sad, but after what that old bastard did to me, I can't shed the same tears as Freddie and Ma.

Part Three

The Only Child
LaPrairie Township, Wisconsin

Sherry

Chapter Thirty-Three

July 4, 1951

For as far back as I can remember, my parents took me to Sunday school and then church at the Shopiere Congregational Church. On one Sunday each month, as soon as church let out, we left to drive to Evansville to have dinner with Grandma and Grandpa Derr as well as Uncle Freddie and Aunt Leona.

If I close my eyes, I can still see the house. When we entered the house, it was directly into the living room. To our left was the library table piled high with newspapers and magazines along with bowls of tangerines and salted peanuts in the shell. I don't ever recall stopping to sit down in the living room, since Mom always went out to the kitchen to help Grandma get dinner on the table and like a good daughter, I followed my mother. I know Leona was always at the table, but I never remember her helping with anything in the kitchen.

Dinner was always the same. Grandma served chicken, in one form or another, mashed potatoes, brown n serve rolls, canned asparagus, and a molded jello salad, from the grocery store. The best part was always getting to pick a can of pop, and a store bought angel food cake with strawberries for dessert, as well as windmill cookies that Grandma took from a package. Since my mother and Grandma Howard were both excellent cooks, having store bought cookies was a real treat.

After dinner, the men would go into the living room to talk while we women went out to Grandma's small kitchen to clean up. I was

245

usually under everyone's feet and eventually went to sit on my dad's lap. It was during those times that I got to see the roomers.

The upstairs bedrooms of the house were rented out to single men who roomed there. Each one of them was special to me, but none as special as the man who lived in the basement apartment, Bert. I never knew his last name, but he made a lasting impression on me. He occupied the small apartment and to my delight he had an old upright piano. Of course I'm ahead of myself in this story.

With the dishes done, Grandma, Aunt Leona and Mom would join the men in the living room and sit on the straight chairs from the dining room set in the parlor. I never knew what the men talked about, but I do know Grandpa sat next to the coal pail by the stove so he could easily spit his tobacco juice into it.

Behind where the women sat was the mysterious room Grandma called the parlor. I remember it always darkened with heavy lace curtains. The only furniture in the room consisted of the dining room table that went with the chairs we sat on in the doorway, a daybed and the mysterious china closet with pictures taped to the front glass. The pictures of the two little girls along with the two women standing by a young man I didn't recognize. I later learned the man was Uncle Freddie and the two pretty women were my Aunt Harriett, Grandma's only daughter, and my Aunt Marion, Freddie's first wife. I also learned the little girls were my cousins, Beverly and Donna Jean. I didn't learn their complete stories until I was much older and better able to understand. Still those pictures always intrigued me.

At some point in the afternoon, we would walk the two blocks uptown to look into the shop windows. I think Mom enjoyed it, since living on a farm there was little chance for anything like that at home. If we were really lucky, Grandma would let us go and visit her friend, Maude Lewis.

Maude lived in Tower House and Grandma cleaned for her. She was a sweet lady who, after an accident where her husband had been driving, was confined to a wheelchair. I thought she was one of the prettiest women in the world. Her house was filled with photographs taken by Maude's father who had been a famous photographer, or at least that's what she told me.

By the time we finally returned to Grandma's house, Daddy would be anxious to head for home. His excuse was always the same; he needed to get back in time for evening chores.

* * * *

I was about five when Grandma persuaded Mom and Dad to allow me to come up to Evansville and spend the Fourth of July with them. I was excited about going, but I know my mother and Grandma Howard fretted about me being away from home for several days.

Since it was the middle of summer, my dad said he couldn't take me to Evansville until after evening chores, so it was decided Uncle Freddie would come down to get me. With a lot of tears from my mother and grandmother, Freddie bundled me into the car and headed toward Highway 14.

We were just north of Janesville when Freddie told me he had to stop and talk to someone and I was to stay in the car. I now realize he stopped at a tavern to get a drink. Of course, a five-year-old child has no idea about such things. I do remember him saying I shouldn't ever tell my parents he stopped to talk to the man.

Before we got to Evansville, Freddie stopped at his farm to pick up Aunt Leona. She had cookies baked, but they weren't like the ones my mother made. I still ate them because it was getting close to noon and I was very hungry.

Staying overnight at Grandma and Grandpa's house was very exciting. I got to sleep in Grandma's big bed in a small bedroom I hardly knew existed. It was off the parlor and since I never went into that room it was very intriguing to me. While I slept with Grandma, Grandpa slept on the daybed in the parlor.

The next morning, I awoke to a breakfast far different from any I'd ever had at home. Grandpa, who was a very slender man, sat down to a breakfast of half a pound of crisp bacon, eggs and cereal with chocolate milk. I was in heaven when Grandma served me cereal with chocolate milk just like Grandpa's. I knew this was a special treat.

To my delight, one by one the roomers came down to breakfast and then left to do whatever it was they did each day before returning at night to sleep. I loved seeing these older men and not having to share their attentions with the usual adults at Grandma's house, was delightful.

After everyone finished breakfast, Grandma and Grandpa took me up to Leota Park for the Forth of GI celebration, as that was what the City of Evansville called their observance of the holiday.

At the park, I felt like I'd walked into fairyland. Flags depicted the patriotism connected with the celebration and booths were set up everywhere. I'm certain there were carnival rides, but I don't remember them being there. The most important booth to me was the Klinko booth. Here, the adults pitched nickels toward a board with different prizes named in the hopes of winning them. Since I was so small, Grandpa lifted me up so I could sit on the two by four making up the barrier between the customers and the people running the booth. To my delight, I won several prizes before it was time for us to go home for the night.

The next morning, I waited for my parents to arrive for Sunday dinner. I could hardly wait for them to see my winnings, which included pieces of carnival glass, plaster of Paris animals and even an Indian blanket.

My father looked at my treasures skeptically, but Grandpa assured him, I'd won them playing Klinko. I doubt my father believed I actually won the prizes, but he never said anything about it. Of course, by sitting on the counter I was actually cheating, but I think the man who ran the booth might have been a friend of my grandparents and bent the rules for me.

Chapter Thirty-Four

In 1952 I turned six and starting school as well as piano lessons excited me more than I can begin to say. One of the first people I told about the piano lessons was Bert. Since he had a piano, he told me I could come down to his apartment every time we visited with Grandma and Grandpa so he could hear what progress I was making.

After the lessons, I know my parents were getting tired of listening to me practice and making the same mistakes over and over again. Grandma Howard always complimented me, but as an adult, I can only imagine her cringing at every clinker I hit.

In Evansville, Grandma and Grandpa as well as Uncle Freddie and Aunt Leona were only mildly interested in my childish excitement. I'm sure they were more than ready for me to go down to visit with Bert so they could concentrate on adult talk without my monitoring their every word.

Bert always greeted my timid knock at his door with a broad smile and an affectionate hug. "What did you learn this week?" became his standard greeting once I started my lessons.

"I brought the new music my teacher gave me on Wednesday night. I hope I don't make too many mistakes."

"Don't worry about the mistakes, Little One. If we don't make mistakes, how can we ever learn?"

I remembered beaming at his words and taking my place on the piano stool. For me that was a great treat, as Bert was the only person I knew who had a piano stool and not a bench. Grandma had a bench where she kept all her sheet music and my teacher had a bench so she could sit next to me and correct my mistakes.

As soon as I finished, Bert got to his feet and clapped his hands. "Bravo! Bravo! You are becoming a very promising musician. Are you enjoying your lessons? Are you doing well in school?"

I turned to face him, still sitting on the piano stool and told him about everything that had happened at school as well as at my piano lessons. My parents always asked how my day went, but they had other things on their minds. In this little apartment, I was the center of Bert's world. Even though he was an adult, he reveled in my childish explanations about the important events in my life.

As with any child, I became used to my meetings and special talks with Bert. I couldn't begin to tell you when they stopped, but one Sunday when we arrived at Grandma and Grandpa's house, I hurried through dinner so I could go down to play my new, more difficult piece, for Bert.

"You won't be able to go down to see Bert today," Grandma said.

Immediately my world was shattered.

"Why can't she go down?" my dad asked.

"Because Bert moved out this week."

"Moved out?" Daddy echoed. I could see the astonishment on his face. To him, Bert was just another roomer, but he also knew the kindly older man had become important to me and therefore someone one different from the other men in the house.

"Leona and I are going to be moving into that apartment. I'm just not making any money farming. Since it's close to the first of March, my landlord didn't have a problem finding someone to take over the farm. As a matter of fact, his new tenant has offered to buy my half of the cattle as well as my machinery. We're just going to need some help this week moving the household stuff. Do you think you can come up and help us out?"

I know Daddy agreed to help Uncle Freddie, but didn't care. I'd lost my friend and the one adult I could talk to about what was going on in my life and understand what I was saying.

"You know I'll help you out. I just wonder what you're going to be doing with your time. I mean you have to work and working for someone else will be a lot different from farming."

"I've thought about that," Uncle Freddie replied. "I heard they were hiring over at Highway Trailers in Edgerton. I'll be starting to work over there a week from tomorrow. It's forty hours a week and possibly some overtime."

"Do you think you can handle it?"

"I'll have to."

That afternoon, just as we were getting ready to leave for home, Grandma handed me a little book. She said it was a present for me from Bert. Upon closer inspection I saw it was an early edition of Robert Lewis Stevenson's A Child's Garden of Verses. It became the only reminder of my short-lived relationship with one of the gentlest men in the world. As much as I always wanted to know what happened to Bert, his name was never mentioned again. He was the first real loss in my life.

* * * *

Christmas at Grandma and Grandpa Derr's house was so different from the one I shared with my parents and Grandma and Grandpa Howard. It was like a usual Sunday, but after we ate dinner we all went into the living room to exchange presents. I know I received presents from Uncle Freddie and Aunt Leona but what I remember the most was the presents from Grandma and Grandpa Derr. Grandma always gave me a dress from a children's store called The Juvenile Shop and Grandpa would hand me a jar of dimes he'd been saving throughout the year. Like the nickels for Klinko on the Fourth of July, I knew he saved them especially for me. Since the Christmas program at church was always held on the night we went to have Christmas in Evansville, I always had a new dress to wear.

Grandma bought me so many of the expensive dresses that when I was probably five or six I was asked to be in a fashion show for the shop.

At Christmas time when I was maybe seven or eight, Mom and Grandma did a lot of whispering, but until I got my present from Santa

I didn't know what it was all about. Since that year Santa brought me a pair of ice skates, the week after Christmas I went up to Evansville to stay with Grandma and Grandpa so I could learn how to skate on Lake Leota where Grandpa ran the warming house.

On the morning we were to go to the lake, Grandpa assured me the ice on the lake was perfect for skating. I was so excited to be going with my grandpa. Once we got there, he sat me down on a bench at the side of the lake, put on my skates and helped me to my feet. Then he motioned for an older girl to come and help me skate while he went back into the warming house. I was so disappointed I wanted to cry, but I didn't. More than anything else I wanted to learn how to skate and be like the ice skaters I'd seen on television.

In the past I'd gone out to the driveway in my boots and slid around on the frozen puddles and pretended to be one of the graceful skaters I so envied. Now on the narrow blades, I realized I wasn't anywhere near perfection. I was exactly what Uncle Freddie told me I was. His exact words had been "There's our three belly Sherry." According to my mother, as a toddler I'd always been so thin she didn't like putting me in sun suits or other summer clothing because I was so skinny. Well, by the time I went to school, I'd started to grow taller and pack on the pounds. I never recall a time when I was the smallest girl in school. Now, out on the ice, I was even more conscious of being heavy than ever before.

Around me other girls glided past me. The girl who helped me skate was older than me and so patient. Unfortunately, I can't remember her name but she did teach me how to do the one thing I wanted to do so badly.

The time I'd looked so forward to being with my grandfather paled from my expectations. I thought he'd be teaching me to skate. Instead, he sat in the warming house keeping the stove going. When I came in to be with him, he scolded me and told me I was the one who wanted to learn how to skate and I couldn't do that if I stayed in the warming house with him. To say I was crushed would be a gross understatement. In the future, I never returned to Lake Leota to go ice-skating.

The only other memory I have of spending time at Grandma and

Grandpa Derr's house was after Freddie and Leona moved to town. I went up to spend a few days in Evansville in the summer. Instead of sleeping in Grandma's bed, I was told I'd be bunking in with Aunt Leona. I didn't like sleeping in the same bed with Aunt Leona, but I said nothing about it.

The nicest part of the visit was when Freddie came home. Through the week he didn't smell bad like he did when we came up on Sunday. I later learned he'd curbed his drinking to starting on Friday night right after he finished work and not stopping until bedtime on Sunday night. Miraculously, he was able to stay sober throughout the workweek.

While I was staying with Grandma that summer, she took me with her when she went to clean houses. While she cleaned at young Dr. Gray's house, his wife let his daughter and me have a lemonade stand out on the sidewalk. I don't know if we made any money, but the memory of the experience stuck with me all my life. Being a farm girl, I thought I'd died and gone to heaven.

During that same stay we stopped to see Maude Lewis. Of all the people Grandma cleaned for, she was my favorite. I know I spoke of her before, but going to her house was like entering fairyland. She had several china closets all filled with knick-knacks and because I was coming with Grandma, she had a tea party for me. The tea, as I recall, was apple juice and she had little cookies to go with it. They weren't like the windmill cookies Grandma always had. These were little coconut macaroons. Whether she bought them at the grocery store or had someone make them I didn't know, but it was like eating food fit for fairies.

Chapter Thirty-Five

I remember the night Daddy got the call from Evansville saying Grandpa was dying. We'd been up to visit the day before and I knew things were bad. I was only eleven at the time, but I knew the man I called Grandpa was no longer there. He had no idea who I was even when I stood next to the daybed in the parlor and held his hand.

The next morning, my parents said I wouldn't be going to school for the rest of the week because Grandpa had died. It wasn't my first brush with death, since we'd still been living on the farm with Grandma and Grandpa when my Great Uncle Norm was killed in a fire. I remembered Uncle Norm and although I felt bad that he was dead and had gone to heaven, he wasn't my grandpa.

I stayed with Mom's friend, Kathryn Schroeder, while Mom and Dad went to Evansville to help plan the visitation as well as the funeral. To be truthful, I don't remember going to the visitation, but on Friday I did go to the funeral. I was sitting next to my father and at the front of the funeral home was a casket. I'd looked into it before the service started and was startled to see my grandpa looking like he could get up and talk to me, unlike he'd been on Sunday when he really wasn't there.

As the minister started the service, Daddy leaned over to me and whispered in my ear. "Don't you dare cry. For what that old bastard did to me, he doesn't deserve your tears." I never knew exactly how my father felt about his family, even though our Sunday visits were strained, I just thought that was the way things were supposed to be,

254

especially since we'd lived with my Grandma and Grandpa Howard. As long as I live I will never forget those words or the impact they had on me. I sat through the entire service dry eyed and never really understood why I couldn't cry for him until I grew up and learned more and more about my father's life before he met my mother.

After the funeral, we had one more grave to decorate on what Grandma called Decoration Day, now it's known as Memorial Day. I was now old enough to understand the gravestone with the name of Marion belonged to Freddie's first wife and Beverly was his daughter. Although the particulars of their deaths were the unknown at the time, I knew we took lilacs and tulips to those two graves as well as to one for Harriett and Donna Jean every year. The flowers were always put in mason jars in water and I'm sure by the next day they were completely wilted, but it didn't matter, we'd decorated the graves. The only difference the next spring was that we took four jars of flowers to the cemetery and Grandma looked at each of the gravestones with a look of sorrow on her face. I think those were the only times I ever saw emotion on her face. I can never remember seeing her smile.

Sunday dinners at Grandma's changed as well. Now it was my father who sat at the head of the table, leaving Mom and me with more room on the side we'd always sat on. After dinner, Freddie now sat in Grandpa's chair next to the stove and the coal pail to spit his tobacco, while Daddy sat in Freddie's chair. It didn't take long for Daddy's chair to become piled high with papers.

I can't remember how old I was when Freddie said he had something in the basement apartment he wanted to show me. I wasn't thrilled about going down stairs, but what teenager would be? Reluctantly I followed him to his apartment. As I did, I remember how neat and clean it always was when Bert lived there. What I found was a cluttered mess and I couldn't see anything Freddie would consider worth showing me.

After cleaning off the day bed he asked me to sit down. Once I was seated, he put his hand on my knee and ran it up my leg almost all the way to my panties. As he did, he told me this was what boys did to girls and he wanted to show me how good it felt. I was so frightened I pushed him away and ran back upstairs. Until the day he died, I never told my father what Freddie did to me. It was like Freddie stopping at the tavern for a drink when I'd been too little to understand what he was doing. If I'd told my dad, he would have killed Freddie and Grandma would have blamed him for yet another death in the family.

* * * *

With each trip to Evansville, I realized just how much Freddie was drinking. I think it was mainly because I was getting older and as a teenager, I heard my friends from high school talking about going to Fort Atkinson or Jefferson to the eighteen-year-old beer bars and getting drunk. I was beginning to realize Freddie was getting drunk, not because he was a kid trying something new, but because he was an alcoholic.

I was a senior in high school and engaged to be married when Daddy got a call one Sunday night to come down to the Sheriff's Department and get Freddie, since he'd been picked up for drunk driving. To be truthful I was horrified. Derr was a very uncommon name and I was certain the kids at school would think Freddie was my dad and it would be terribly embarrassing to me. I don't know how my dad did it, but somehow he managed to keep the arrest out of the paper and off the news.

I graduated from high school on June 4, 1964 and was married two days later. Bob Wille and I had been dating all through high school and getting married was a natural progression of things. At the time I wanted nothing to do with any of the Evansville family, but they all came to my wedding. I was aware of Freddie being drunk and Leona being obnoxious. Even Grandma Derr didn't seem to be happy about being there, but at least they came to the wedding.

It must have been about 1971 when we received a call saying Freddie had been taken to University Hospital and was asking for me to come up and see him. Mom and Dad went with us while my husband's mother stayed with our kids, Robin, Steven and Sandra.

I was totally unprepared for what I saw at the hospital. Freddie finally managed to burn up his brain with the alcohol. When we walked into the room, he looked at me and began to smile.

"I knew you'd come, Donna Jean. I knew you wouldn't let your old uncle down. They told me Beverly couldn't come, couldn't come for her own father."

Tears welled in my eyes and threatened to cut off my words. "I'm not Donna Jean, Uncle Freddie. I'm Sherry. Do you remember me?"

Freddie closed his eyes and thought for a minute. "Oh, yes, Sherry and Bob. I thought you were Donna Jean, but she's up in the cemetery with Harriett, Marion, Beverly and Pa, isn't she?"

"Yes, she is, but I'm here."

Freddie continued to ramble, often calling me Donna Jean and at one point he even called me Beverly. To my amazement, he remembered my husband, Bob, and son, Steven, perfectly.

When Freddie was finally released from the hospital, he was admitted to Evansville Manor Nursing Home. There he was alcohol free but the damage had been done.

Within a little over a year, Grandma Derr was also living in the nursing home, leaving Leona alone in the house on Madison Street.

* * * *

In early 1973, the nursing home called my parents to tell them Daddy had to come up to Evansville and see Grandma because she was not doing well. My husband and my mother thought Daddy and I should go up alone, so we drove up together.

Grandma was in bad shape and really didn't know we were there. After stopping at her room, we went to see Freddie. To our surprise there were some people visiting him.

Freddie was so excited to introduce us to Ann and her husband, but from the look on their faces I knew they were shocked to be meeting my dad.

"Are you Ralph's second wife?" Ann asked once we were outside the room.

"Second wife?" I echoed. "I'm his daughter."

"Oh, we must have read your wedding announcement incorrectly."

"Just who are you?" Daddy asked.

"I'm Ann Dobson and this is my husband Cecil. We're your cousins on your mother's side. We came today because we heard Aunt Amy was very sick."

"Are there any other cousins?"

I could tell by the sound of Daddy's voice this the new information came as a shock.

"My sister, Flossie, lives close to us," Ann continued. "We were so shocked when Freddie told us who you are because when your daughter got married, Amy sent us an announcement of the wedding saying you'd died and her mother was a widow."

"Well, as you can see, I'm very much alive. What I don't understand is why I know nothing about you or Flossie?"

We followed Ann to the sitting area and waited for her to start the story that by the time she finished seemed too strange to be true.

"Several years ago, we read about the accident that took Harriett's life along with the two little girls. It was big news all over the state. After a proper time, a little over a year, we found Aunt Amy and Uncle Ruben. We were so excited to find more family that I suggested we have a family reunion the following summer. I told Aunt Amy to be sure and include you in the invitation. She just shook her head and told us you'd gotten married and your wife was high society and didn't want anything to do with the rest of the family. After that we never questioned her. They came over to Boscobel a couple of times a year, but until your daughter got married we never heard anything about you.

"After the wedding, Amy sent us the wedding announcement saying Sherry was getting married and she was the daughter of Mrs. Ralph Derr and the late Ralph Derr. I think I still have it at the house. At the time I told Flossie it was a shame for two of Amy's children to die at such young ages."

"I don't understand any of this," Ralph replied. "Ralph Totten used to come over to the house on Sunday. Certainly he must have told you about Norma and that I wasn't dead."

"Ralph Totten," Ann repeated the name as though trying to remember the name. "Oh yes, he was my mother's half brother. I do remember our mother talking about him, but we never met him. She said since he wasn't really her brother, he didn't matter. He was related to Aunt Amy but not to us."

Within the week, Grandma was dead and we were once again planning a funeral. Freddie was in no shape and Leona was far from competent. Daddy was told although Grandma had a small life insurance policy it wasn't enough to cover the cost of the funeral. He also learned her will read Freddie was to get everything and my father was to get the bills.

Although the will came as a shock, she already told us she'd arranged a quick claim deed so the house would go immediately to Freddie upon her death.

After making the arrangements, Daddy went to the house to talk to Leona. At that time, he demanded the family Bible, the wedding ring I'd never seen Grandma wear, and the pendant watch belonging to his mother. Leona didn't want to part with them, but he didn't feel she was entitled to them so he took them anyway.

On the day of the funeral, there was no admonishment about not crying for my grandma. I was able to cry, not for my grandma, but also for all the things she'd deprived my father of over the years.

After the funeral, we went back to Leona's house. She was preparing to sell most of Grandma's furniture. Although I'm sure he paid too much for it, my dad bought us the dining room table that had always been in the parlor along with the extra chairs. He also bought me Grandma's refrigerator, as Leona only wanted to have her small refrigerator in the kitchen.

She did allow Mother to go through Grandma's linens. It nearly broke my mother's heart to see all the beautifully embroidered and crocheted linens she'd give her mother-in-law over the years packed away and never used. Needless to say, she brought them all home with her and put them to the use they'd been meant for over the thirty-four years of her marriage.

We were just about to leave when Leona brought out a box with my name on it. I wanted to open it then and there, but Daddy said that could happen later. Once we were in the car, I opened the box to find a fine china dresser set. Each piece matched perfectly and the set included a large tray, a hatpin holder complete with hatpin, a powder pot, hair receiver, ring tree and small tray. I was certain I'd been given a special gift.

The one thing I did learn was my name had never been written in the family Bible. When I called my pastor to vent my anger over not being acknowledged by my own grandmother his reply was maybe she didn't have time. I screamed back at him that in twenty-seven years she could have found the time.

On closer inspection, we found the papers bonding my grandmother to Joseph Coble in 1892. Since her early life was such a secret, we could only imagine what it had been like growing up in that kind of a household.

Over the next months, Daddy managed to bring home several pictures of the family, especially the ones from the china closet. By the end of September, 1973 he was finally able to breathe a sigh of relief, as it was six months after Grandma's death and any unpaid bills were no longer his responsibility.

Chapter Thirty-Six

Grandma's death brought several changes. We no longer went to Evansville on a monthly basis, and neither did my parents. Daddy often got calls from Leona demanding he come up and bring her money. He did manage to go to Evansville but it was to see Freddie and not to stop at the house on Madison Street.

When he did stop, he learned she'd become a ward of the county due to her mental handicap. My mother often said how sad it was Leona had someone who came to the house to give her a bath, clean the house, bring her meals and she'd never worked a day in her life. Leona also bragged how an antique dealer came to the house and bought all of Grandma's antique furniture for a hundred dollars.

At Christmas, we went up to see Aunt Leona and were shocked to see the condition of the house. The parlor had no furniture in it whatsoever. Even the china closet with all of the old glassware was gone. Grandma's bedroom was empty. In the living room, the only furniture was the three dilapidated chairs and a TV tray. Gone were the cluttered library table and the side table from beside Freddie's chair. The dining room was just as stark. It had been stripped of Grandma's second dining room set and replaced with a card table and four folding chairs. Also gone were the roomers who lived at the house for as long as I could remember. In their place were younger men of Leona's choosing.

In 1975 we received news of Freddie's death. Leona carried on, but my father had long since ceased listening to her ranting.

After the funeral, my father would take us to Evansville on Mother's Day to decorate the graves, but he would never stop at Leona's house. Feeling obligated, I continued to go up to see her at Christmas, although my kids really didn't want to go.

My father passed away in 1996 of a massive heart attack and my mother followed him, after a long illness, in 2001. By that time, Leona no longer lived in the house on Madison Street. I learned she'd been taken to an assisted living center on the east side of Evansville and she now had a caregiver.

I know it wasn't a very Christian thing to do, but I just couldn't bring myself to visit her. When the end came in 2008, her friends paid for her funeral and the luncheon afterwards. It was a very small gathering. The only family in attendance was my husband and myself along with our daughter, Robin. Otherwise, the mourners were people who'd looked after Leona and of course the two young men who took rooms in her home after Grandma died.

An era had ended. The members of my father's family all rested in either the Evansville or Janesville cemeteries.

With no one left to consult about the things that happened to my grandmother and father I decided I needed to put down the facts as I'd heard them and embellish them as I imagine things happened. I do not want these stories to become lost when I am gone.

This has been a long soul-searching process and one I have taken on because people should know how orphans were treated in the late nineteenth century and what effect those actions had on the next generation as families struggled with the Great Depression and World War II.

THE END

AUTHOR'S NOTE

This story has been very different as well as very difficult for me to write. I am the only child of Ralph and Norma Derr as well as the only grandchild of Amy and Ruben Derr. What I thought was normal as I grew up, I have since learned was nowhere near normal.

The secrets that were revealed concerning my grandmother were not known prior to her death and then we learned of them by accident.

As for my father's story, I heard him talk of his childhood as well as the years of his young adulthood so many times I could repeat them word for word.

These are stories of how life was in the late nineteenth and early twentieth century in Southern Wisconsin. For those people who did not live through such things I know they are hard to believe, but they happened and must be told so they will not be forgotten.

My main objective is to unburden my soul about what my life was like but also to hopefully find any living family related to Ruben Delos Derr or Amy Belle Totten Derr. Since I'm the last of my family, maybe this book will bring forward someone who knows more of my family history.

It is my hope that I have given my own children, Robin Turner, Steven Wille and Sandra Brown, as well as my grandchildren, Faith Turner-Skinner, Matthew Ehr, Morgan Brown, Steven Brown, Vaughan Turner, Alex Brown, Miles Turner, Tanner Brown and Tyler Brown better memories of the past than my father carried with him all his life. Without my husband, Bob Wille, coming to grips with the past and giving our children a future would not have been possible.

FAMILY TREE

Ruben Delos Derr – b – June 9, 1880 – d – October 1, 1957
Married: Amy Belle Coble (Anna Belle Totten) December 14, 1910

Amy Belle Coble (Anna Belle Totten) – b – February 3, 1889 – d – February 23, 1973

Freddie Ruben Derr – b – June 22, 1911 – d – 1975
Married: Marion Walmer February 20, 1934
Marion Walmer Derr – b – 1916 – d – February 23, 1938
Daughter: Beverly Leila Derr – b – December 28, 1934 – d – October 2, 1938
Married: Leona Hosley February 27, 1939
Leona Hosley Derr – b – 1920 – d – 2008

Harriett Leila Derr – b – August 2, 1919 – d – October 2, 1938
Married: Ted Bumgartner August 24, 1935
Daughter: Donna Jean Bumgartner – b – July 21, 1937 – d – October 2, 1938

Ralph Eugene Derr – b – August 12, 1921 – d – February 15, 1996
Married: Norma Jean Howard December 9, 1939
Norma Jean Howard Derr – b – May 11, 1923 – d – May 6, 2001
Daughter: Sherry Lee Derr – b – April 24, 1946
Married: Robert John Wille June 6, 1964
Robert John Wille – b – May 16, 1942

Daughter: Robin Dawn Wille – b – August 13, 1966
Married: Jeffrey Michael Schmitt December 1, 1984 – Divorced 1987
Son: Brandon Jeffrey Schmitt – b – April 4, 1986 – d – April 26, 1986
Married: David George Turner June 14, 1992 – Divorced 2004
Step Daughter: Faith Turner Skinner b – November 1982
Daughter: Julia Skinner – b – September 13, 2010
Son: Vaughan David Turner – b – November 3, 1994

Sherry Derr Wille

Son: Miles Robert Turner – b – November 5, 1998

Son: Steven Dale Wille – b – August 7, 1969
Son: Matthew Ehr – b August 16, 1987
Daughter: Alyssa Mae Ehr – b October 30, 2006
Daughter: Sandra Lynn Wille – b – September 30, 1971
Married: Michael Brown May 31, 1995
Step Daughter: Morgan Brown – b – July 2, 1990
Step Son: Steven Brown – b – August 30, 1991
Son: Alexander Michael Brown – b – September 15, 1996
Son: Tanner John Brown – b – June 16, 2003
Son: Tyler Scott Brown – b – June 16, 2003

About the Author

Mild Mannered wife, mother and grandmother by day, Sherry Derr-Wille spends her nights writing and writing and writing. Having been inspired by an English assignment in her sophomore year of high school, she had never quite finished the assignment. New stories pop into her head every day with never enough time to write them all.

A Wisconsin native, she grew up a country girl, but enjoys her "city" home. She and her husband of over 40 years, Bob, live in a mid-sized town close to the Illinois border, where she works as a receptionist for an insurance office and he is retired. Deeming Bob "A Saint" for putting up with her she has never regretted marrying her high school sweetheart just two days after graduation in 1964.

www.derr-wille.com